a Dear Daphne novel

Lock, Stock, and Over a Barrel

MELODY CARLSON

a Dear Daphne novel

Lock, Stock, and Over a Barrel

B&H
PUBLISHING GROUP

Nashville, Tennessee

978-1-4336-7930-8

Published by B&H Publishing Group,
Nashville, Tennessee

Dewey Decimal Classification: F
Subject Heading: ADVENTURE FICTION \ INHERITANCE AND
SUCCESSION—FICTION \ WILLS—FICTION

1 2 3 4 5 6 7 8 • 17 16 15 14 13

Chapter 1

When Daphne Ballinger graduated top of her class with her degree in journalism, in the memorable year of 2000, she had promptly moved to the city to launch her illustrious career writing for *The New York Times*. And why not dream big? Because really, how many grads landed such an impressive job straight out of college?

Her plan had been to work hard and quickly scale the ladder to success. By thirty she would have a corner office with a window overlooking the river as well as an apartment on the west side. By her midthirties, she would have published her first book. But similar to the plans of mice and men, Daphne's best-laid schemes had gone awry.

She stuffed a worn pair of brown Prada pumps into her Hermès bag (splurges she'd indulged in back when she still believed you should dress for the job/life you wanted). Then she sat down to put on her comfy-yet-unfashionable white sneakers. After tying the first shoe, she sat up straight and looked around the messy apartment.

Daphne knew it was cliché but, on gloomy days like today, it truly did feel like the walls were closing in on her. Most of the time, she could overlook the crowded space. She could walk right past piles of papers and miscellaneous pieces of clothing and empty take-out boxes . . . and not even notice. But this morning, the apartment actually seemed to stink. When was the last time they'd really cleaned this place?

She shared this three-bedroom apartment with Greta and Shelby. And in previous years Greta, the lease owner, had always proclaimed April as spring-cleaning month. But it was already mid-May and no one had lifted a finger. And Greta, obsessed with a new job promotion, hadn't complained once. Daphne's gaze skimmed over gritty windows, dingy curtains, dust-covered surfaces, piles of clutter, sun-faded carpet. . . . How had she stayed here so long?

"I can't promise to be here more than a year," Daphne had informed Greta Phillips when she first moved to the city right after graduation.

A coworker at *The Times* had tipped off Daphne about a friend looking for a third roommate for an apartment in Brooklyn. And although the location was lackluster, it was near the subway and the rent was affordable. Besides, it would just be a temporary stop— the bottom rung on her ladder to success—or so she had naively believed.

"And *after* a year?" Greta had asked Daphne with a single arched brow.

Daphne simply smiled . . . perhaps a bit smugly upon reflection. "Oh, I plan to move into my *own* place by then."

"Your *own* place?" Greta seemed humored by this declaration. *"Really?"*

"Oh yes. This is just the first step for me."

"Well, I still need you to sign a one-year lease. After that, we'll see."

Daphne had hesitantly signed that "confining" lease, wondering how Greta would react if she was forced to break the contract before the year was up. Although numerous other roommates had come and gone during the next thirteen years, climbing their own ladders to success, Daphne had stayed . . . and stayed . . . and stayed. Remembering the arrogant assumptions of her youth was embarrassing.

"Hey, Daphne," Shelby called out cheerfully. Shelby was the most recent roommate, less than six months ago she'd moved here straight from her family's Connecticut home. "I'm heading out early this morning. So you'll have to put Oliver in the bathroom. Okay?"

Daphne looked over to see Shelby looking sparkly and stylish as she opened a golden shoe box. After tossing the lid, tissue paper, and red shoe bags aside, Shelby extracted a dark-colored shoe with a sole that flashed like a stoplight. Shelby slipped on the first high-heeled pump, pointing her toe to admire the sleek black patent leather. "Classy, huh?"

"*Another* pair of Louboutins?" Daphne frowned, knowing she probably sounded like somebody's mother. But really, Shelby couldn't afford such extravagances.

"Yes. Can you believe it?" Shelby giggled. "I think I'm going to need a twelve-step program before long."

"Or a raise."

Shelby waved a hand, hopping on one foot as she tugged on the other shoe. "I'd rather settle for a nice, big diamond." Shelby was obsessed with Marilyn Monroe, and sometimes Daphne worried that the pretty young woman had seen *How to Marry a Millionaire* one time too many.

"So how is that working for you?" Daphne knew Shelby had been flirting with her boss's son for the past several weeks. She also knew the boss's son had recently divorced his second wife.

Shelby stood up straight, pushing her short, sassy blond hair back into place with a confident-looking grin. "As it turns out, John Junior is taking me to Club 21."

"21?" Daphne was impressed. The whole time she'd been in New York, she'd only been there once. And here Shelby was going after just a few months. This girl worked fast.

"Yes. I told John Junior that I'd been dying to go there ever since I moved to the city. And we're going there *tonight*. Can you believe it?"

"Can you believe it" was Shelby's favorite expression and sometimes, after hearing it a few dozen times in the course of an evening, Daphne sometimes wanted to gag the girl. "That's wonderful, Shelby." She stood and smiled. "I hope you and John Junior have a lovely time." Did Shelby really call him *John Junior*—to his face?

"Oh, we will." Shelby reached for her hot pink umbrella, holding it in front of her like a scepter. "The weatherman predicted showers this morning. So don't forget your umbrella."

"I hope the rain doesn't ruin your pretty new shoes."

"No worries." Shelby shrugged. "John Junior is picking me up in his car this morning."

"He's driving you into Manhattan at this time of day?"

"No, silly, that would be insane. He's giving me a ride out to his parents' home in the Hamptons. John Senior is working at home today, so I'll be working there too."

"Oh . . ." Daphne nodded. That explained the new shoes, stylish suit, perfect hair. Shelby was out to impress Mrs. John Senior. "Well, have a good day."

"Oh, I'm sure I will." Shelby opened the door to peek out. "There he is now—right on time. You should see his car, Daphne." She stepped outside, then looked back in. "Don't forget to put Oliver in the bathroom."

Daphne went over to the front window, watching as Shelby skipped down the cement stairs in her new shoes, swinging her bright umbrella in time with each step. Sometimes it was as if Shelby were starring in her own movie. She paused midway down the steps, waving to the man who was just getting out of the silver Jaguar in front of their building. From her vantage point, Daphne could see the balding patch on the top of the man's dark hair, and for some pathetic reason this comforted her.

Still, as she stepped away from her voyeurism, she didn't wish ill for young Shelby. If John Junior was truly a nice guy, she hoped he would produce a diamond . . . in due time. Daphne hadn't known Shelby long, but she knew the old-fashioned girl dreamed of a big white wedding and a houseful of kids. It was sweet, really.

"Oliver," Daphne called out as she grabbed a yogurt carton from the fridge. "Here, kitty-kitty." She reached into Greta's bag of kitty treats, singing out enticingly. "Here's a treat for you, Oliver. Here, kitty-kitty."

She was not fond of Greta's fat gray cat and, unfortunately, Oliver seemed to sense this. Still, she kept her voice sugary as she walked around calling for him, "Come on, Oliver, come get your yummy-yummy kitty treat."

She eventually found him hunkered down in Greta's bedroom with a guilty expression, but if he was doing something he shouldn't, Daphne did not want to know. She had learned the hard way to keep her own bedroom door closed. For some twisted reason Oliver sometimes preferred a nice soft bed to his smelly litter box in the bathroom.

"There you are, you darling little scoundrel," she said in a saccharine tone. As he looked up, she curled her arm around his hefty midsection. "Got you." Then she quickly packed him off to the bathroom, tossing in the treat with him behind it. "Have a good day, you spoiled fat cat." Daphne closed the door firmly. It wasn't that she disliked cats in general. She just didn't care much for Oliver.

By the time Daphne locked up the apartment and was on her way to the subway, it was already starting to rain. And despite Shelby's reminder, Daphne had set off without her umbrella and there wasn't time to run back and get it now. Consequently, as the clouds opened up and let loose, she got thoroughly drenched in the short distance to the subway. Waiting with the other dampened commuters, she tried to shake off some of the moisture before the train arrived, then she hurried in with the crowd, finding a spot in the back of the car where the air was smelly and muggy and close.

Firmly planting her feet, Daphne held tightly to a pole and, shutting her eyes, attempted to imagine herself in a happier, cleaner, dryer place. Like the Grand Canyon where her dad had taken her as child one summer. She breathed deeply as she recalled the beautiful painted mountains changing hues of golds, reds, and russets at sunset.

This was a trick she'd taught herself years ago, her way to combat the claustrophobia that she sometimes suffered in the city. One would think she'd be over her dislike of tight spaces by now, but on days like today the anxiety seemed to lurk just below the surface. She remembered when she had been in love with New York. Some called it the Big Apple Honeymoon Phase, but it had lasted several years for her. However, like so many other things in her life, it had gotten a little tarnished and dull over the years. And as she emerged from the subway, back into the drizzling rain and noisy traffic, she didn't much like the city.

By the time Daphne reached her cubicle at *The Times* and peeled off her soggy jacket and slushy sneakers and stashed them in a sodden pile in the corner, her long auburn hair, which she'd spent thirty minutes straightening this morning, now resembled Bozo the Clown. Not that anyone would particularly notice or care since most of her day was spent on her own.

Daphne was a wedding writer—one of several—and she had been doing the same thing for more than ten years. She could write one of these pieces in her sleep. In fact, sometimes she did. Oh, not for the paper, but she would lie in bed writing another piece. They ran about 250 words, five or six paragraphs, all meant to impress the bride and the groom and their family and friends.

She turned on her computer and perused her e-mail, sifting through junk and flagging some, and then on to read today's assignments. This time of year was usually fairly busy, but to her surprise there was only one happy couple waiting for the spotlight, and she managed to spend two whole hours on making them seem larger than life. Hopefully they would appreciate her efforts.

Then with still an hour until lunch, she imagined what she'd write for Shelby's wedding announcement, and because she was bored and didn't like to appear idle or get caught playing Spider Solitaire, she decided to hack a phony baloney announcement for her romantic roommate.

Miss Shelby M. Monroe and John Junior Millionaire were married on Friday night in May at Club 21 in downtown Manhattan. Family friend and celebrity entrepreneur Donald Trump, who became an ordained

*minister for this monumental occasion, officiated the extravagant
event where no expenses were spared.*

*The beautiful bride, twenty-three, and the prematurely balding bridegroom,
of undetermined age, met at the bride's place of employment, which is also
the bridegroom's father's multimillion-dollar investment corporation.*

*Miss Monroe, who will not be keeping her name since it's not really her
name, will give up her career, which wasn't really a career, in order to
raise a houseful of boisterous children. She is the daughter of a once-
prestigious family who resided in Westport, Connecticut, until her father's
investment corporation was dissolved in a scandal involving insider
trading. Now, despite some diminished wealth, the bride's parents are
enjoying an early retirement abroad.*

*Mr. Millionaire, who goes by John Junior, holds some mysterious position
in his father's corporation, where not much actual work is required of
him. John Junior graduated from some Ivy League school,
where his family probably had some really good connections.*

*Following an over-the-top honeymoon, which probably involved
a beach in an exotic locale, the happy newlyweds will reside
in a penthouse apartment on the upper west side.*

*The bridegroom's first two marriages ended in divorce.
Hopefully the third time will be the charm.*

Feeling a bit juvenile, not to mention catty, Daphne hit the select
all and delete buttons. Best not to leave something like that lying
around for too long. She was about to shut down and go to lunch
when her cell phone rang. She got up and grabbed her bag. After

digging for her elusive phone and expecting it to be Beverly since they were meeting for lunch today, she was surprised to discover it was actually her father. He rarely called her in the middle of the day. Not unless something was wrong.

"Dad?" she said with concern. "What's up?"

"Hello, Daphne. I'm afraid it's bad news."

"What?" Her throat tightened. He'd had some health issues last winter. Hopefully it wasn't worse. She'd lost her mother as a small child. Dad was all she had left of her immediate family.

"It's Aunt Dee . . . she passed away this morning. Her lawyer just called to inform me, and I thought you'd want to know."

"Aunt Dee." Daphne sank back down in her chair. "Oh, I'm so sorry to hear that, Dad. I know how much you loved her. I loved her too. And I'd been hoping to get out there to visit you and her this summer. I can't believe she's gone."

Tears filled her eyes as she suddenly recalled the summers she'd spent at Aunt Dee's house as a child when Dad was busy with work. Aunt Dee had tried to make up for Daphne losing her mother. Daphne and Aunt Dee had always enjoyed a special connection and a shared name.

"If it's any consolation, she died peacefully. In her sleep."

"How old was she?" For some reason, Daphne couldn't recall her aunt's age. She knew she was older than Dad, but in a way Aunt Dee had seemed timeless. Maybe it was her youthful spirit.

"She would've been ninety-one in July."

"Ninety-one? Wow, I had no idea she was that old."

"Yes. She never really told anyone her real age. But she enjoyed a good, full life." He sighed. "Even though she never married or had children, she seemed to have a good time in whatever she did. She traveled. Had lots of friends. Dee lived life on her own terms. And she always seemed happy."

"She did—didn't she?" Daphne let out a choked sob as she reached for a Kleenex, wiping the tears now streaming down her cheeks.

"I'm sorry, honey. I hate to be the bearer of sad news. But I knew you'd want to know."

"Yes. I appreciate that. I don't know why I'm taking this so hard." She blew her nose.

"Will you be able to make it out here for her memorial service?"

"Yes, of course, Dad." She reached for another tissue.

"Oh, good. I'm in charge of everything. And I could really use your help with the arrangements. I mean, if you can come out here soon enough . . . I'll understand if you can't drop everything." His voice sounded tired and weak, but maybe it was just sadness.

"How are you feeling? I mean, with your heart and cholesterol and everything. Are you okay?"

"Oh, sure, honey. I'm fine. Don't worry about me." He sighed. "When do you think you can get away?"

"I'll find out as soon as we hang up. And I'll get right back to you," she promised.

"Thanks, Daph. I can't wait to see you."

They said good-bye, then she grabbed her purse and hurried up to her boss's office, feeling she'd get better results if she asked in person. Hopefully Amelia wouldn't have left for lunch yet. However, when she got up there, Daphne could tell by the darkened office that Amelia was already gone.

"Amelia left early for a lunch meeting," her assistant told Daphne. "Want me to leave her a message for you?"

"No. I'll come after lunch. When do you expect her back?"

Fiona shrugged. "Well, you know how those working lunches can drag on forever. I wouldn't expect her until three or maybe even four."

"Thanks. I'll stop by later." Daphne headed out to meet Beverly, calling her as she walked toward their favorite dining spot. She left a message saying she was running late. Then she called Dad and explained that her boss was out. "As soon as I know, I'll call," she assured him.

Fortunately, the rain had stopped and the clouds had cleared and the city, now scrubbed fresh and clean, should be shimmering in the sunshine. And yet, as Daphne hurried down the street, everything around her still felt dull and gray and dismal.

Chapter 2

Beverly already had a table when Daphne arrived at the busy restaurant, and after their preliminary greetings were over, Daphne explained about her aunt and her dad and why she was late.

"I'm so sorry." Beverly reached over and put her hand on Daphne's. "I've heard you mention her before. Didn't she help you get your job at *The Times*?"

"Yes. Strangely enough, Aunt Dee knew someone there back then. I'm not even sure who it was or what the connection was . . . but she did put in a good word for me when I graduated college."

"And wasn't she a writer too?"

"Yes. But you know, I've never actually read a thing she's written. I think she did some kind of technical writing. Like manuals or textbooks or something pretty dull. When I was a kid staying with her, she'd hole up in her study for several hours in the afternoon, pounding away on her old electric typewriter." She shook her head. "Can you imagine writing a textbook on a typewriter?"

"No way."

"She had a fear of computers and I suppose they were a little hard to use back then. But sometimes I'd sneak in and ask her if I could read what she was working on. But she'd just laugh and say something like, 'Oh, it's so doggone boring, darling, it would put you to sleep faster than a glass of warm milk on a cold winter's night.'"

They both laughed.

"And then as if to make up for it, she'd find me some wonderful classic book to read. Aunt Dee's the reason I learned to love reading. She started me out on *Little House on the Prairie* and *Anne of Green Gables*. Then she introduced me to Jane Austen and the Brontë sisters later. And she made me keep a journal while I was at her house. I learned to love writing because of her."

Beverly smiled. "It sounds like she was a wonderful influence on your life."

"She was. Everyone in her town loved her. I'm sure she will be missed a lot." Daphne explained her plan to go back to help her father with the funeral plans. "I just hope Amelia doesn't mind."

"Well, she shouldn't mind," Beverly declared a bit hotly. On a regular basis, Beverly told her that Amelia took unfair advantage of Daphne's loyalty. "You work harder than any of her staff. And you never take sick days. You must have plenty of vacation time coming."

Daphne nodded. "I do."

"Then take them. And I know I've said this before, but I'm sure it's because of Amelia that you never get promoted." Beverly rolled her eyes. "But don't get me going on that."

"Trust me, I won't."

Ever since Beverly had quit working for the paper more than five years ago, back when she married their friend Robert and started freelancing from home, she had gotten quite comfortable at taking potshots at certain department heads, including Amelia. In an effort to preserve their friendship, Daphne had proclaimed discussions on the paper to be off-limits—it was a no-fly zone. And most of the time, Beverly respected it.

"Okay, you're right. Let's change the subject." Beverly's tone turned cheerful. "I was going to tell you something . . . although in light of your bad news, I suddenly feel a little guilty. Maybe I should—"

"What is it? *Tell me,*" Daphne demanded. "And really, it's okay. Did you sell your book?"

Beverly giggled. "No, no. I wish . . . I mean that would be really good news. But this is actually much better . . . in a different sort of way." Her eyes twinkled.

Daphne studied her. Something seemed different about her friend. "Is it . . . I mean are you . . . Beverly, are you expecting?"

With an ear-to-ear grin, Beverly nodded eagerly. "It caught me by total surprise. You know how we'd been trying . . . and how my biological time clock was ticking. . . . But I'd gotten so caught up in the feature I was writing this spring. And it kept taking longer than I expected, it's like I lost track of my own body. And last month I realized that I was late. I mean very, very late."

"And you didn't even tell me then?" Daphne felt slightly hurt.

"No way. I didn't tell anyone. Not even Robert." Beverly took in a deep breath. "You remember when I lost the other baby after only two months and we were all so devastated? Well, I was determined to make it three months before I told anyone." She beamed at Daphne. "And I did that last week. And the doctor says everything looks really good. I should go full term."

"I'm so happy for you. You've waited so long. You really deserve this. Both of you." More tears filled Daphne's eyes. But these were tears of joy . . . at least that's what she told herself. The truth was, she didn't know for sure. Her best friend was married and soon to have children . . . they would undoubtedly drift apart.

"As you can imagine, Robert is over the moon," Beverly said. "He's already looking for houses, if you can imagine."

"Houses?"

Beverly waved her hand. "Oh, you know Robert. He's a country boy at heart. He's certain we can't raise normal, healthy children in the city."

"So you're really going to move?" Daphne tried not to imagine what it would be like living in the city without her best friend nearby.

"Oh, not right away. Unless Robert finds something too great to pass up."

"Well, it is a buyer's market."

"That's what Robert keeps telling me. He keeps saying things like we have to strike while the iron's hot." Now Beverly described some of the charming properties Robert had found, some that actually had white picket fences, explaining how Robert might start working from home part-time to help her with the baby. It sounded like they were about to become such a delightfully happy little family that it took all of Daphne's self-control not to burst into uncontrollable full-blown sobbing.

She nodded and smiled as she picked away at her flat-tasting chicken salad, trying to act supportive and interested in her best friend's perfect life. How was it possible that in just one day, one's entire life could turn upside down and sidewise while the rest of the world just kept chugging merrily along?

Amelia had been surprisingly agreeable to Daphne's sudden need for time off from work. "Take as long as you need," she told Daphne. "No problem."

Daphne should've felt relieved as she buckled her seat belt on the plane the next day. Instead she felt dispensable. Of course, *The Times* could get by without her. They'd gotten by without her for over 150 years. They wouldn't even notice she was gone now. Beverly was right—Amelia did take Daphne for granted.

As she looked out the window, staring blankly at the clouds, Daphne decided that when she returned to New York, she would confront Amelia and insist on discussing a promotion. Beverly had been telling Daphne to do that for years now. It was high time Daphne grew a backbone and did it.

She thought about Aunt Dee. Wasn't that what she would tell Daphne? Grab life by the horns and live it fully? And truly, that was what Daphne had thought she was doing back in 2000 when she'd first come to New York. She had felt like she was reaching for the stars and dreaming big. But somewhere down the line, she'd given up . . . but why?

The sun broke through the clouds with blindingly bright light, and Daphne quickly slid down the window covering, and leaning back she sighed. She knew exactly why . . . as well as when and where and how and who.

She'd given up on her dreams after Ryan broke her heart.

Although he was seven years her senior, Ryan Holloway had come to work at *The Times* a couple years after Daphne—shortly after she'd been promoted to writing engagement pieces and was just starting to feel more confident. Previous to *The Times*, Ryan had been the sports editor for a small newspaper out west, but he'd showed enough promise and potential to secure an impressive job as a sports writer for *The Times*. And to Daphne's amazement, she was the girl who had caught his eye. Ryan didn't know about her ugly duckling past. He'd never seen the gawky, skinny, redheaded girl who never fit in—the girl with freckles and braces and eventually zits.

Instead, he looked at her with hungry eyes. He was the first man—the only man besides her father—who told her she was beautiful. "Who can resist a long-legged beauty?" he'd say as he dropped a long-stemmed red rose on her desk. "Here's one hot number for another," he'd say as he unexpectedly delivered a cup of steaming mocha. It wasn't long before they were dating—steadily. And right from the start, the relationship had been magical, wonderful, amazing.

In some ways it had probably appeared similar to Shelby's seemingly charmed life now. There had been many incredible moments when Daphne and Ryan, feeling young and in love and invincible, ran around the city with abandon. It had felt like she was starring in her own wonderful movie. A romantic love story that was so totally unlike her previous life—the life where she'd taken everything far too seriously and made all her choices much too carefully. But with Ryan by her side, she threw caution to the wind. She dove into romance, and the water was fine. Sometimes it all seemed too good to be real. Unfortunately it was.

Everything came to a screeching halt when Daphne discovered Ryan was already married. They'd been dating for a year and the whole time she had absolutely no idea, not an inkling, that Ryan had a wife waiting for him back in Idaho. And not just a wife. Two small children as well.

Because he traveled a lot for sports events, she had never questioned his absences. And when he returned to New York, he always seemed as thrilled to see her as she was to see him. Really, if not for that one unforgettable phone call, they could've gone on like that for ages.

Ryan had left his cell phone on the table while they were having a late dinner one night. He'd been paying close attention to his phone because he was waiting to hear about a big assignment from his boss. So when the phone rang, thinking it was Rich at *The Times*, Daphne answered. In retrospect, she wondered why she hadn't let it just go to voice mail . . . but perhaps she'd intuited something. Maybe somewhere deep inside she had known that something was amiss . . . too good to be true. But sitting in the plane, thirty-five thousand feet over the Midwest, Daphne still remembered the phone call like it was yesterday.

"Who is this?" a female voice demanded. "I'm trying to reach Ryan Holloway and I know this is his number."

"I'm sorry," Daphne said. "This is Ryan's phone, but he's in the restroom at the moment, so I answered for him. Is this Rich's assistant?"

"No, this is *not* Rich's assistant. This is Ryan's *wife*. Who is *this*?"

"I—uh—I—uh . . ." Daphne felt like someone had just pushed a diabolical button causing the floor beneath her to vanish, like she was tumbling down into some deep, dark bottomless abyss. "Pardon me?" she said meekly, hoping she'd heard this angry-sounding woman incorrectly.

"I said this is Ryan's wife. Belinda Holloway. What I want to know is *who are you*? I know Ryan's been seeing someone. And since it's nighttime, I'll bet that makes you that someone. Tell me, are you the other woman? The one who's been stealing my husband's affections? The home wrecker who doesn't even care that Ryan has two young children? Tell me the truth!"

Without saying another word, Daphne closed Ryan's phone, set it back down on the table, and slowly stood. She gathered her bag and jacket and, on shaking legs, walked out of the restaurant, got on the subway, and went home.

Ryan had called her again and again, but she didn't answer her phone. And she didn't go into work either. Not for three days. Then following a weekend intervention from Beverly and Greta and their other roommate at the time, Daphne returned to work the following Monday. Humbly going to Amelia, who was threatening to fire her, Daphne groveled and apologized, promising to do whatever it took to make it up to her, including bringing her coffee, taking the worst assignments—kissing her feet whenever she walked by. Daphne managed to keep her job. And, indeed, she had been making it up to Amelia ever since.

Because he'd been out on assignment and Daphne had become quite adept at making herself nearly invisible—which wasn't easy for a tall redhead—their paths didn't cross for nearly two weeks. And naturally, by then he had put two and two together and concluded his wife had figured him out.

"Our marriage was already over," he told Daphne after he coerced her into meeting him at Central Park—he'd told her it was either there or the workplace, and Daphne couldn't risk her job.

"If it's over, why are you still married?" she frostily demanded.

"Because it was just a matter of time."

She was avoiding looking at him, worried he would soften her resolve to never speak to him again—after this meeting.

"Honestly, I don't love Belinda anymore. I planned on telling her it was over."

She turned and glared at him. "And your two children? Is it over for them too?"

He groaned. "I know, I know . . . it's not fair to them. But is it fair for me to remain in a loveless marriage?"

"Was it fair to me for you to pretend you were single and hurt me like this?"

"I know I've made a mess of everything. But I love you, Daphne. I really do."

"I don't want to hear it." She stood. "You are married, Ryan. No matter how I feel about you, I refuse to be involved with a married man."

"But I'll divorce her. I promise I will."

She took in an angry breath, controlling herself from pummeling his chest and screaming. "Do you really think that's what I want? To think I'm the reason you left your wife and young children? Do you really think I can live with that? Do you?" She turned and walked away.

Less than a month later, she learned that Ryan had taken a job with another newspaper on the other side of the country. As much as she appreciated that, she was so deeply wounded that it took years for her to get over him.

Even now, replaying all this in her head, she wasn't completely sure that she was. Because as much as she hated him for deceiving her, a small part of her still had feelings for him. And that just made her feel angry.

At Beverly's recommendation, Daphne had attended a group-therapy session for a year or so after the breakup. It was kind of like a twelve-step group for the "brokenhearted." The sad little band of lonely hearts met in a church in Brooklyn, sharing their problems and praying for each other. And finally after nearly a year, Daphne felt she was ready to move on from the group. The best thing she'd learned from her brokenhearted friends was that she needed to forgive Ryan, as well as his angry wife.

And equally important, she needed to forgive herself.

So whenever thoughts of Ryan came up after that, sometimes not for weeks or even months at a time and sometimes right out of the blue, she'd promised herself she would pray for him and his children, who were probably teenagers by now. And that was just what she was doing as the flight attendant announced it was time to prepare for landing. And just like always, that did the trick. Somehow just praying for him and his kids seemed to make the pain and heartache go away and she was able to move forward again . . . one step at a time.

Chapter 3

Even though she had assured her dad that she could get a taxi to take her the twenty miles to Appleton, Daphne was very glad to see him waiting for her in baggage claim. She hugged him tightly then stepped back to give him a good, long look. He seemed to have aged a lot since she'd last seen him nearly two years ago.

"You look as pretty as ever," Dad said as he reached for her bag. She started to protest that he might strain himself but stopped, knowing that would hurt his feelings.

"Thanks, Dad. You're looking good too." She looped a strap of her carry-on over her shoulder.

He patted his flattened midsection. "The doctor made me lose some weight."

"Good for you."

"And my cholesterol has gone down some too."

"Even better."

"I thought maybe you'd want to stay at Dee's house," he said as they walked through the parking lot.

"Not with you?"

He shrugged. "Well sure, you can stay with me if you want, but the place is a mess."

"A mess?" That didn't sound like her neatnik father.

"Truth is, I've been going through some old stuff—you know, getting rid of junk."

"Junk?"

"Oh, just the stuff that piles up over the years. Worthless things you wouldn't want, Daphne. The Realtor suggested I thin things out."

"The Realtor?"

Dad opened the trunk of his old blue sedan, set her bag inside, then closed it. He turned and gave her a sheepish smile. "I plan to move into a condo. At Green Trees."

"A condo?" She frowned. "Really?"

They got in the car. "I'm not getting any younger, and that house needs a lot of upkeep. The roof will need replacing in a few years. The gutters always need cleaning out. The deck and fence are getting old. And the grass—did you know that grass needs cutting two times a week in the summer?"

"You could get a landscaping service," she suggested.

"I'll have landscaping service at Green Trees."

"So your mind's made up?"

"Yep. I've got an offer on a unit right now. I made it just last week . . . before Dee passed away. Karen, she's my Realtor, is certain she can find a buyer for me. She plans to have an open house as soon as I get it cleared out a little. I've gotten a little distracted . . . you know, because of Dee's death. But I plan to have the house listed by early June."

"Wow." Daphne just nodded, taking all this in. "I had no idea."

"I know, honey, but it just seemed to make sense. As you know, I'll retire this fall on my seventy-second birthday." He chuckled. "Some people, the ones who want my job, say I should've retired a long time ago. I thought why not make a fresh start? And there are a lot of retired folks living at Green Trees. Although Karen lives there and she's not even sixty. But she loves it too."

That was the second time he'd mentioned this Karen person, and something about the way he said her name made Daphne curious. Still, she didn't want to be too nosy. Not yet anyway.

"There's a pool and a game room and some other amenities. Plus the country club is less than half a mile away. Some of the condo people own golf carts and take a little trail over there to play golf or tennis or just have lunch."

"That sounds like fun."

He nodded. "Yeah, it sure does. And the old neighborhood has changed so much over the years, Daphne. You'd hardly know it anymore. None of the old neighbors live there now. Young families have moved in, and they've all remodeled or built additions onto their houses. It kind of makes our old house look like it's stuck in a time warp. But Karen thinks that's a good thing. You never want to have the nicest house in the neighborhood."

There he was talking about this Karen again. "Well, it sounds like you've given it plenty of thought, Dad."

"I sure have. I just had no idea I'd accumulated so much junk over the years. And now that you're here, you might want to go through some things too. I started a pile for you." He stopped for a traffic light, then turned to look at her. "Sorry to break it on you like this, honey. I was going to talk it over with you first, but I know how you're so busy with your big New York City life. Working for *The New York Times*." He grinned. "It's always fun telling my friends about my daughter the famous journalist. Anyway, I didn't think you'd care too much one way or another about our little old house."

She didn't bother to correct his perception of her illustrious career—why burst his bubble? "Well, it sounds like a smart move for you." But even as she said this, she felt incredibly sad. First losing Aunt Dee . . . and then hearing Dad was selling the house she'd grown up in. It all felt so final, like she was being neatly dissected from her childhood and past. And what did she really have to replace it with? As Dad pulled through the intersection, the lump in her throat grew hard as a rock and she dug around her purse for a tissue, quietly wiping the tears slipping down again.

At the next stoplight, Dad looked over at her. "Oh, Daphne, are you missing Aunt Dee too?"

She sniffed and blew her nose. Although that was only one part of her sadness, she had no intention of going into all that right now. "Yes . . . I wish I could've spent more time with her. Sometimes it seems like things change so quickly."

"Well, if it makes you feel any better, Aunt Dee was very proud of you. Do you know she actually got *The New York Times* on the Internet? I think she read almost everything you wrote."

"Seriously?" She tucked the used tissue back into her purse. Her aunt must've been awfully bored.

"She said you were doing a fine job."

Daphne shrugged. "I only write wedding announcements. It's no big deal."

Of course, this only invited her father to sing her praises. She let him go on for a bit before she changed the subject. "Will you miss working at the bank, Dad?"

He laughed. "Just like you'd miss a bad headache after it went away."

"Really? You used to love running the bank."

"Banking has gotten more and more challenging, Daphne. Certainly, the sluggish economy hasn't helped. But honestly, it seems like every time I turn around, we're being inspected or audited or scrutinized. It's like no one trusts banks anymore." He let out a long sigh. "Take it from me, no one will be happier than me when I hit seventy-two and call it quits for good."

"Will you be in your condo by then?"

"I hope to close the deal within a month. I've got some financing lined up in case the house doesn't sell right out of the gate. And Karen says it'll be easier to show the house if I'm not living in it. She has this friend with a business—where they bring fancy new furnishings and lamps and paintings to make the house look like a model home. I think she called it 'staging.' You ever heard of that?"

"Yes, I know exactly what staging is and it really does work to sell houses."

Daphne had never admitted to all the hours she'd spent watching home improvement shows on HGTV. Sometimes she'd spent whole weekends vegetating in front of the little TV in her bedroom. She secretly rationalized it was her way to "vicariously nest" while stuck in the Brooklyn apartment. Especially since she'd learned long ago that Greta wanted everything to remain the same. Besides her ten-by-ten bedroom, Daphne had no control over the depressing decor of the shabby flat, nor did she particularly care to.

Before long, they were in Appleton and Dad was turning onto Huckleberry Lane, entering the neighborhood where Aunt Dee had resided for as long as Daphne could remember. "I always loved this part of town." She admired the maple trees lining the street. "All these old houses are so unique and beautiful." She pointed at a recently painted Victorian. "Look at how they fixed that one up. The plum-colored gingerbread is so perfect against the olive and sage greens. How fun."

"It must've been a bear to paint." Dad shook his head. "Makes my little ranch house look pretty low maintenance."

He pulled up in front of Aunt Dee's Queen Anne Victorian now. "Here we are."

"Oh, it's exactly the same as I remember." She smiled up at the gracious white house with its front bay window and rounded turret on the second floor. Pink roses were already climbing prettily over the arbor that linked the kitchen to the carriage house that served as a single-car garage. Daphne gazed fondly at the overflowing flower beds. "And her yard looks gorgeous. How did she manage that at her age?"

"She hired a yard man about ten years ago. Although she still kept her finger in it—I should say her green thumb. But the yard man did the heavy work. And Dee had been planning to have the house painted again this summer. She'd even been considering using a color besides white this time, if you can imagine."

"I cannot imagine. It's always been white . . . and white just seems right."

He turned off the car's engine and sighed. "I still can't believe she's gone."

"I know." Daphne got out of the car, and as she caught a whiff of the blooming jasmine and lilacs growing along the sides of the house, she was immediately transported to another era . . . a happier time. As much as she loved her dad and the house she'd grown up in on the other side of town, it always felt like coming home when she arrived at Aunt Dee's.

"You sure you don't mind staying here on your own, because I can still carve a place for you at home if you want. Your room's piled high right now, but the guest room isn't really too bad, if you don't mind making a trail through the boxes."

"No, Dad. It's okay, I want be here. It's perfect, really. And it'll allow me to remember Aunt Dee . . . and to say good-bye." She felt the lump again.

He wheeled her bag up the walk and onto the porch, then unlocked the door. "I cleaned things a little," he said as he opened the massive door. "Not that it needed much. Despite her age, your aunt was a good housekeeper. But there were some dirty dishes in the sink . . . some laundry in the hamper . . . that sort of thing. And Mrs. Terwilliger has been seeing to the cats."

"Dee still has Ethel and Lucy?"

"Yes. But they must be getting up in years."

As she looked around for the cats, Daphne remembered when she'd gone with Aunt Dee to get the pair of kittens at the animal shelter. Her aunt had claimed that she was getting them to take Daphne's place since she was going away to college.

"They must be about sixteen years old," she told her dad. And Just then an orange cat, followed by a stripy gray cat came around the corner from the kitchen.

"Hello, girls." Daphne knelt down, waiting as Lucy, the orange cat, cautiously approached her. "I'm sorry for your loss," she said as she scratched Lucy's head. "I know you will miss her." Now Ethel joined her, rubbing against her legs and insisting on being petted too. "What will become of these sweet kitties?" she asked Dad as she stood.

He shrugged. "I don't know. But Green Trees doesn't allow pets." He chuckled. "Which is just one more thing I like about the place. My neighbor's terrier thinks my front yard is his personal restroom. It gets old after a while."

"I suppose I could take the cats back to New York with me. But I doubt they'd like being cooped up in the apartment all day. Plus Greta has a mean old cat that would probably make these sweet girls miserable." She walked through the front room, pausing to open the drapes as well as a window. "Everything looks clean, but I think the house could use some air."

"Good idea." He went to the other side of the room and opened another window to create a breezeway. "We've had good weather this spring—everything is in bloom."

She glanced over to the closed bedroom door, suddenly feeling like an interloper, as if Aunt Dee might suddenly appear and be surprised by this unexpected intrusion. "You say she died in her sleep?"

He rubbed his chin as he studied the tall paneled door. "Yes. Mrs. Terwilliger found her on Tuesday morning. She said she was worried when Dee didn't put her trash out for pick up. She called to remind her it was garbage day, and when Dee didn't answer the phone or the door, Mrs. Terwilliger got worried. She used the key under the flowerpot and let herself in and found Dee in bed. She said Dee looked so peaceful that she thought she was asleep and almost left. But then she realized something wasn't right . . . and that's when she called me."

Daphne pressed her lips together. "I'm glad she died peacefully."

Dad put an arm around her. "Yeah . . . me too."

Daphne got her things settled in the front bedroom upstairs, the one with the turret and the place she'd always claimed as her own as a child. To her relief not much had changed up there either. She ran her hand along the smooth cherry banister as she came down the stairs. How many times had she slid down that?

They took a little tour of the backyard that, like the front, looked better than ever. And then Dad insisted on taking her to dinner. "Anywhere you want to go," he told her as they went around to the front. As they stood by the car, he listed all the restaurant options and many were places she'd never even heard of before.

"Sounds like the town has grown."

"Oh, yeah. We had that building boom shortly after you moved to New York." He unlocked the car. "But it's been a lot quieter these past few years."

"You know what I'd like to do?"

"What?" He opened the car door for her.

"I'd like to walk downtown and eat at Midge's Diner. Just like I used to do with Aunt Dee sometimes."

He grinned as he closed the car door. "Sounds good to me. Let's do it."

Before they left, Mrs. Terwilliger hurried out, expressing her sympathy to Daphne and asking Dad about the upcoming memorial service.

"I've scheduled the church for Monday morning at ten," Dad told her.

"And will you need help with a meal afterward?" she asked hopefully.

"Maybe so. We'll let you know as soon as we get all the details figured out." He tipped his head to Daphne. "She's going to help me get organized."

"And I'll be staying here at Aunt Dee's," Daphne assured her. "So I'll take care of the cats."

Mrs. Terwilliger nodded. "Oh, good. I know they've been lonely. And maybe you can come over for coffee or tea tomorrow." She made a sad smile. "I'm sure going to miss Dee. She was my favorite neighbor."

Daphne reached over and grasped Mrs. Terwilliger's hand. "I'm sorry for your loss too. I know you were a good friend to Aunt Dee."

"And she was a good friend to me . . ." She sniffed, retrieving a hanky from her pocket. "Sometimes I forget . . . we're all getting older . . ."

As Daphne and her dad walked toward town, she admired the old houses along the side street, commenting on how their homeowners were keeping them up. "It looks even nicer than it did when I was a kid. It's like people have realized the value of these sweet, old houses and decided to invest in them."

Downtown looked pretty much the same, although there were a number of new businesses. Midge's Diner had big flower boxes by the door as well as some outdoor seating. But they went inside and Daphne was surprised to see it wasn't very busy, but then it was just a bit past five and a little early for dinner. To her relief everything looked exactly the same inside—only better. From the gleaming black-and-white floor tiles to the chrome-trimmed tables and bar stools to the shiny fire-engine red upholstery—it still looked straight out of the fifties and just as Daphne remembered it. The only thing missing was Midge. But then she'd retired when Daphne was a teen.

"Who owns this place now?" she asked her dad after a waitress seated them in a booth by the front window.

"Ricardo Martoni. Didn't you go to school with him?"

"Sure. I remember Ricardo." Daphne didn't admit that she used to have a huge crush on the handsome boy. Naturally, he probably didn't even know she existed. Why would he? Back then she thought he resembled Charlie Sheen. What did he look like now?

"Speak of the devil." Dad pointed to a dark-haired man coming into the restaurant. "Hello, Ricardo."

Smiling, Ricardo came over to their table and shook Dad's hand. "Good to see you, Mr. Ballinger." He was dressed casually in neat-looking jeans and a blue plaid shirt. And although he didn't look as much like Charlie Sheen as she remembered, he was definitely attractive in that dark Italian way.

"Remember I told you to call me Don." Dad nodded to Daphne. "And you remember my daughter, Daphne, don't you?"

"Oh, he probably doesn't. I was a couple years younger and—"

"Sure I remember you." Ricardo smiled and reached over to shake her hand. "Daphne Ballinger. Your aunt lived a couple houses down from us and you used to spend a lot of time there. In fact, did I just hear she passed away?" His smile faded.

They filled him in and he expressed his sympathy and then, to change to a happier subject, Daphne complimented him on the fine condition of his restaurant. "It looks like you've made a lot of nice improvements. And yet you've kept things the same too."

"Oh yeah, you can't mess with a classic. Even though I've reno-vated, I've tried to stay true to its history. I loved this place when I was growing up."

"Well, it's very nice. It feels like coming home."

"And the food's better than ever," Dad told her. "And healthier too."

"We try to offer a heart-healthy menu." Ricardo released a sheepish smile. "Although we still have to offer the old burgers, shakes, and fries." He lowered his voice. "But we try to use healthier ingredients."

The restaurant was getting busier now and Ricardo excused himself, going over to play host by the front door. Everyone seemed to know everyone by first name here. And as they came in and were seated, the restaurant felt more like a private home having a social gathering than a place of business. It felt comforting.

"That Ricardo is a good businessman," Dad said quietly. "He came in for a loan and I was very impressed. Good head on his shoulders."

"He always seemed smart in school." Daphne opened her menu. "And he's *still single*."

She glanced up. The way Dad said the words *still single* was obviously some kind of insinuation. But not wanting to go there, she turned her attention back to the menu. "How's the meatloaf?"

"It's delicious. Ricardo makes it himself."

Dad was grinning, like he was enjoying a private joke.

"Maybe I'll try it." She closed the menu.

"The meatloaf or Ricardo?" Dad chuckled like this was hilarious.

"Dad." She scolded him, shaking her head.

He made an innocent look. "Hey, you can't blame an old guy for trying. After all, Ricardo's a respectable, hard-working young man. I'm surprised some smart young lady hasn't snatched him up by now." He shrugged. "Besides, you could do worse."

She gave him a tolerant smile. "I guess I should be thankful we don't live in the same town, or I'd probably have to put up with this all the time."

His lower lip protruded as if her words had cut him deeply, although she knew better. She and her dad had always enjoyed a little good-natured teasing—especially when it came to her marital status. "Somebody's got to look out for your interests," he said. "You heard Mrs. Terwilliger's insinuation. None of us are getting any younger. And just so you know, some of us are hoping to get some grandchildren before he's too old to enjoy them or remember their names."

Daphne suppressed the childish urge to smack her father over the head with her menu. But she didn't want to create a spectacle or disrupt their fellow diners. Sometimes, just sometimes, she was tempted to enroll her father in a sensitivity training seminar—the remedial class!

Chapter 4

It was a lot to take on, but Daphne insisted on hosting a luncheon in the house following the funeral service. So many friends and neighbors and family members had offered to bring food, and it just seemed fitting to celebrate Aunt Dee's life in the home she had loved. Of course, Daphne hadn't realized what a chore it would be to get everything organized and ready for so many guests.

"That was a lovely service," Aunt Louisa said to Daphne as they strolled through the backyard, admiring the flower beds together. "And a very nice luncheon too." Louisa Ballinger, in her late eighties, was Aunt Dee's sister-in-law. She'd been residing in an assisted-living facility since her husband, Uncle Dennis, had passed away several years ago.

But their two children, Martin and Marlene, as well as their spouses and children and their children's spouses and grandchildren—numbering more than twenty—had all shown up to show their respect to Aunt Dee. Combined with friends and neighbors, Daphne estimated there were more than a hundred coming and going through the house throughout the afternoon. Still, it was worth the effort. Daphne imagined her aunt smiling down on all the people milling about, visiting, reminiscing, and enjoying a big reunion in her honor.

After several hours, and after all the neighbors and friends had gone their separate ways, Daphne was a bit surprised to see all the family members seemed to be lingering. It was touching to think that they loved Aunt Dee so much that they didn't want to leave, but some of the small children seemed to be getting tired—and getting into things. Daphne had already hidden the terrorized Ethel and Lucy in an upstairs bedroom. And now some of her cousins' older kids were taking a toll on the flowers as they improvised a game of soccer in the backyard.

"Why are they staying so long?" Daphne whispered to her dad as they cleaned up in the kitchen.

"Oh, didn't I tell you?"

"Tell me?" She rinsed a platter and set it in the dishwasher.

"Dee's attorney is coming at four."

Daphne looked at the kitchen clock. "Well, it's nearly four now. What is the attorney going to do?"

"The reading of the will."

"Oh . . ." Daphne closed the dishwasher. "And everyone is staying for it?"

"Yes." He frowned. "Martin asked that it be read with everyone present."

"I see . . ." Martin was Louisa's oldest son, and although he was an attorney, he had not been Aunt Dee's attorney. Daphne knew this because she'd heard him complaining about it earlier.

"Did you notice that Ricardo Martoni and his mother came by to pay their respects?" Dad hung up a dish towel.

"Yes. I had a nice little chat with Maria. I didn't realize she was widowed." She elbowed her Dad in a teasing way. "Pretty good-looking too for being in her midsixties. Maybe you should give her a call."

Dad looked embarrassed. "Well, you did meet Karen, didn't you? I thought I saw you two talking."

"Oh?" She tilted her head to one side. "Does that mean you and Karen are getting serious?"

Unless she was mistaken, her dad was blushing.

"Sorry. It's really none of my business."

He nodded. "But I'm curious . . . what did you think of her?"

Daphne thought about the energetic blonde Realtor who had chatted with enthusiasm about what kind of price Aunt Dee's house might fetch in today's market. "Sure, I liked her. She seems intelligent and motivated and interesting."

Dad smiled. "Yes, she is, isn't she?"

"Hello?" called a male voice. "Don, are you in there?"

Dad called back, and now a man wearing a dark gray suit came into the kitchen. He had thick, dark hair with a speckling of gray. "Oh, you must be Daphne." He reached out for her hand, firmly shaking it. "I'm Jake McPheeters."

"Aunt Dee's attorney," Dad explained.

"I would know you anywhere." Jake released her hand.

"Really?" She was surprised.

"Absolutely. Dee told me you looked like Lucille Ball in her younger years. And I must agree with her."

Daphne felt her own cheeks flushing now. "Well, that's flattering, but I don't know . . ."

"Speaking of that, how are Lucy and Ethel faring?"

"They're okay," she told him. "I tucked them into a quiet bedroom for safekeeping."

"So, want to round up the relatives?" Jake held up his briefcase. "This really shouldn't take long."

"Sure." Dad nodded. "I'll go tell everyone to gather in the front room."

"You ready for this?" Jake asked Daphne.

"Sure." She turned on the dishwasher, then gave the counter a swipe. "Let's get it over with."

Before long, all of the adults and many of the children were crowded into the front room. Some were sitting on chairs, some on the floor, and a few of the younger ones were standing. Jake went over to the foot of the staircase. He had a buttoned-down look, like he belonged in Manhattan or *GQ*. He opened his briefcase, slid out a file, and removed a single piece of paper.

"As I just told Don and Daphne in the kitchen, this shouldn't take long. In fact, I wouldn't have bothered to gather everyone together like this, but Don told me it was the family's request." He held up the page. "As you can see there's not much to read. And interestingly, as much as Daphne Ballinger loved words and writing, her last will and testament is surprisingly brief and succinct."

He cleared his throat and began to read the traditional beginning of a will, stating Aunt Dee's full name and that she was of sound mind . . . but Daphne's mind wandered as she noticed one of her second or third cousins on the other side of the room. The mischievous boy was stripping the lower leaves off of Aunt Dee's beloved philodendron plant and piling the big glossy leaves on the floor in front of him like he intended to make a campfire. Why didn't someone stop him?

"What on earth?" a woman spoke sharply, and Daphne looked up

from the naughty boy and over to where Marlene and her husband were sitting on the sofa next to Aunt Louisa. They all looked upset.

"How can she do that?" Marlene demanded. "It's not fair."

"Dee expected she'd be met with some resistance. But I assure you, we've written it all up very tightly."

"You're saying that *everything* goes to Daphne?" Martin asked him. "Did I hear you correctly?"

"Everything." Jake looked at Daphne. "You and I can go over the other details of her will later . . . privately."

A shockwave ran through Daphne. What had she missed?

"But how could she do that?" one of the other cousins asked. "We were all as much related to Aunt Dee as Daphne was—why does Daphne get everything?"

"Because *that* is what Dee wanted." Jake slid the paper back into the file folder and back into his briefcase.

"But what about this house?" another cousin said. "Wasn't it in the family? Didn't Aunt Dee inherit it from our grandparents? Shouldn't it be shared equally with all the descendants?"

"Dee purchased this house herself," Dad firmly told them. "Our parents' house was on the other side of town—the three children, Dennis and Daphne and me, we all inherited equal thirds of that house when Mother passed away." He looked at Aunt Louisa. "Surely you remember that? You and Dennis used your portion to go to Europe. Remember?"

Aunt Louisa looked confused. "I . . . I don't really recall."

"Anyway, it wouldn't matter where Dee's money came from," Jake told them. "This house and all of Dee Ballinger's property belonged to her and to her alone. And now it will all belong to Daphne."

"But that's so unfair," someone else said.

Jake came over to Daphne. "Care to make an exit with me?" he said quietly.

"But I should—"

"Go ahead, Daphne," Dad said urgently. "I'll take care of things here. I'll lock up."

"Come on." Jake took her by the arm. "Let's get out of here."

"I don't get this," someone said loud enough for Daphne to hear as Jake led her to the front door. "Daphne moves away from Appleton and hardly ever comes back. Meanwhile I came to visit Aunt Dee at least once a month and now Daphne gets everything."

"It's not fair," someone said again.

Jake firmly closed the door. "My car's down the street. I was afraid it would go like this."

"But I don't understand." She looked over her shoulder. "Just moments ago we were all friends and everyone was so nice and—"

"It's always like this. Following a funeral, families are congenial and pleasant—and then the will is read and suddenly they all turn against each other." He shook his head as he opened the door to a tan SUV. "It's sad."

She slid onto the leather seat, trying to comprehend what had just transpired. Aunt Dee had left her house to her? It was very sweet . . . but why didn't she just leave it to all the cousins? Really, that would've been more fair.

"How about if we get coffee?" he said as he drove away.

"Sure." She studied his handsome profile, trying to determine his age. Although his thick, dark hair was peppered with gray, she didn't think he could be much over forty.

"And I'll explain it all to you."

Before long they were seated at the Red River Coffee Company.

She'd never even seen this place before, but with its recycled wood floors, retro collectibles, and old-fashioned overstuffed furnishings, she found it cozy and charming. With her hand wrapped around her mug of latte, she asked Jake to explain her aunt's thinking.

"Obviously, Dee loved you, Daphne. You were her namesake . . . and something more."

"Something more?"

Jake began to tell her the story of Dee as a young woman in college more than seventy years ago. "As you can imagine not too many women continued their education back in the forties. But Dee was a smart, determined woman."

"Yes, I know about all that. Aunt Dee told me—"

"You don't know all of it, Daphne. Dee had a secret." He chuckled. "In fact, she had a lot of secrets."

"What do you mean?"

"Dee became pregnant in her second year at the university."

"Really?" Daphne blinked. "Aunt Dee has a child?"

"Yes. Your father."

"Dad?" Daphne tried to wrap her head around this. "But Aunt Dee was his sister . . ."

"Yes, that's what Dee's parents led everyone to believe. I'm not even sure of all the details, but according to Dee, her parents relocated to Appleton shortly after your dad was born. Daphne returned to college and her parents raised your father as their son. It was just simpler for everyone that way."

Daphne could partially understand this. It made sense on a number of levels. "That would explain the age gap between Aunt Dee and Dad."

"And why Dee favored you. You're her granddaughter."

"Does Dad know about this?"

He shook his head. "Dee wasn't sure she wanted him to know. She was worried that he'd feel disappointed in her . . . or that his life was a lie. She didn't want to hurt him. But she seemed to feel that you would understand."

Daphne pressed her lips together, trying to imagine how it must've been for Aunt Dee, knowing that Dad was really her son, Daphne was her granddaughter, and yet for her entire life, she played that she was only a sister and a spinster aunt.

"This is a lot to take in," Daphne admitted. "But in hindsight, it all adds up. I could always tell that Aunt Dee favored Dad over Uncle Dennis. And I was closer to her than my cousins. I suppose that's why." She smiled. "It's actually sort of cool to think that Aunt Dee was really my grandma. No wonder we were so close." Her smile faded. "I sure wish the rest of the family knew about her secret. . . . It might make this whole thing easier."

"I suppose it's up to you whether you disclose this or not. I know Dee wasn't eager to make her past public. But she has entrusted all her secrets to you."

"If my cousins knew Dee was my grandmother, they might not be so angry at me for inheriting everything."

"Well, if it's any comfort, once they recover from the surprise of not getting a piece of the pie, they will probably return to normal . . . in time. Unless your lawyer cousin Martin tries to contest the will. Dee was worried he might."

"I wouldn't be surprised."

"It'll be a waste of his time. Trust me, this will is airtight."

She took a slow sip of coffee. "So that wonderful house really belongs to me." She shook her head. "Wow."

"It's actually a bit more involved than that."

"What do you mean?" She set her cup down.

"Well, we don't have to go over everything today. I mean, I'd understand if you're feeling overwhelmed. It's a lot to take in and I'm not sure how you'll react to the rest of the news. So I'm glad to meet with you another time to go over—"

"No, I think I'd like to hear it all today. If you don't mind." She forced a smile. "Did Aunt Dee have a pile of debt? Unpaid taxes? Some other skeletons in the closet?"

"Not exactly." He offered an uneasy smile. "It's just that your inheritance has some strings attached. Some very specific strings."

"What kind of strings?"

He pulled something more bulky out of his briefcase now. "It's all written up in legal language, but if you like I can explain it in plain English first. And then you can read through the whole will at your leisure."

"Yes please, do give me the condensed version." She nodded eagerly. "I think my brain is a little fuzzy after all the funeral preparations and decisions for the burial service and preparing the luncheon. Keep it simple."

"Okay." He held up one finger. "First of all, you have to be willing to take over Dee's advice column."

"Advice column?" She frowned. "You mean she wrote something for the local paper?"

"Yes, as a matter of fact, it does run in the local paper." He grinned. "As well as the paper you work for."

"*The New York Times?*"

"Have you ever read *Dear Daphne?*"

"*Dear Daphne?*" She felt her eyes getting large. "Seriously?"

He nodded. "Yep."

"Are you saying that Aunt Dee—I mean, my grandmother—was Daphne Delacorte? She wrote—*Dear Daphne?*" She stared at him in wonder.

"Uh-huh. Dee started writing it back during World War II. So many couples were in tricky relationships, men overseas, women working like men at home, hasty marriages—it was a perfect setup for an advice column. And Dee had a knack for coming up with good answers. Her column was a hit and started getting picked up by other papers. It became syndicated in the fifties, and she's been writing it ever since. Although I've notified the papers that she's on hiatus, so they will be running some of her old pieces for the next couple of weeks."

Daphne put a hand to her cheek. "I cannot believe it. I've always loved that column. My best friend in New York used to give me a bad time for liking it so much. She thought it was hopelessly old-fashioned. Sometimes she'd tease me, saying that since my name was Daphne and I worked for the newspaper and was a little old-fashioned myself, that I should take over the column."

"Interesting." His dark eyes glimmered with amusement.

"Why is that interesting?"

"Because Dee wants you to quit your job in New York and write her column."

Daphne frowned. "You're kidding?"

"No. Dee was very loyal to her readers. She wanted the column to live on after she was gone. She felt that you have what it takes to do it."

"I don't know . . ."

"I'm sure you think it was presumptuous of her. The truth is, I actually tried to talk her out of it. But she wouldn't hear of it. Your grandmother had an iron will."

Daphne nodded. "Yes. I know once she made up her mind about something . . . you couldn't talk her out of it."

"So what do you think? Are you amenable to this?"

"I'm curious . . . what if I'm not?"

He grimly shook his head. "Then Dee's entire estate will go into a trust fund for the Cat House."

"The *Cat House*?"

"The pet shelter where she adopted Lucy and Ethel. She's been a contributor to them ever since."

"Oh yes, I remember the Cat House now. Aunt Dee really liked that they never euthanized cats. And they ran free spay and neuter clinics for impoverished families. I guess it's not surprising she would remember them in her will." Daphne hated to imagine how her relatives would've reacted if all of Aunt Dee's estate had been left to the Cat House. Martin would probably claim that Aunt Dee was senile.

"So what do you think about the first stipulation?"

She shrugged. "Well, I am a writer . . . and I wouldn't mind trying to write *Dear Daphne*." She frowned. "But what if I'm no good at it? Or the readers hate me? And the newspapers cancel and—"

"She only expected you to try, Daphne. And to do your best." He smiled. "She believed in you. She assured me you could do it."

"I'll try."

His cell phone rang. "Excuse me, I promised to take this call."

She nodded and, leaning back with her now-lukewarm coffee, attempted to replay the strange things she'd just heard about Aunt Dee . . . a.k.a. Grandma Dee as well as the Daphne Delacorte of *Dear Daphne*. It was all rather mind-blowing.

She tried not to eavesdrop on Jake's conversation, which was difficult. But if he didn't want to be overheard, he should've left the table. As it was, she could tell he was talking to someone named Jenna, and based on what she was hearing, she suspected Jenna was his "significant other" and that she was worried that Jake was going to be late for something this evening.

Was Jenna his wife? Although he had no wedding ring and for some reason, perhaps just hopeful thinking, she had assumed he was unmarried. Perhaps Jenna was a fiancée or girlfriend. Perhaps it was none of her business.

Chapter 5

After he hung up, Jake apologized for the interruption but offered no explanation for who Jenna was. And really, why should he? And why should she care?

"Do you want to finish up our condensed version of your grandmother's will?"

"If you have time." She glanced at her watch to see that it was getting close to six. "Maybe you need to be home for dinner."

"I think we can wrap this up in about five minutes. There are only two other conditions." He held up two fingers. "Which brings us to the second one. Fortunately, it's fairly straightforward. Dee wanted you to live in her house and take care of Lucy and Ethel for the rest of their natural lives. After that, you are free to sell the house if you want."

"That's not too much to ask."

"Really?" He looked surprised. "You don't mind moving back to Appleton? I thought you adored living in New York. That's what Dee told me."

"I used to . . . but I actually think I'm ready for a change. Just being here these past few days has made me appreciate Appleton in a brand new way." She sighed. "You know, I think I was secretly wishing for this."

He released a relieved smile. "This is going better than I expected."

"So, is that it? Anymore strings?"

"Just one more." He seemed to grimace. "However, this one might be problematic."

"What?"

"And believe me, I *really* tried to talk Dee out of this one. We went around and around for quite some time because I thought it unreasonable. But that iron will of hers had kicked in and she wouldn't back down."

"What?"

"I honestly hate to tell you."

"What is it?" Daphne pressed. "Just get it over with—like ripping off a bandage."

He nodded grimly. "Dee stipulated that within one year of signing the agreement to inherit her entire estate, you must get married. Or else you will lose her house and her column and—"

"What?" Daphne felt angry now. "Is that even legal?"

He sighed. "It was *her* estate, Daphne. She could do with it as she pleased. This was what she wanted."

"But why?" Daphne hit the table. "Why would she do something like that? It seems heartless. And mean."

"More than anything Dee wanted you to be happy. She hoped you would fall in love and get married, within her lifetime."

"Oh . . ." Daphne remembered the conversations she'd had with

Aunt Dee about Ryan . . . back when Daphne was still oblivious and in love. Aunt Dee had been so thrilled for her. She'd even talked about hosting a wedding in her house, saying how lovely the roses would look in June.

Daphne had never told her the truth, that Ryan was married. In fact, she'd never really told her about the breakup. She didn't want to disappoint her. But over the years, she simply assumed that Aunt Dee would figure things out. After all, Daphne never mentioned Ryan's name anymore. She never brought him home for a holiday. Wouldn't it have been obvious?

"For some reason Dee was convinced that you would be happiest if you were married. I suppose this was just her way of helping you."

"So that's it? What I have to do to remain in her house?" Daphne bit her lip. This was so ridiculous. Why was she even having this conversation? It was impossible. "Well, I'm sorry, but that's asking too much. Way too much."

"I know." He nodded. "I agree."

"How can I promise such a thing? It would be disingenuous on my part." She twisted the napkin between her fingers. "And how could she even ask it of me?"

"I'm sure it's because she regretted never marrying. She confided to me it was the one thing about her life she never fully resolved herself to. She said she had pretended to be content in her singlehood, but if she could've done it again differently, she would have. And she was afraid you were going to make the same mistakes that she made."

"But she seemed truly happy to me. She was in control of her life. She lived it on her own terms."

"Part of her act, I'm sure. And as she got older . . . and she saw you getting older—not that you're old." He smiled. "But Dee worried that she'd set you a bad example. Just last Christmas, she confided to me that she always wished she'd married her college love—the father of her child."

"Oh . . ." Daphne sighed.

He straightened the stack of papers on the table. "Dee was the most eccentric client I ever had. And I'm sure going to miss her. But I promised to do all I could to ensure that you inherit her estate, Daphne. That's what she wanted."

"Well, as much as I'd love to live in her house . . . and to care for the cats . . . and even write the advice column, it feels impossible. Seriously, how can she expect me to get married within a year? I don't even have a boyfriend."

"You don't?"

"No. I don't." She narrowed her eyes.

"Dee seemed to think you did. She thought you'd been involved with the same man for quite some time. She hoped this would encourage you to tie the knot."

"Well, she was wrong. I haven't been in a serious relationship for years. I might not have told her about the breakup, but it was only because I didn't want to worry her."

"Maybe if she'd known about your current dating status, you know before she died, maybe she would've left that part out." He shrugged. "Or maybe not. As I said, her mind seemed to be made up. Regardless, it doesn't change anything."

"So when did she actually make this will?"

His brow creased. "Originally? Oh, about seven years ago, as I recall. We made a few revisions here and there. Don't worry, it's all still very official."

"And if I *don't* marry?" Daphne set the twisted napkin down. "It all goes to the Cat House?"

He nodded.

"Oh, those lucky kitties."

"But you have a whole year, Daphne. You can live in her house and write her column . . . and who knows what might happen a year from now?" He smiled. "You're an attractive, intelligent woman. What guy wouldn't be happy to snag you?"

She rolled her eyes. "You sound like my dad now. Trying to get me married off."

"Thanks. I'll take that as a compliment."

The wheels were turning in her brain. Or maybe it was the caffeine making her mind spin. "So, let me play devil's advocate. Say I found someone . . . someone I could pretend to love, someone who I could pay to pretend to love me . . . and what if I married this person just to inherit the estate—then divorced him afterward?" Even as she said this, she knew it went against everything she believed. She couldn't do it to Aunt Dee or to herself.

"Well, as you read the will in its entirety, which I encourage you to do as soon as possible, you'll see everything is clearly stated. You must legitimately fall in love and marry. And she made me promise to hold you to it. And even though I feel it's a bit unfair to you, I will honor my promise to her."

She let out a long sigh. "Are there any other strings?"

"As a matter of fact, there is a little something you should know about. Not exactly a string. Just a rather interesting ingredient of Dee's rather interesting estate."

"What?" She braced herself.

"Have you ever heard of Penelope Poindexter?"

She frowned, trying to remember why the name was familiar. "It rings a bell, but I have no idea why."

"Penelope Poindexter is a certain romance writer who became popular during the sixties and remained popular into the midnineties. She wrote about a couple dozen books."

"Now that you mention it, I do recall that name. I'm sure I've seen her books in grocery stores. And probably even in Aunt Dee's house. As I recall, she liked reading those pulpy bodice-ripper sorts of paperbacks. I suppose it was how she took a break from all that technical writing she did."

"Did you ever read any Poindexter books?"

Daphne wrinkled her nose. "No, of course not, never. As a child I preferred the classics. Now I prefer mysteries. Penelope Poindexter was definitely not my cup of tea."

"Well, Penelope Poindexter was a pseudonym."

"Yes, it rather sounds like a pen name."

"A pen name for Dee Ballinger."

Daphne's jaw dropped, but she was too stunned to speak.

He just nodded. "Yep, you heard me right."

"Seriously? You're saying Aunt Dee wrote steamy romance books?"

He chuckled. "Yep."

"Those sleazy-looking books with bare-chested pirates and busty maidens in distress, those were written by my aunt—I mean my grandmother?"

"That's right."

"But I don't understand." Her voice grew weak, almost like a little girl. "I thought she wrote textbooks or instruction manuals or something respectable . . . and boring."

"Everyone thought that."

"So she wrote *Dear Daphne* but kept that a secret . . . and she wrote romance novels and kept them secret . . . she was really my grandmother, but she kept that secret." Daphne put a hand to her forehead—this was all starting to make her head throb.

"Dee concealed her identity at the recommendation of the newspaper back in the forties. This is a small town and the editor wanted local folks to feel comfortable writing to an anonymous Daphne. And she did a fabulous job of keeping it all under wraps. No one has ever guessed she was Daphne Delacorte of *Dear Daphne*. Then when Dee contracted her first romance novel back in the sixties, she was concerned about how friends and family would react if this became commonly known. Again, it was the small town concern. And to be fair, consider your own reaction just now. Multiply that times the population of Appleton."

"I suppose that makes sense."

"And as you can imagine, it was important to Dee that you continue to protect her anonymity. As well as your own."

"I don't think that will be a problem." Daphne couldn't imagine wanting to tell anyone about the smutty Poindexter books. "Although there's my dad . . . it seems a little unfair to leave him in the dark. Do you really think I should continue keeping all this from him too?"

"I guess that's up to you. I'm sure you wouldn't do anything to disrespect Dee's memory. She felt certain you would know how to handle all this."

"I wish I had as much confidence . . ."

"And there's one more thing."

A rush of panic blazed through her. What more could he possibly dump on her? Perhaps Aunt Dee had been a double agent working for the CIA.

"You should know that Dee's estate consists of more than just her house and her cats and the advice column." He laid a bulky manila envelope in front of her now. "It's all summarized in here, statements and bank records. You see, Dee still gets royalties on some of her books and they've actually been picking up with the recent e-book craze."

"Oh . . ." Daphne was relieved that Aunt Dee hadn't been involved in international espionage. She slid the other papers into the envelope. She would have lots of reading to do tonight.

"Your grandmother left you a fairly hefty inheritance."

Daphne sighed. "You mean *if* I should marry? Otherwise the Cat House will be building some very deluxe kitty suites. Or maybe they can outfit their cats in diamond-studded collars. Perhaps install an indoor pool, although most cats don't go in much for swimming."

He looked slightly amused as he held his palms up in a helpless gesture. "I'm sorry there's nothing I can do to change that. I suppose, as they say, therein lies the rub."

Daphne picked up the thick envelope, still trying to absorb all the information Jake had disclosed. Aunt Dee was not her aunt but her grandmother, as well as Daphne Delacorte, *and* she wrote steamy romance books? It felt crazy. Certifiably nuts. But the wildest part of all of this was the expectation that Daphne could fall in love and get married within a year's time. Only a crazed romance writer could possibly conjure up such a twisted plot.

Jake's brow creased as he looked at his watch.

"I'm sorry to keep you so long." Daphne stood. "I know you've got something you need to do this evening."

"It's all right." He closed his briefcase and stood. Smiling, he straightened his tie. "I knew this was going to take some time. It's a lot to take in."

"Well, I appreciate you taking the time to explain things." She forced a stiff smile. "And I appreciate that you were a friend to Aunt Dee . . . I mean, my grandmother." She started for the door, still feeling a bit like she'd just gone through the looking glass.

"And if you have any questions about anything in that packet, feel free to call," he told her as they went outside. "My business card is in there. After you've had a chance to read everything, I have some papers for you to sign."

She thanked him, but as he opened the car door for her, she waved her hand. "No, thanks. I can walk home. You go do whatever it is you need to do."

"You're sure?"

She nodded. "A walk might help clear my head."

His face broke into a relieved smile. "Great. Jenna will appreciate that."

She waved and said good-bye, and with the oversized envelope under her arm, she continued on down Main Street. She knew it was none of her business, but she was mildly curious as to who Jenna was—wife, girlfriend, fiancée? But more than that she was curious as to how she would present this strange news to her father. Because he had a right to know. He would want to know. And besides, she needed someone to talk to.

She was ready to call him and ask if he'd like to have dinner with her, but realized that in her haste to exit Aunt Dee's house, before her relatives strung up a rope to lynch the unexpected heiress, she hadn't thought to grab her purse.

She walked past several businesses that were closed for the day. But when she came to Midge's Diner and delicious smells wafted her way, she realized that she'd barely eaten today. So caught up in getting things ready and playing hostess, she hardly touched the food.

If she had her purse, she'd be tempted to go into Midge's Diner and order takeout, but that seemed extravagant in light of the fridge full of food at home. Of course, the irony of her being concerned about extravagance in light of Aunt Dee's generosity—at least for the year anyway—did not escape her. Perhaps her best way to get even with an eccentric aunt (a.k.a. grandmother) would be to live it up for the next twelve months. She could travel the world, buy a new wardrobe, get herself a Porsche, dine on caviar and champagne for breakfast, rent a yacht. . . . However, she knew herself well enough to know she wouldn't do any of these things.

Aunt Dee had her pegged. She must've known that Daphne's careful, conservative nature would play right into her diabolical plan. Daphne would not waste a penny of Aunt Dee's money. She would take excellent care of her cats. She would do her best to continue the advice column.

As for marriage . . . well she had 365 days to figure that out. And perhaps it was true that miracles still happened. God was capable of doing anything—but would he want to help her find a husband in order to keep a house? She wasn't sure.

The only thing she felt certain about was that it would take a miracle to satisfy the conditions of Aunt Dee's will.

Chapter 6

Daphne was relieved to see Dad's sedan was still parked in Aunt Dee's driveway but dismayed to see that a shiny yellow Mustang convertible, with its top down, was now parked behind it. Hopefully it didn't belong to one of her irate relatives, lingering on to give her a piece of their mind. It wouldn't surprise her if Martin owned a showy car like that.

"Hello?" she called as she entered the house. "Dad, are you still here?"

"Back here." He stuck his head out of the kitchen. "I didn't see a car drive up. Didn't Jake drive you home?"

"No, he had to meet someone named Jenna."

"Oh, that's his daughter. She's a real sweetheart." Dad stepped aside as she came into the kitchen. "And Jake's a devoted dad."

Daphne looked around to see that the countertops and stove and even the deep white sink was sparkling. "You finished cleaning up for me?"

"Last load's in there." Dad pointed at the dishwasher.

"But I could've done it."

"It's okay. Karen helped me."

Karen joined them. "This is such a fabulous kitchen," she told Daphne. "Especially considering the age of this house. Your aunt put a lot of money into top-of-the-line appliances and finishes. It's all just stellar. And yet she never compromised the integrity of the house." She patted the Wolf gas stove. "This baby alone will fetch you top dollar if you decide to list."

"Karen says the timing is good to sell a house like this. There aren't many on the market right now," Dad told her. "I let her look around and she was impressed with how well Dee maintained the place."

"Yes," Karen said eagerly. "It wouldn't take much to get this place ready for an open house. Just thinning out some personal things. And I have a gal who could do that for you. But right now the yard and flower beds look fabulous. And summer buyers are just starting to shop."

"I told Karen you planned to head back to New York on Wednesday," Dad said. "That's when your flight's booked, right?"

Daphne set the big envelope down on the pine kitchen table, then sat on one of the wooden chairs, letting out a long, weary sigh. "It seems my plans have changed."

"Really?" Dad hung up the dish towel, then came over to peer curiously at her. "Are you okay, honey? You look tired."

She nodded. "I think I am tired."

"Maybe we should let her have some time to herself," Karen said quietly to Dad. "And don't forget, Gene and Marsha are probably already there."

"We have a standing date for bridge at the country club," Dad explained. "Monday nights at seven. But I can cancel if—"

"No," Daphne said. "Karen's right. I am tired and I could use some time to myself. I have a lot to think over right now."

"But you said your plans have changed? Does that mean you're going to stick around awhile longer? To figure out what you'll do with Dee's estate?"

"Yes." She nodded. "I will definitely be around." She forced a smile. "So, no worries, Dad. You and I will have plenty of time to talk later. Go ahead and meet your friends. I think I'll just grab a bite to eat, then do some reading and go to bed. Thanks for cleaning up."

"All right." Dad looked a little uncertain, but Karen nudged him, pointing out that they were already late. And without further ado they left. Daphne watched out the kitchen window as Karen got into her flashy Mustang, backed up quickly and confidently out of the driveway, and then drove at what seemed a fast speed for this neighborhood. Dad followed along at a distance and, predictably, at a much slower speed. Like the tortoise and the hare.

It wasn't that Daphne didn't like Karen. Except that she just didn't. But, more than that, she didn't quite trust the fiftysomething fast-talking blonde. Daphne might be wrong, but it seemed that Karen's energy was linked with opportunity. And Daphne couldn't help but wonder if the vivacious Realtor would've befriended Dad if there hadn't been some real estate involved.

Normally Daphne liked to believe the best in people and she didn't like to pass judgment on anyone. But this was her down-to-earth dad—the slow-moving, good-hearted Donald Ballinger. The rules all changed on the home turf.

Daphne kicked off her pumps and peeled off her black suit jacket, but before she started raiding the fridge, she remembered the girls. "Lucy," she called, "Ethel, where are you?"

She realized they must still be locked in the spare bedroom, so she went up to rescue them. But as she went up the stairs, running her hand along the smooth cherry banister, it began to sink in . . . this could all be hers. If only.

"There you are," she said as she opened the door and the two cats shot out. "Sorry about that, girls." She went in and fetched the litter box and water dish, carried them downstairs, then set them back into place in the laundry room, where the cats were now milling hungrily around their food bowls. She knew the girls were agitated from all the noise and activity today . . . and for all she knew, they could be grieving for their mistress too.

After feeding them, she filled herself a plate of leftovers and zapped it in the microwave. Then she sat down at the kitchen table and, watching out the window, she slowly ate. How many times had Aunt Dee sat here doing this same thing? Daphne had decided to continue calling her Aunt Dee. It was just too hard to wrap her head around calling her "grandmother."

Grandma had been the wrinkled white-haired woman who lived in a nursing home just outside of town. She'd been placed there shortly after Grandpa died. Dad had taken Daphne to see Grandma occasionally, but all Daphne remembered was the pungent aroma of overcooked vegetables combined with other smells she didn't care to think about and that Grandma could never remember her name. She couldn't even remember Dad's name. Daphne later learned that the poor old woman had dementia. Perhaps even Alzheimer's, although Daphne didn't recall anyone using that term back then.

Of course, Daphne wasn't quite seven when Grandma died. And after having lost her own mother just two years earlier, Daphne had drawn the childhood conclusion that all adults would die before long. She expected that Dad and Aunt Dee wouldn't be around for long either. As a result she lived in an almost-constant state of anxiety and fear as a child. And it didn't get much better as she grew older. She still had a fear of her loved ones leaving her.

It was about three years after her breakup with Ryan that Daphne began seeing a therapist. With Sylvia's help Daphne had made great strides, working her way through this phobia. Sylvia had shone the initial spotlight on Daphne's own personal fear of dying young . . . like her mother. They talked things through and Sylvia helped Daphne to incorporate some positive thinking into her life, utilizing everything from uplifting and lighthearted music, to biofeedback CDs before bedtime, to meditative prayer and memorizing favorite Scriptures. All of it had helped. And for the most part Daphne felt perfectly normal. Except for when she didn't. Like now.

Daphne sat there, poking at her warmed-over chicken-and-broccoli casserole, listlessly staring out the window and feeling completely out of sync with the world. Or perhaps she was simply out of sync with Appleton. Really, how would she ever fit in here?

She imagined Dad and Karen happily playing cards at the country club with their friends Gene and Marsha. She imagined Jake enjoying time with his daughter, Jenna, and presumably his wife as well. Then she imagined Ricardo Martoni cheerfully greeting patrons at his restaurant, where everyone seemed to know everyone. Even when she imagined her disgruntled relatives, it seemed they all had other family members to go home with. Thomas Wolfe was probably right. "You can't go back home."

Daphne considered New York now. Wasn't that supposed to be her home? At least that's where her return address had been listed for more than a dozen years. But when she thought of her dead-end job as Amelia's grunt-girl, or her dismal apartment in Brooklyn, or her preoccupied roommates, or even her pregnant best friend, who was suddenly ready to build her nest in the suburbs, it didn't feel very welcoming. Seriously, who wanted to go "back home" to that? Maybe she didn't fit in anywhere.

A lump grew in her throat as she pushed the barely touched plate from her. She jumped in surprise as Lucy gracefully leaped onto her lap and started purring loudly. Meanwhile, down under the table, Ethel was rubbing against Daphne's bare legs. It was as if the cats wanted to comfort her. Or maybe they just missed human companionship. Or more likely, they were grateful she'd fed them. Whatever it was, it made her feel better.

As she petted the cats, talking to them like old friends, she wondered if she was destined to become just like Aunt Dee. Maybe it was something woven into the depths of her DNA. And really, was it such a bad sort of life? Alone and independent, coming and going as she pleased. Even if she turned out to be a spinster too, what was wrong with living out the last of her days in this sweet old house with—?

"Wait a doggone minute!" She eased Lucy from her lap and stood. "I can't even do *that*." Thanks to Aunt Dee's airtight will, Daphne would be tossed out of this sweet old house just a year from now. Lucy and Ethel would be sent to the Cat House, where they would surely live in high feline style. And then Daphne would do what? Return to New York to beg for her job back? Go live with her father in the old folks' condo units? Become a thirty-four-year-old bag lady in Appleton?

"Oh, don't be such a silly goose." She scraped the food from her plate into the garbage disposal. "You're overdramatizing again. What would Sylvia say?" As she rinsed the plate, Daphne could just hear Sylvia. She'd be telling Daphne to make the most of this. She would say something like, "Enjoy this year in Appleton. See it as God's way of giving you a much-needed vacation. Take time to figure out what you want to do next in your life. No one has a guarantee of what tomorrow will bring—you only have today. Why not live it to the fullest?"

Feeling slightly heartened from her make-believe pep talk, Daphne considered poking around and exploring the house, but it was such a lovely evening outside, she decided to do something far bolder. But first she changed her clothes, replacing the serious black business suit for khaki pants, loafers, and a mossy green cashmere sweater set. The look wasn't as fun and lighthearted as she wished, but it was what she had packed for casual wear and it would have to do.

Next she grabbed her purse and went to the laundry room, where she opened the little door that concealed the spot where Aunt Dee hung all her spare keys on little brass hooks. And there, sure enough, was what Daphne knew was the old car key. Hopefully the old car that went along with it was still here. She removed the key marked *carriage house*, a.k.a. the garage, and went outside and unlocked the double doors, letting them swing open to expose just what she hoped to find.

Shrouded in old sheets with faded red roses printed on them was the shape of a classic Corvette. Daphne's heart beat a little faster as she slid the sheets off to reveal the gorgeous convertible. Using the wadded-up sheets, she dusted the car, starting with the ivory-colored convertible roof to the sleek, long hood that still reminded Daphne of a shiny new Lincoln penny. Aunt Dee had purchased this car straight from the factory in 1955, long before Daphne was even born.

"A very limited number of copper-colored cars were produced," Aunt Dee had told Daphne years ago. "So Bonnie is very special." Daphne had thought nothing was strange about naming a car Bonnie. And looking at Bonnie today, the name seemed as fitting as ever.

"Want to take a spin, Bonnie?" Daphne tossed the sheets aside.

Hopefully the car still ran. And knowing Aunt Dee, who rarely drove the car but was a firm believer in regular maintenance, there was a good chance that Bonnie was raring to go. The odometer had less than twenty-eight thousand miles on it, which meant Aunt Dee averaged less than five hundred miles a year.

Of course, that made sense considering that Aunt Dee walked everywhere. Even to the grocery store. Daphne wondered if she remembered how to put the top down and although it took a few minutes, she eventually got it. Now the car looked sleeker than ever.

Daphne felt a shiver of guilt as she slid into the driver's seat. Like the rest of the car, the upholstery was in mint condition. She slipped in the key and, holding her breath, turned the starter and stepped on the gas, just the way Aunt Dee had taught her to do nearly twenty years ago. And to her delight, after a couple of tries, the engine roared to life. Aunt Dee was the one who taught Daphne to drive—and in this very car. And today, since it had been years, Daphne hoped that driving was like riding a bike.

She tried not to remember the reason that Bonnie had been completely repainted back in the nineties. After Daphne, then sixteen, had scraped the passenger door against a cement post at the gas station, Aunt Dee had been understandably distressed, but she quickly recovered. She made a few phone calls and eventually reassured a sobbing Daphne that Bonnie would look better than new with a gleaming new coat of paint. And indeed she did. She still did now. However, the unfortunate incident had taken away some of Daphne's enjoyment of driving. As much as Aunt Dee would encourage her to take out the car, Daphne was always hesitant. Not tonight.

Daphne put the gearstick in Reverse and carefully backed out, and just like that she was driving down Huckleberry Lane—and sitting on top of the world. She even turned on the radio, which was still tuned to Aunt Dee's favorite station, a station that played music from Bonnie's era—the fifties. Not exactly Daphne's favorite kind of music, but in honor of Aunt Dee, she left it playing as she cruised around town.

To her surprise, the old car garnered a few waves and honks and definitely turned a lot of heads. And that was fun. Then as she was making her second run down Main Street, her stomach began to rumble and she realized she was ravenous. And there, with a parking spot right in front, was Midge's Diner.

She pulled right into the parking spot, near a couple who were dining outside. The woman's back was to her, but the guy gave her a solid thumbs-up. "Perfect set of wheels to park in front of a fifties-style diner."

"Thanks." She smiled, but as she got closer to the door, she noticed the woman's profile and paused. "Olivia?" she asked cautiously.

The petite brunette turned around, then leaped to her feet. *"Daphne!"* Now they were hugging and exclaiming and trying to figure out why they were both in Appleton. So Daphne explained about Aunt Dee, and Olivia admitted that she lived here in Appleton now.

"I just got back from a weeklong business trip this afternoon, so I only just heard about your aunt passing," Olivia said. "I'm so sorry."

"She had a good, full life." Daphne suppressed the urge to go into detail about how full it was. That had to remain her secret.

"Do you remember Jeff Sorenson?" Olivia finally appeared to remember the guy with her. "He graduated from ASH too. He was a senior when we were freshmen."

Daphne studied his bright blue eyes and billiard-ball smooth scalp. "I don't really recall."

Olivia laughed, smoothing her hand over Jeff's shiny head. "Yeah, that's because he had hair back then."

"I still have hair," he protested. "But this is my low-maintenance do."

"Low maintenance?" Olivia shook her head. "That is a big, fat lie. He shaves it almost daily and when he thinks I'm not looking, he oils and polishes it. That head gets more attention than I do."

Jeff frowned. "And how much time do you spend on your hair, Livvie dear?"

"Never mind." Olivia turned back to Daphne. "Are you eating here?"

"Yes. I was just going inside—"

"Eat with us," Olivia insisted.

"Oh, I don't want to intrude. I can just go—"

"No, no, we *want* your company. Don't we, Jeff?"

"You bet. I want to hear more about that stunning Corvette. What a sweet ride."

"Please," Olivia begged. "We can catch up."

"All right," Daphne conceded. "If you're sure."

"I'll go tell Ricardo," Jeff said as he ducked into the diner.

Olivia was already dragging another chair over to the table. "Here you go."

"Thanks." Daphne sat down and took in a deep breath. "I actually wanted to eat outside tonight, but I was afraid it would look pathetic. You know, a lone woman eating by herself out here."

"Well, I don't think that's pathetic. But anyway, you don't have to worry about that now." Olivia smiled. "You look great, Daphne. Very sophisticated. That must be from living in New York all these years. How exciting!"

Daphne shrugged. "To be honest, it was starting to get old."

"Oh, you're just saying that to make me feel better. The closest I got to living in a big city like New York was Omaha." She laughed. "But the truth is, even that was too busy for me. I moved back home four years ago . . . when my sister got sick."

"Your sister?"

"Remember Bernadette?"

"Of course. How could I not?" Bernadette had been two years ahead of them in school, she'd been class president, and admired by everyone.

Olivia's dark eyes grew sad. "Bernie passed away three years ago. Pancreatic cancer. She didn't even know she had it until it was virtually untreatable."

"Oh, I'm so sorry. I never heard about that."

"I know . . ." Olivia sighed. "We lost touch."

Daphne reached for Olivia's hand. "You know how many times I thought of you . . . and wondered how to get in touch . . . but then life would get busy."

"Yeah. I know. And I'm one of the few people on the planet who has not succumbed to the social network."

"I tried it for a while. But really, I just don't see the point."

"Sorry to take so long." Jeff handed Daphne a menu and napkin and silverware, but he didn't sit back down. "But I was talking to Ricardo in there. And then he noticed your car—and knew it was you." Jeff gave Daphne a sly look. "And he asked if he could join us."

"Yes!" Olivia nodded eagerly. "Tell him absolutely."

Ignoring her, Jeff turned Daphne. "I think he wanted your approval, not Livvie's."

"Oh, sure," Daphne said. "Of course he can join us. It's his diner."

Jeff laughed. "Yeah, well, I don't think Ricardo uses that as his invitation to sit down and dine with all his customers. But I'll go let him know you girls gave him the green light."

"A double date," Olivia said happily. "Who knew?"

Daphne nodded as she laid the napkin in her lap. Yes, who knew? And although she was flattered that Ricardo wanted to join them, she suddenly felt suspicious. Had her dad said something to him? She remembered how Dad had gone on and on about Ricardo being such a hot bachelor commodity in this town, as if he was ready to play matchmaker for her. Was it possible Dad had already known about the strange conditions of Aunt Dee's will?

Chapter 7

"I feel like a party crasher," Ricardo apologized as he joined them.

"No, I was the party crasher," Daphne told him.

"Here's to crashers." Olivia held up her water glass.

"And here's to Appleton High alumnus," Jeff added.

"Yes, this is like a mini-reunion." Daphne smiled at her friends as they clicked glasses.

They paused as a pretty blond waitress named Kellie came out to take their orders. She reminded Daphne of Shelby back in New York, and she vaguely wondered if Johnny Junior had popped the question yet. But for some reason it all seemed like another world right now and very far removed.

"And remember, no check," Ricardo quietly told Kellie. "This is on the house." Naturally they all protested but he insisted. "Hey, if I can't treat my friends at my restaurant, what's the point in being the owner?"

"Good point," Jeff said. "And now I think I'll have the steak and lobster and a bottle of your finest pinot noir."

Ricardo laughed. "I think you've got Midge's confused with The Zeppelin."

Kellie finished taking their orders and Daphne looked around the table with a happy smile. "This is so great. You guys are making me feel right at home." She waved to where the old-fashioned iron streetlights were just starting to come on, glowing warmly in the dusky blue light. "And the town looks so beautiful. I never remembered it being like this before."

"When do you have to go back to New York?" Ricardo asked.

Pressing her lips together, Daphne set down her glass, deciding how much she should tell them. "Well . . . I might not be going back to New York at all. Other than to pack my things to bring back here."

"*What?*" Olivia's eyes lit up. "Are you moving back home too?"

Daphne nodded. "Do you think that's totally nuts?"

"No," they all said simultaneously.

"Of course not," Ricardo said. "Otherwise, we'd all be crazy. Right?"

Jeff nodded. "When I left Appleton after graduation, I thought I was never coming back here. But after seven years in the Silicon Valley I couldn't wait to come home." He grinned at Olivia. "And then I found the love of my life right here in Appleton."

She patted his cheek. "My prince came and rescued me just in the nick of time."

"What do you mean?" Daphne asked.

"Jeff came home about the same time Bernadette started going downhill," Olivia said quietly. She glanced at Ricardo as if something about this topic made her uncomfortable with him. And now there was a short silence.

"Olivia was taking care of Bernadette twenty-four/seven at the end," Ricardo explained to Daphne. "But she was at the end of her rope by then. I tried to help out when I could, but Olivia was really handling most of it. I was so happy for her when she and Jeff started dating. She needed a spot of brightness in her life."

"Oh . . . yes, I can imagine." Daphne was still confused as to Ricardo's role. "And that was so generous of you to help Olivia like that," she told Ricardo. "If I'd been around, I would've helped her too."

"My mom did what she could," Olivia said, "but she's not real good around sick people. I was overwhelmed. I couldn't have gotten through it without Ricardo's help."

"You see, Bernadette and I had just gotten engaged and then she got diagnosed." Ricardo clarified for Daphne's sake. "I still wanted to get married, but she insisted we should wait. She truly believed she was going to beat it . . . and get better."

"But that never happened," Olivia said sadly. Jeff reached over and grasped her hand tightly in his.

"It was a rough time," he told Daphne.

"I'm so sorry," Daphne said for the second time, but this time to all three of them. "Bernadette was such a good person. I always admired her."

"It wasn't easy losing her," Ricardo admitted. "She was a vital part of this community."

Olivia pointed across the street. "See that—Bernie's Blooms—that was the florist business she started a few years before she got sick."

Daphne peered at the quaint little shop. With its green-and-white striped awnings and dark green flower boxes overflowing with blooms, it was absolutely charming. "I admired it from the street. I had no idea that was your sister, Bernadette. It's adorable."

"I run it now," Olivia said proudly.

Ricardo pointed to his own flower boxes. "And she maintains most of the flowers along Main Street, including these."

"Well, not me personally. Not all the time anyway. I have a couple of girls working for me."

"See that pink bicycle with the big basket?" Jeff nodded toward the flower shop. "That's how they make most of the deliveries. As I recall some of them went out for your aunt these last couple of days."

"What a fun job to deliver flowers on a bicycle," Daphne said. "I would've loved working there when I was in high school."

"That reminds me," Jeff told Olivia. "Jenna dropped off a job application when I was helping out there on Saturday. She wants to work for you this summer."

"Jenna McPheeters?" Daphne asked impulsively.

"Yes, do you know her?"

"Not really. But her dad is my—I mean he's my aunt's attorney. He helped her with her will and her estate. We met earlier today to go over it."

"Ooh, did Aunt Dee leave you anything good?" Olivia's dark brows arched with interest.

"I see you're driving Dee's old Corvette. I remember washing and waxing that car when I was a kid." Ricardo sighed wistfully. "And how I used to wish it was my car."

Daphne blushed to remember how she'd daydreamed about Ricardo back then, probably when he was washing the car, secretly wishing he was her boyfriend. "Yes, Aunt Dee dearly loved that car. She named her Bonnie and I was the one to put the first ding on her. Actually it was more than a ding. The whole car had to be repainted."

"But it's the original color," Ricardo told Jeff. "Only fifteen Corvettes were made in that copper." He looked back at Daphne. "Let me guess, your aunt left *that* to you?"

"No kidding?" Jeff turned to admire the car again. "She's a real beauty. Any interest in selling her, Daphne? I'll give you a fair price."

"No way," Olivia answered. "Daphne needs to keep that car. I can just imagine how hot she must look behind the wheel. I mean, seriously, it goes with her hair color and everything. You better keep her, girlfriend."

"Don't worry. The car will stay with the house."

"Meaning you got the house too?" Olivia blinked. "I have always adored that Queen Ann Victorian. And the gardens are to die for. You better let me know first off if you plan on selling it."

"Oh, listen to you." Jeff elbowed his wife. "I can't even attempt to buy her car, but here you are about to make an offer on her house. Nice going, babe."

"You two sound like you've been married for twenty years," Ricardo teased. "Instead of just two."

"But we're still just as much in love as ever." Jeff reached over to give his wife a squeeze and she responded by gazing into his eyes and suddenly they were kissing.

Not comfortable with public displays of affection, Daphne picked up her water glass and looked out upon the street, but her gaze seemed to get stuck on the sign over the flower shop. It was still hard to believe that Bernadette, the vivacious girl who'd always been so full of life, had passed on.

"Bernadette was the first business owner to leave a water dish on the sidewalk for dogs," Ricardo told Daphne. "And she even kept a cookie jar of doggy treats in there. That was just one of the trends she started."

"She was so thoughtful." Daphne turned back to smile at him. "I'm sure you must still miss her a lot."

He nodded. "But like so many things, it does get better with time."

"So back to you, Daphne," Olivia said suddenly. "Are you really not going back to New York? You're going to live here in Appleton for good?"

Daphne gauged how much to say. "I have to admit, it's not a very well-thought-out plan . . . but yes, I think I'll give my boss my notice tomorrow." She bit her lip. "Do you think it's a mistake?"

"No," they all said simultaneously again.

Ricardo laughed. "You guessed it, we're all card-carrying members of the Appleton Chamber of Commerce. And whenever anyone wants to move to town, we automatically turn into the town's loudest cheerleaders."

"That's not true," Olivia said. "We only sing the town's praises when we *like* someone. If we don't care for them, we act like Appleton's not all that great. Right?"

The guys laughed.

"But that's only because we love this place so much that we want to protect it," Jeff clarified. "And we want to see it grow in well-thought-out ways."

"What will you do for a living?" Olivia asked her.

Again, Daphne had to be careful with how much information

she disclosed. "Well, don't laugh . . . but I think I'd like to try writing a novel."

"Good for you," Ricardo told her.

"Yes," Olivia said. "You were always a good writer. And you've been writing for *The New York Times* for ages."

"You write for *The New York Times*?" Jeff looked impressed.

"Not anymore." Daphne laughed nervously. "How about you? What do you do here in Appleton?"

"Jeff has the kind of job he can do anywhere," Olivia explained. "He designs software."

"And I help with the flower shop sometimes too," he reminded his wife.

Kellie returned with their orders, carefully setting them in place and taking time to smile warmly at her boss. But unless Daphne was imagining something, the look Kellie gave her was a trifle frosty. Still, Daphne simply smiled back, politely thanking the pretty waitress. Then as they all dug into their meals, the conversation lulled slightly.

Daphne paused for a moment, glancing around the table and marveling at how these three people had made her feel more at home than she'd felt in years. Maybe forever. Perhaps Aunt Dee knew more about what she was doing in crafting that will than Daphne had assumed.

After dinner, Ricardo insisted that everyone have dessert.

"It's his famous Appleton deep-dish pie," Olivia told Daphne after Ricardo cleared their table and went inside.

"With his killer handmade vanilla bean ice cream." Jeff smacked his lips like he hadn't just consumed a Reuben sandwich and sweet potato fries.

"I guess I'll have to take over the deliveries tomorrow," Olivia confided to Daphne. "To bike off all these extra calories."

Jeff leaned forward. "So, tell me, what do you girls think of Kellie?" he asked quietly.

Olivia rolled her eyes. "Jeff is just certain that this new waitress is crushing on Ricardo."

"She's very pretty," Daphne said.

"But if you ask me, she's not really the waitress type." Olivia tossed Daphne a knowing look. "If you know what I mean."

"She seems intelligent and well spoken." Daphne tried to act nonchalant, but she was surprisingly disappointed to think that Ricardo and Kellie were this close to becoming a couple. Not to mention a bit chafed at Dad for acting like Ricardo was unattached.

"And Ricardo must like her or he wouldn't have hired her," Jeff pointed out.

"She's good at her job," Daphne added with feigned enthusiasm.

"That's true." Jeff nodded. "And you can tell she's really into Ricardo."

"I thought I noticed that too," Daphne admitted.

"But she's so not Ricardo's type," Olivia told Jeff. "And I don't want to see you encouraging this. Seriously, you stay out of it."

"But it would do Ricardo good to have a girlfriend," Jeff said. "He hasn't dated once since Bernadette died."

"That's because he's putting all his energy into the diner. Just leave well enough alone."

"And here comes the man of the house now," Daphne announced. "And that dessert looks lovely."

"Kellie is bringing our coffee." Ricardo set a dish in front of each of them. "I had her brew a fresh pot of decaf." He grinned at Olivia. "Because I know you don't do caffeine at night."

She beamed at him. "Thank you." Now she turned to Daphne. "I still pretend that Ricardo is my brother-in-law."

"And you keep on doing that." Ricardo reached into the center of the table to light the votive candle. "You can't go through what we did without becoming family."

Although she didn't feel hungry, Daphne took a bite of dessert and couldn't believe how delicious it tasted. "Oh, Ricardo. This dessert is fabulous. Honestly, this might be the best apple pie I've ever eaten."

"Really?" He looked hopefully at her. "I mean, you're the New Yorker girl. I'm sure you've eaten at a lot of fine restaurants."

"I don't know about that. But really, it's fabulous."

"I've been telling Ricardo that for years," Jeff said. "I've dined at some pretty posh LA restaurants but never had anything like this."

"And I've eaten at some of Omaha's best," Olivia chimed in. "This beats them all hands down."

Kellie came out with coffee, taking her time to arrange their cups and the sugar and cream. "I don't believe I've met you," she said as she filled Daphne's cup with steaming dark brew.

"I'm sorry, Kellie," Ricardo said. "This is Daphne Ballinger. We went to school together. Her aunt and my mom are neighbors."

"I came home for my aunt's funeral," Daphne added.

"Oh, I'm so sorry for your loss," Kellie told her.

"Thank you. She was quite elderly. But I still miss her."

"I can imagine." Kellie finished filling Olivia's cup. "So I assume you won't be around for long?" Kellie moved on to Jeff.

"Daphne just told us she's planning to relocate here," Ricardo informed her. "Moving from New York. She plans to live in her aunt's house and write the great American novel." He grinned at Daphne. "Can't wait to hear more about that."

Kellie looked surprised—or was it displeased—as she stepped next to Ricardo. Then placing what seemed a possessive hand on his shoulder, she slowly filled his cup. "I hope you enjoy our quiet little town, Daphne. I'm sure it will seem like small potatoes compared to the big city lights you must be used to."

"Actually, I grew up here," Daphne said. "But it's not nearly as quiet as it used to be. Our little town seems to be coming along quite nicely."

Without responding to her, Kellie turned to Ricardo and smiled prettily. "Can I get you anything else?"

"No, this is fine, Kellie. Perfect. Thank you." He smiled warmly, and with the coffee carafe in her hand and a confident smile on her pretty pink lips, Kellie strutted back inside.

Daphne was certain Olivia and Jeff were right. That girl was definitely crushing on Ricardo. And it wouldn't surprise her if Ricardo was enjoying it. What did surprise Daphne was that she felt jealous . . . and a little territorial.

Chapter 8

By the time Daphne got home, she had convinced herself that her unexpected reaction to Kellie and Ricardo was all just a figment of her overactive imagination. Good grief, she simply enjoyed dinner with old friends and the next thing she knew she was hearing wedding bells? Perfectly ridiculous.

As she closed and locked the garage door, thankful that she hadn't put any new scrapes or scratches on Bonnie, she told herself that she had simply been caught up in Aunt Dee's last will and testament. Which reminded her, she wanted to read through it tonight.

She considered going into Aunt Dee's study to sit at the big desk to read it, but for some reason—probably because that had always been her aunt's private "do-not-disturb" space—Daphne was reluctant to trespass there now. Instead she made herself comfortable in the big front room, reading the pages carefully, one by one, and spreading them all around her. She was no legal expert, but it did seem that Aunt Dee had carefully covered everything. And Jake would have no reason to convince her that the will was airtight if it wasn't.

"All right, Lucy," she nudged the cat off of a pile of papers, "find someplace else to sleep." She gathered all the papers, stacked them neatly, then shoved them back into the envelope. What was done was done. And she had a year to figure it all out.

As Daphne got ready for bed, she thought about Ricardo again. He was so sweet and thoughtful and generous. She could imagine being happy with a guy like that. Plus he wasn't too hard on the eyes. Of course, that could be a challenge in itself. A guy as handsome as Ricardo, working around pretty waitresses like Kellie . . . was that a formula for disaster? What would Dear Daphne say? While brushing her teeth, she began penning a letter in her head.

> *Dear Daphne,*
>
> *I'm interested in a man who is a great guy but very attractive. In fact, he's attracted the attention of one of his employees. And that scares me. Would I be foolish to get involved with a guy like that? What if he broke my heart?*
>
> *Afraid in Appleton*

She turned off the tap and stuck her toothbrush back in the glass. This was silly and futile. Even so, she was curious as to how Dear Daphne would respond. As she washed her face and applied moisturizer, she constructed a response.

> *Dear Afraid,*
>
> *Just because a guy is attractive doesn't mean he will break your heart. Have you taken time to get acquainted with the true character of this man? Before you get your heart involved, why not get to*

know him better? Before you give him up, why not
give him a chance to show you what he's really made
of? You might be surprised.
    Daphne

She briskly rubbed lotion into her hands. Why was she even thinking about Ricardo like this? Just so she could secure her aunt's inheritance? What kind of character did that reveal in her? And how would Ricardo feel if he knew she was considering him all because of Aunt Dee's will? And what about Jake? She'd been obsessing over him just a few hours ago, fretting over who the mysterious Jenna was, when she was only his daughter. Seriously, Aunt Dee had created a real quagmire for Daphne. In a way, she had turned Daphne into an ironic sort of gold digger.

But instead of fretting over all these questions, Daphne played one of her favorite biofeedback audios on her iPod. And when that didn't work to put her to sleep, she went downstairs and drank a glass of milk. And finally, she was back in her bed.

God, please lead me safely through the year ahead. She knew she would sign the paperwork that allowed her twelve months of playing the heiress. What happened at the end of that time was still a mystery.

The next morning, she got up with the sun. This was her first official day of knowing that she truly was mistress of the house. At least for a year—but she was not going to think about that now. She happily tended to the cats, chatting cheerfully with them. Then she returned to the kitchen and ground the Red River blend coffee beans and made some delicious-smelling coffee.

And since it was sunny outside, she took her coffee out to the private backyard where, still wearing her silky nightgown and robe, she made herself comfortable on the padded lounge chair. She peeled off her robe and soaked in the sun as well as the flowers and greenery and chirping birds. She felt like she'd landed in paradise. And really, it did feel like a vacation—a much-needed vacation!

"Whoa!" a man said.

She nearly spilt her coffee as she looked up to see a tall man in a light blue chambray shirt and blue jeans smiling down on her.

"Who are you?" She set down her coffee and grabbed up her robe, holding it in front of her like a shield.

"I'm sorry to disturb you," he said with what sounded like a British or perhaps it was an Australian accent. "I'm Mick Foster. Who, may I ask, are you?"

She checked him out more closely now. His heavy brown boots were scuffed and his brown hair needed a trim. But all in all, he was strikingly handsome in a rugged sort of way. He looked a bit like Matthew McConaughey, and she could almost imagine him posing for a cover of one of the steamy romance novels penned by Penelope Poindexter a.k.a. Aunt Dee a.k.a. her grandmother. Standing, she pulled on her robe and tied it tightly about her waist. "I'm Daphne Ballinger."

He frowned. "Wh—*what?*"

"I'm Dee Ballinger's niece," she explained, backing toward the house.

"Ah, well, yes, that makes sense. But the name threw me. I knew you couldn't be Dee Ballinger, but I know her name is Daphne." A smile lit his face. "Although, now that I think on it, I reckon Dee's mentioned you a time or two. You're the niece who lives in New York City."

She decided to use a no-nonsense tone now—her way to put the brakes on what felt like a far-too-personal encounter. "Is there something I can help you with?"

His smile only grew bigger. "Well, I'm not too sure. But I'd certainly be willing to find out."

She suspected he was flirting with her. And understandably so. Finding a girl sunbathing in a skimpy nightie probably seemed like something of an invitation. "I'm sorry, Mick." She narrowed her eyes. "But I don't recall if you mentioned what your business here is." Her hand was on the knob of the back door now and she was ready to bolt.

"Oh yeah, sorry about that. My bad manners. I'm Dee's groundskeeper."

She relaxed a little now. "Oh, my dad mentioned that my aunt had help with her gardens. I've been admiring how gorgeous everything looks. I've never seen her yard looking better."

"Thanks. I appreciate that." He glanced over to the hedge in back. "Then you probably noticed that the veggie garden still needs some attention. I got some of the spring plants set a little more than a week ago, before I had to go to Brookdale to work on a big new project, but there's still lots to be done if Dee wants to pick her tomatoes in time for—"

"Didn't you hear?"

"Hear what?"

Daphne sighed. "My aunt passed away. Less than a week ago. We had her funeral service yesterday."

He cocked his head to one side with a furrowed brow. She could tell he was both saddened and shocked. "Dee's passed on? *Truly?*"

"Yes, she died in her sleep."

"And she and I were just out here, just last Monday, walking about her yard, talking and laughing and making plans." He shook his head. "I can hardly believe it."

"She was quite elderly."

"Dee?" He rubbed his chin. "Well, yeah, I suppose she was getting up there in years. But she had a youthful spirit." He peered at her. "Don't you think?"

"I always thought that. In fact, I was kind of shocked to hear how old she was. Ninety-one."

"No kidding?" He blew out a long sigh. "Well, I got to give it to her. The old girl knew how to live. I reckon we can all take a lesson from her."

She just nodded, unsure of how to proceed. "So, I suppose you can still do whatever it is you wanted to do to her yard . . . or garden or whatever."

"Yeah, I reckon I could. But you see, I don't work for just *anybody.*" He folded his arms across his front, studying her. "I decided a while back that life's too short to work for the wrong people. Or in the wrong yards."

"Really? You can afford to be that choosy in a small town like this?"

"So who would I be working for now? If I decided I wanted to continue here."

"For now, you'd be working for me." She held up her chin, looking evenly at him, almost as if challenging him to walk away.

But instead his blue eyes twinkled with interest. "Well, I reckon

I can handle that." He tipped his head to one side. "That is, unless you're awfully bossy. Are you?"

She shrugged. "I don't know much about gardening so it's unlikely I'd try to tell you what to do."

"And there's another thing," he said as she opened the door.

"What's that?"

"Dee always invited me in for tea or coffee. Sometimes she had cookies. Or else she'd bring lemonade out here for me. It wasn't just a business relationship. It was a social one too. How do you reckon you'd deal with that?"

She couldn't help but smile as she imagined Aunt Dee looking down right now and chuckling. "I think I'd be okay with that."

"Right." He stuck out his hand. "Then I reckon we can seal this deal with a handshake."

She gave him her hand and was surprised at the warm tingly rush she got as he firmly shook it. "Well, if you will excuse me, I'd like to go get dressed."

"No worries, Daphne, but I reckon you look just fine as is." He grinned, then turned and walked away.

Her cheeks felt flushed as she went into the kitchen. As she got a cool drink of water, she looked out the kitchen window to see his truck in the driveway. She didn't know what year the olive green truck was, but she could tell it was from the fifties. And it was in perfect condition. Wooden rails ran along the sides of the bed, where it looked as if gardening tools were stored. On the cab's door it said *The Garden Guy* in neat white letters. Was that Mick or perhaps the name of the landscaping business he worked for?

She watched as he gracefully hoisted a wheelbarrow from the back of his truck. He was easily six foot four, and although she wasn't sure, she suspected he was about her age. Anyway, he was probably thirtysomething. For some reason, probably the way he was looking at her, she suspected he was a bachelor. However, she knew better than to make that assumption . . . again.

Shaking her head, she set down the glass and hurried upstairs to get dressed. She wished she'd packed some more casual clothes—like the jeans and sweatshirts she often wore at home during the weekends. Right now the best she could do was her khaki pants and a white shirt. Not exactly gardening clothes. But then it wasn't as if she was going to help him out there. All she had committed to was coffee or lemonade.

But first she decided to e-mail Amelia, giving her notice that she was quitting. She carefully worded the letter, thinking that she didn't want to burn any bridges, especially since she had no idea how she'd be feeling one year from now. But when she hit Send, she felt confident that she'd made the right decision. The question now was whether Amelia would try to talk her out of it. Or if she would demand that Daphne give her two more weeks of work. Daphne had offered to work from Appleton or, if necessary, to come back in—but only for two weeks.

With her laptop on the kitchen table, Daphne peeked out the back window to see if she could spy on Mick, but he must've been working behind the hedge. She was eager to see what the vegetable garden looked like and was about to go out when she heard her computer ping announcing she had mail. Surprised to see that Amelia had already responded, Daphne braced herself for her boss's demands.

No problem. Resignation accepted. Come in and clean out your desk. Or I'll ask Fiona to do it for you. Contact

Fiona with your forwarding information and where to send
your last check.

Amelia

Daphne tried not to feel overly slighted as she snapped her laptop shut. Really, she should be relieved. But it stung slightly to be so
dispensable—and after all these years too. It was humiliating. And
it hurt.

"Where's that lemonade?" Mick hollered into the house.

She went to the opened door where his head poked through. "I
don't have lemonade, but I think there's some punch leftover from
yesterday. And I do have coffee already made. Or I can make tea."

"What's the matter with you?" He stepped into the house now,
peering curiously at her. "You look like you lost your best friend."

She shrugged. "I just gave notice on my job."

"Oh yeah, that's tough. Change is always hard at first."

"That's not it," she confessed. "I think I'm ready for change."

"Oh . . . what's the problem, then?"

"The problem is that my boss didn't even care. She was like, *no
problem*, like *what took you so long to quit?*"

"That is rough." He made a half smile. "But aren't all New
Yorkers a bit like that? Rather abrupt and sharp and impatient?"

She didn't answer.

"Although you don't seem like that. I reckon you didn't really fit
into the big city life. Not really."

"No, I suppose not." She was caught off guard that a yardman's
consolation could bring such comfort. "I'll be out with your coffee.
How do you take yours?"

"Cream and sugar, please. I'll be out in the veggie garden. I'd like your opinion on some things."

She made their coffees, then went outside. As she walked through the yard, she wasn't sure what to make of Mick Foster. On one hand, he was a little rough around the edges, yet on the other hand, he seemed to have some depth to him. And she got the impression that Aunt Dee and he had shared some special sort of relationship. That alone made her curious. Plus, he was very easy on the eyes. And she loved the accent!

"Here you go," she said as she found him sitting in a white Adirondack chair looking over what appeared to be a well-laid-out garden with raised beds. Already a lot of bright green plants were growing nicely. "This is wonderful back here." She sat on the other chair, just taking it all in.

"Thanks. It was a fun little project."

"I had no idea anything this lovely lay behind that hedge. When I was a little girl this was just a wasteland of weeds and blackberries and tall grass. Aunt Dee called it no-man's-land and the one time I came back here, I was frightened off by a big black-and-yellow snake."

"Probably a garter snake. Not dangerous."

"Still it was scary to a little girl." She took a sip of coffee.

"So what scares the big girl?"

Caught off guard again, she wasn't sure how to answer.

"I reckon giving up your big New York City job is a bit frightening."

"To be honest, it's a little unnerving. But it's even more upsetting to think that what I've invested myself into—for all these years— really doesn't matter. My boss knows I'm replaceable."

"Then you should be thankful you're not there anymore." He took a sip. "Good coffee."

"Thanks."

"The only thing worse than being stuck in a bad career is not having the good sense to get out." Mick grinned. "And now you're out."

"You sound like you've had some experience in a bad career."

"Oh yeah, I have. I spent more'n my fair share of time in the corporate world."

"What did you do?"

"Investment broker." He shook his head. "Family corporation. Where the money was. After university, I got stuck in an office in Sydney for ten long years that I'll never get back."

She nodded. "Sounds vaguely familiar."

"I'd escape my corporate prison on weekends by hanging on the beach—surfing all day and staying out all night. Then I'd go back into the office on Monday with a nasty disposition and by Tuesday I'd be counting the days until the next weekend."

"Sounds delightful," she said sarcastically.

"Delightfully stupid." He shook his head. "Best thing that ever happened to me was when the economy started to unravel. I wished my dad good luck and kissed my mum good-bye and set off to find a life."

"And that brought you here?"

"Not directly. I did some traveling first. And I noticed a pattern—wherever I went, no matter what kind of amazing sights there were to see, more than anything I wanted to visit the local gardens. I've toured gardens all over the globe. And each time I'd talk to gardeners and groundskeepers, when there wasn't a language barrier, and they all seemed to have one thing in common."

"What's that?"

"A sense of contentment and peace. Something I was lacking."

"But you've found it?"

"Yeah. Nothing makes me happier than having my hands in the dirt, making things grow, planning new green spaces." He grinned. "It's all good."

"So The Garden Guy is your business?"

"Sure is."

"And what made you pick Appleton?"

"Well, I fell in love with the States straight off. And it was just far enough from my family that they couldn't attempt to drag me back into the business. Then I did some research, trying to find an area with good soil and a climate conducive to gardening, and I visited a few towns, but Appleton just seemed to stand out."

"So you could've lived anywhere in the world and you picked Appleton?" For some reason this stunned her. As much as she loved her hometown, she had always taken it for granted.

"Yeah. I picked Appleton. And I have no regrets."

"Do you do a lot of people's yards around here?"

"Not really." He finished his coffee and stood.

"How did my aunt discover you?"

"Now that's an interesting story." He set his cup down. "But I'm not sure I have time to tell it to you this morning. Right now, I'd like to get your opinion on some things." He pointed over to a wood frame. "I want to put in berries over there, but I need to know which you prefer." He listed off berry varieties.

"Raspberries," she told him. "I don't even care what kind. Whatever you think is best. But I love raspberries."

"Good on you." He walked her over to an area that hadn't been planted and listed vegetables he thought would do well there. Eventually they decided on a number of things. "And the salad garden." He took her to where some plants were growing. "Do you want anything besides the lettuces, radishes, green onions, carrots—?"

"I love all and any kinds of vegetables. I can't even imagine how heavenly it'll be to come out here and pick them from my own garden."

His brows arched. "So are you the new owner, then? Did Dee leave this all to you? Or are you just temporarily holding the fort?"

"I plan to be around for a year. We'll see after that."

"All right then, we should discuss the herb garden over there." He pointed to a smaller bed. "Dee had asked me to start on that. How do you feel about herbs?"

"I adore herbs."

As he began listing off herbs, she imagined all the cooking she could do in Aunt Dee's kitchen, with access to herbs out the back door. Really, it felt almost too good to be true.

Chapter 9

"Hello?" called a man from somewhere on the other side of the hedge. "Anyone home?"

"We're back here," Daphne called out. "That sounds like Jake McPheeters," she told Mick. "My aunt's attorney."

"Go through that green gate to get back here," Mick said.

Soon Jake joined them, looking out of place in his tidy navy suit and neatly striped tie. But he just smiled, taking time to shake hands with Mick before turning to Daphne. "Sorry to drop in on you like this, but the court case I'm working on took a recess until after lunch, and I tried to call you but no one answered. So I thought I'd just pop over and see if you wanted to sign the papers I sent home with you yesterday."

"Yes. I read through them last night." She looked back at Mick. "Do you need anything more from me?"

Mick's eyes lit up. "Not at the moment, but I'll be more than glad to take you up on that offer later."

Her cheeks warmed at the suggestion in his tone. "Thanks, Mick, I'll keep that in mind." She turned back to Jake. "Should we go inside?"

Jake chuckled as they went into the kitchen. "You certainly don't waste any time," he said as he closed the back door.

"What?" She set the coffee cups in the sink and rinsed her hands.

"I mean regarding Dee's marital challenge."

She narrowed her eyes as she dried her hands on the dish towel. "What are you insinuating?"

He held up his hands. "I'm not trying to insult you, Daphne. After all, you're a pretty young woman and you're new in town. It's no wonder you've already attracted some admirers."

"What do you mean by that?" She picked up the envelope of papers she'd set on the china hutch as well as a pen, then went over to the kitchen table and peered curiously at him.

"Sorry." He smiled apologetically. "I didn't mean to sound like that."

She frowned. "I still don't get what you're saying."

"I happened to drive by Midge's Diner when I was taking Jenna home last night."

"Oh?"

"I noticed Dee's Corvette parked out front. So I took a second look and saw you enjoying yourself with Ricardo—"

"And Olivia and Jeff," she added crisply. "I just went to get a bite to eat and Olivia insisted I join them. And then Ricardo joined us. It wasn't as if it was a premeditated date."

He laughed. "No, I'm sure it wasn't. But it did appear as if you were having a good time. Nothing wrong with that."

"Oh, good. I'm relieved to know I'm allowed to have a good

time." She didn't know why she was being so defensive. But something about his tone was really irritating.

"Of course you're allowed. Dee would be pleased to see you're making such progress in such a short amount of time."

She glared at him. "What are you insinuating?"

He shrugged. "I was just a little surprised to find you and Mick in the garden this morning."

"You make it sound like we were having a little tryst." Her defenses were up now, but at the same time she was thankful Jake hadn't happened on them when she'd been conversing with Mick in her nightie. That would've given Jake plenty to tease her about.

"Forgive me, but I'm only saying that for all your protests against the unfairness of the conditions of Dee's will, you seem to be making good progress with two of the town's most eligible bachelors. You work fast, Daphne."

She bristled as she pointed to the table. "Do you want to sit down while I sign the papers?"

"Thank you." He sat down.

"Would you like some coffee?" She considered dumping a cup right over his head.

"No, thank you. I've already had more than enough."

So had she. But she controlled herself from saying it as she pulled the packet of papers out of the envelope.

"As you surely noticed when you read these last night, this is only an agreement for the next year, giving you the use of Dee's estate for the duration of twelve months and—"

"Yes, I read the contract carefully. I understand the conditions." She clicked the pen impatiently. "I realize that I have no right to any capital gains from interest or royalties or property or anything. I will only get a monthly stipend, which is actually quite generous, and the use of Aunt Dee's house and car. I understand that you will continue to act as my aunt's trustee." She narrowed her eyes. "And my Big Brother, keeping a close eye on my transactions to be sure I don't try to embezzle any funds or sell off—"

"That's a little harsh. I'm only doing what Dee asked me to do." She twisted her mouth to one side.

"I'm sorry, Daphne." He laid both his palms on the table. "I think I offended you with my comments about Ricardo and Mick. And in retrospect, I can see that I was out of line. Will you forgive me?"

Taken aback and somewhat disarmed, she blinked. "Yes, of course I forgive you. And I'm sorry I was coming across so defensive just now." So she explained about giving notice on her job this morning and how Amelia so easily dismissed her. "I suppose I was already out of sorts. But your insinuation about me being a fast mover—well, that hurt."

He nodded. "I really am sorry. The truth of the matter is, I was probably just jealous."

"Jealous?"

A sheepish smile tipped the corner of his mouth. "Yes. Ricardo and Mick were already making headway with you. Maybe I was jealous."

She cocked her head to one side. "But aren't you married? I mean, Dad told me that Jenna is your daughter and, well, I assumed you had a wife."

"I was married. But Gwen and I have been divorced for some time." His brow creased. "Jenna was about seven then."

"Oh . . ." Daphne sighed. "Well, I'm sorry. That must be hard . . . I mean having a child . . . and being divorced."

"It's not so bad. Gwen and I have managed to get over a lot of our differences over the years. And we share joint custody of Jenna. And thankfully neither of us wanted to move away. All in all, it's a fairly congenial relationship."

Daphne nodded, but she really didn't get this. A congenial divorce? It sounded like an oxymoron to her.

"Anyway, no hard feelings?" he asked.

"Yes. No hard feelings."

He showed her where to sign and before long they were done, and he gathered up his set of papers and handed her back hers. "Now, you have exactly one year from today's date to figure it all out. May the best man win."

She wondered at his words. Win what? Her? Or Aunt Dee's estate? Suddenly everything about this arrangement felt murky and confusing. "Does anyone else know about this?" she asked as she walked him to the door. "I mean besides you?"

"No one."

"And you won't tell anyone?"

"No, of course not. Why would I?" He peered curiously at her. "If news like this got out, you'd have no end of characters knocking on your door."

"Yes . . . I suppose so."

"As it is, you will have to be careful. Many will make the assumption that you're fairly well off. Kind of like the wealthy widow, if you know what I mean."

"Yes, that just occurred to me."

"So just be watchful." He smiled pleasantly. "And just for the record, as far as I know, both Ricardo and Mick are good upstanding guys. I suppose that's what aggravated me." He chuckled. "Your comment about Big Brother was slightly on target. But not the Orson Welles type. I'd rather think of myself as your friend, appointed by Dee, to watch over you for your welfare." He stuck out his hand. "Friends still?"

She shook his hand. "Yes. Friends. Absolutely. I appreciate it."

"Good. And if you have any questions, feel free to call—anytime. In the meantime, I'll try to stay out of your hair as well as your love life." Then he tipped his head and made his exit.

But that last comment about staying out of her hair and love life bugged her. One minute he seemed to be coming on to her and the next minute he was backing off. What was up with that? She wondered what Dear Daphne would say. And once again, she found herself constructing a letter in her head.

> *Dear Daphne,*
> *There's this guy I'm mildly interested in, and at times it feels like he's interested in me as well. But the next moment, he's acting like he only wants to be friends. I feel like a Ping-Pong ball getting bounced back and forth. How can I determine what he really wants in our relationship?*
> *Annoyed in Appleton*

As she rinsed out the coffee carafe, she imagined what Dear Daphne would write back.

> *Dear Annoyed,*
> *You say you want to determine what this guy wants in a relationship, but maybe you need to figure out what it is you want. You need to ask yourself*

what this man has to offer you and whether or not
you're really interested. Perhaps when you settle this
question, your fellow will stop acting so wishy-washy.
     Daphne

She chuckled as she washed down the kitchen table. Dear Daphne was probably right. Instead of worrying about Jake's intentions, she should figure out her own feelings. Besides, it was sweet of him to offer his big brotherly friendship. She needed someone she could trust.

She looked at her laptop and considered e-mailing Fiona back at *The Times* with her forwarding information like Amelia had advised her, but instead she decided to call. It might be interesting to hear what was going on there.

"Amelia Jones' office, this is Fiona," Amelia's assistant said pleasantly.

"Hi, Fiona, this is Daphne. Amelia told me to call you."

"Oh yeah, I heard you quit. Everyone was pretty shocked. I mean, you were like a fixture around here. No one ever thought you'd quit."

"I was a little surprised too."

"So what are you going to do?" Fiona asked with her usual curiosity. "I mean for a living? Do you have another job lined up?"

"No, not really. Thanks to my aunt's will, I don't need to worry about that right now."

"Oh, man, you're so lucky. Does that mean you're an heiress?"

"Sort of. Mostly I'm just looking at this as a vacation. I plan to take it easy for about a year. Although I do plan to do some writing . . ." She thought about the *Dear Daphne* column, wondering if she would be able to pull it off. "Among other things I might work on a novel I've been noodling on for years."

"What a life. I am so jealous."

They chatted a bit longer, and after enjoying a smidgen of relief to know that someone at the paper seemed to care that she was gone, Daphne gave the forwarding information. It was heartening to hear how Fiona longed to be in Daphne's shoes. By the time she wished Fiona a long and happy future at the paper, ending the conversation, she was glad she'd taken the time to call.

As she hung up, she decided to call Beverly. Daphne was just telling her about inheriting her aunt's house when her friend interrupted her.

"I hate to cut this short," Beverly said curtly, "but I'm right in the middle of an article and I really wanted to finish it before Robert gets back."

"Oh, I'm sorry. I didn't know you were busy."

"Yeah, well, some of us still have to work to pay the bills." Beverly laughed like this was funny. "I'll call you back later. Okay?"

"Sure. Don't let me keep you." As Daphne set her phone aside, she tried not to feel hurt.

She'd been looking forward to confiding in Beverly, hoping that her old friend might even have some advice for her.

And it wasn't often that Daphne went to Beverly for help. Yet how many times had Beverly called Daphne at inopportune times? How many times had she used Daphne as a sounding board, asking her about everything from picking out shoes to menu suggestions? And now Beverly was too busy? How much busier would she be when the baby came? Perhaps it was just as well that Daphne wasn't going back to New York. But she hadn't even been able to tell Beverly that.

Instead of brewing over Beverly, Daphne decided to rebook her return flight, giving herself another week before going back to the city. After that she called and left a message with Greta, telling her the news. Thankfully, the "binding" lease from more than twelve years ago had long since expired.

"But I'll pay next month's rent," she promised. "Or longer if necessary, although I'm sure you'll find a new tenant before long." Daphne didn't feel guilty since Greta never seemed to have a problem finding new roommates.

Daphne spent the rest of the day puttering about the house, enjoying the feeling that she was in control here. Oh, she knew the house wasn't really hers to keep indefinitely, but for the time being, she planned to pretend it was.

But as she began making herself more comfortable, she realized that she still had some legal questions for Jake. Although the contract she signed stipulated that she couldn't dispose of or sell any of Aunt Dee's property, what was she to do with her aunt's personal effects? Wouldn't it be nice to share a few things with some of the family members? Or would that be breaking her contract?

Just as she was pondering this, her dad called to ask how she was doing. She filled him in on a few things, including her changed flight, but the topics she really wanted to discuss with him, details about Aunt Dee's will, seemed to be off-limits. Another question for Jake. So as she was chatting with Dad, she added that one to her growing list.

"I have a meeting tonight," Dad finally told her. "Or else I'd ask you to join me for dinner. Maybe tomorrow night?"

"Sounds good." For the second time today, she felt a bit slighted. But her dad was a busy man . . . he had a life. For that she should be thankful. Besides it was a good reminder to her—she needed to get a life too!

Later that afternoon when straightening out a drawer in the kitchen, she found the paint colors Aunt Dee had picked for repainting her house. Again she wondered about the contract she'd signed. Would that allow her to get the house painted? The colors, a buttery yellow for the body and soft orange and olive green for the trim, actually looked quite nice together. And Daphne could imagine how they would bring new life to the old house, as well as go well with some of the others in the neighborhood. Besides that, she'd noticed that some of the white paint was getting chalky and flaky, and it was obvious that the exterior of the old house needed some TLC. But, of course, as she considered changing the exterior, she couldn't help but wonder about the interior. All those weekends of watching HGTV made her want to try her hand at some things. However, she wasn't sure if she was allowed.

She called Jake's number the next morning, and because he was about to see a client, he recommended they meet for lunch to go over her questions. However, she was a little surprised when he suggested The Zeppelin.

"Isn't that just a dinner place?"

"No, they serve lunch too. I often have business lunches there."

So she agreed to meet him at one. And realizing this restaurant might be more formal than Midge's Diner, she decided to wear her black skirt and moss green sweater set. Her wardrobe choices seemed to be getting more limited with each passing day. Not only that, but she realized that her clothes back in New York might not be appropriate for small-town life either. Might her old friend Olivia be able to give her some pointers? Perhaps after lunch she would stop by Bernie's Blooms and chat with her and reconnect.

After dressing for lunch, Daphne remembered Aunt Dee's pearl necklace. Since she was allowed to use anything in the house, it was permissible to wear her aunt's jewelry as well. And a string of real pearls would go nicely with the cashmere sweater set. But so far there were two rooms in this house where Daphne had been unable to force herself to enter—Aunt Dee's study and Aunt Dee's bedroom. Both of those spaces seemed so personal, so private, and so far she had avoided them.

And now, feeling like an interloper, she cautiously opened the bedroom door and just stood there looking. To her relief, Lucy and Ethel wasted no time, pushing right past her, and entered the bedroom as if they owned the place. They sniffed around and Lucy jumped on the bed while Ethel peeked underneath it, but both cats seemed to have the same curious expression—as if they were asking—*where did she go?*

"She's not here," Daphne quietly told them as she went into the room. "And she's not coming back."

Everything in this room looked exactly as she remembered from childhood: from the rosebud wallpaper to the blond-toned midcentury modern furnishings to the pale blue satin comforter and lace-covered pillow shams. Besides being a little more faded and worn, nothing had really changed. She looked at the aqua blue fainting couch, still positioned by the window that overlooked the backyard, where Aunt Dee sometimes liked to recline after lunch, enjoying a short nap before returning to her "textbooks."

Daphne could almost hear her aunt's voice. "A girl needs to make her surroundings comfortable and reflective of who she is," she'd told Daphne as they put a new set of pink satin sheets on the bed. Her aunt later confessed that the sheets were too slippery. "I felt like I was falling out of bed," she'd said as she bundled up the shiny sheets to donate to Aunt Dee's church's tag sale. "But I wouldn't have known that if I hadn't tried them." Daphne ran her hand over the satin comforter, wishing Aunt Dee were still here to answer all of her many questions.

For instance, what was Daphne supposed to do with all of Aunt Dee's clothes and shoes and hats and things? Because whether Daphne remained here for only a year, or longer, it seemed inevitable that her aunt's personal effects would need to be sifted and sorted and removed from here. One more question for Jake.

She went over to the long dressing table, looking at the many bottles of perfume still arranged on a gilt-framed mirror. Some of them were decades old and some a bit more recent. She slid open one of the drawers where Aunt Dee had kept her jewelry. Other than the pearls, which Dee had explained were "an extravagant splurge from the success of one of her textbooks," Daphne had always assumed that most of her aunt's flashy jewelry was only costume. But now she wasn't so sure. Not much about Aunt Dee would surprise her anymore.

The pearls were right on top, resting in a velvet-lined box, almost as if her aunt had recently worn them. As she picked them up, Daphne wondered if her aunt should've been buried in them. However, Dad had made those decisions before she arrived. He'd taken her clothes to the mortuary on the first day. And Daphne hadn't questioned his choices. As she ran the smooth, cool pearls over the palm of her hand, she knew in her heart that her aunt—grandmother—would be glad for her to have this strand. At least for a year anyway.

She slipped them around her neck, fastened the latch, and then checked her image in the big round mirror above the vanity. Yes, it was just the touch of elegance her conservative outfit needed.

Appropriate for meeting her lawyer at a nice restaurant. Respectable. Her aunt would be proud.

"Aunt Dee," she said quietly. "You really didn't have to die to get me here." She closed the drawer, then picked up a sleek glass bottle of her aunt's favorite fragrance, Chanel No. 5. She removed the top and squirted some into the air, sniffing the familiar aroma. As a child she hadn't been fond of the overpowering smell, but over the years it had grown on her. A sophisticated powdery scent with contrasting elements of dark musk and light sweetness. A bit like her mysterious aunt . . . grandma.

"Are you pleased with yourself now, Aunt Dee? Are you up there chuckling in your sleeve over how you got me over this confounded barrel? Are you impressed with the fact that I have managed to catch the attention of not just one, but two and possibly three men?"

She frowned at her image in the cloudy old mirror, smoothing her auburn hair a bit, not that it made much difference. "But marrying for true love—*really*? That's a tough one. How will I know what's true love and what's not? And what about being true to myself? I know you care about that too. I hope you won't regret this game you created. And I hope you won't be disappointed in me." She turned from the mirror, went over to the window, and opened it up wide to let some fresh air into the stuffy room. Then she shooed Lucy and Ethel back out and closed the door.

She smiled to herself as she fingered the pearls around her neck— somehow she knew that the same aunt who had gotten her into this mess was going to help her get out of it. With God's help.

Chapter 10

Daphne had never been a wallflower exactly. Certainly it wasn't really possible with her height as well as a head of curly auburn hair. But driving around in the copper Corvette only made her even more conspicuous. But why not simply enjoy it? Hold her head high and accept that, like her flamboyant aunt, she wasn't the kind of woman who could go around unobserved? Perhaps she'd managed to lurk in the shadows while working at *The Times*. But those days were over now. It was time to come out of her shell—and live her life. At least for a year.

As she parked her car in front of The Zeppelin, she felt people glancing her way. She could tell they were curious as to her identity—or perhaps they recognized her aunt's car, although that seemed unlikely since Aunt Dee had seldom driven. But it was obvious that she was being watched as she went into the restaurant.

The foyer was bright and cheerful with pale wood floors and sky blue walls adorned with large black-and-white photos of old zeppelin balloons. Fun. She went to the aluminum-topped reception desk, with sides of corrugated steel that resembled something from an airplane hangar and told the hostess she was meeting someone.

"Jake?" The hostess asked with a knowing look.

"How did you know?"

The hostess grinned. "He told me to watch for a striking redhead. I figured that had to be you. Right this way."

Jake stood to greet her as the hostess brought her to the table and pulled out her chair like a real gentleman. Then the hostess took their drink orders.

"You look pretty today," he said after the hostess left. "Those pearls are a nice touch."

She reached up to them, smoothing her fingertips over the silky beads. "Thank you. And that brings up one of my questions. The pearls belonged to Aunt Dee, and I assume since I'm allowed to use everything in the house that it's okay for me to wear them. But I wasn't sure . . ."

He nodded. "It's perfectly acceptable for you to enjoy them. Besides I've heard that pearls keep their patina longer when they're worn. And I'm sure Dee would be pleased to see them on you."

She felt relieved as she turned her attention to the menu. Skimming past the broad selection of tempting choices, she quickly spotted the soup and salad special. For three practical reasons, this was her usual choice when having lunch in New York. (1) It usually had fewer calories, (2) it was usually moderately tasty, and (3) it was economical. She closed the menu and slid it aside.

"That was quick." He studied her. "Already decided?"

"Yes. The soup and salad."

"That's a nice, safe choice. But what about all the other offerings? Don't you care to consider them too?"

"Not particularly."

He started reading from the menu, commenting on which entrées he'd sampled and which ones were his favorites. "You're not really listening, are you?"

She shrugged. "I'm listening. But I just happen to want the soup and salad."

"Really?" He leaned forward, peering curiously at her. "That's what you *really* want? Or what you picked out of habit . . . what you're willing to settle for."

She pressed her lips together.

"So, do you have any idea what Dee would order?"

"Not really. I never ate with her here," Daphne said.

"Sometimes she only wanted crab cakes and a martini. And sometimes she got the portabella sandwich with coleslaw. And sometimes she went all out and got a top sirloin steak—rare, with all the works."

"And your point is?"

"Dee knew how to live."

"Oh . . ." Daphne nodded. "Meaning I don't?"

"I'm not sure." He set his menu aside. "But I have my doubts. And quite frankly, so did Dee."

But the waitress appeared with their drinks and asked if they were ready to order, and suddenly Daphne was flustered—and determined not to settle for soup and salad. She grabbed up the menu as Jake ordered the hazelnut-encrusted halibut. She was scanning over the list, trying to remember what he'd recommended, but everything just seemed to blur in her mind.

"And you, miss?" The waitress looked down on her.

"I'll, uh . . . I'll have . . . hmm . . . the halibut too."

"Very good." The waitress nodded.

Jake chuckled as she left. "Nicely done. Stepping out of your comfort zone."

She rolled her eyes. "You think I'm in my comfort zone? I haven't been in my comfort zone since I left New York."

"Really, you were that comfortable there?"

She considered this. "No, probably not. I simply meant that I had my routine and rituals in New York and I knew what to expect, but to be honest it wasn't exactly comfortable."

"So maybe you're finding your comfort zone here?"

"Maybe. But what you said about Aunt Dee having her doubts about me not knowing how to live. Was that true or were you just trying to get a rise out of me?"

He frowned. "Unfortunately it's true. Dee felt that your life in New York was a disappointment to you. She was worried that you were never going to find fulfillment there."

She sighed. As usual, Aunt Dee was probably right. Not that she planned to admit that to Jake. She had been feeling this way too and her boss's reaction confirmed it.

"Anyway, you said you have questions. I assume about more than just Dee's pearls."

"Yes, but the pearls lead to the next question." She pulled the slip of paper from her bag. "Regarding Aunt Dee's personal effects. I realize I'm not supposed to sell or get rid of anything, but even if I don't get to keep the house—after my year's up or if I give up before then—the house will still need to be cleared out some to be put on the market. That is, unless the Cat House plans to relocate to Huckleberry Lane and I suspect there could be a zoning ordinance problem there."

He grinned. "You're a sharp one."

"Anyway, I wondered if I could at least pack up my aunt's things. Put them in crates and store them until—"

"Actually, if we're only talking about clothes and things of no real monetary value, I see no reason why you can't clear them out whenever you like. You don't need to store them. Just donate them to Salvation Army or the nonprofit of your choice."

"Really? That's okay?"

"Sure. And you're right, you'll be doing everyone a favor in the unlikely event that the house must be listed and sold." He nodded. "Feel free to clean house, Daphne. Just don't profit from it."

"Thank you. And that brings me to the next question. What about Aunt Dee's possessions, the ones that aren't really valuable but might be meaningful to relatives. Like I know my young teenage cousin Mattie collects old costume jewelry. She told me about it the day of the funeral when I commented on a brooch she was wearing. And I honestly don't think she told me as a hint, but even so I'd love to share some of my aunt's old pieces with her. I think she'd appreciate them."

"Mattie? You're not referring to Mattie Stone, are you?"

"Yes. She's Martin's granddaughter. Her mom is Jocelyn Stone. She used to be Jocelyn Ballinger, Martin Ballinger's daughter."

"Okay, that makes sense now. Mattie Stone is also my daughter's best friend." He grinned. "I didn't realize she was Martin's granddaughter."

"Small world."

"And you're right, Mattie does collect old costume jewelry and purses and things. She's even gotten Jenna interested in it too. And fortunately those kinds of fashion accessories aren't as nearly costly as some of the new designer stuff that my ex-wife was into."

"So I can give Mattie those pieces?"

"Sure. Just make sure you don't give her any real jewelry. That could be a problem. At least for the time being. If you choose to give away Dee's jewels after you marry, that's entirely up to you."

She frowned at him. "You seem awfully sure that I'm going to get married."

He smiled. "I think the odds are stacked in your favor. You haven't been here a week and already the men are lining up."

She waved her hand. "Okay, even if I did manage to get a proposal—I mean who knows, miracles happen—but what about the true-love part? Didn't Aunt Dee stipulate I had to fall in love and marry?"

"Yes, well . . ." He gave a reluctant nod.

"How likely do you think that is?"

She watched him as he focused on buttering a piece of sourdough bread. He was nice looking in a sleek New York sort of way. Very lawyerly in his charcoal gray suit and light blue shirt. But if she was his client, wouldn't it be unprofessional for him to get involved with her. Besides that, how could she possibly trust his motives, knowing he was the only person in town—possibly the only person on the planet—who actually knew the value of the fortune she stood to inherit if she married, as well as the conditions attached to it? That alone warned her that of all the eligible bachelors, he was the last one she should consider.

"So, you have more questions?" he asked after a bit.

"Yes." She glanced down at her list. "The house needs painting.

And Aunt Dee had already picked out colors. Is it all right to get it painted?"

"Absolutely. No problem."

"What about any changes or improvements to the interior of the house?"

"Again, I don't see how that can be a problem. As long as the changes and improvements remain with the house in the unlikely event that you and the house part ways a year from now."

"Please, could you stop calling it the *unlikely event*?"

He nodded. "Sorry."

"The changes I make would probably help the house to sell."

"I'm sure they would. I'll create a budget for you from Dee's estate. Just keep track of your receipts."

"Now, about the *Dear Daphne* column. When am I supposed to take that on?"

"There's no hurry. As I mentioned, they're running old columns for the time being."

"I know, but I think I'd like to get started on it anyway. I thought maybe I could practice a little in the upcoming week. Then I could start up for real after I get back from New York and settle in a little."

"When will that be?" She told him a date which he jotted down. "I'll let the appropriate parties know," he said. "Everything, as you can imagine, is sent electronically nowadays. And everything should be on Dee's computer. Did I give you her passwords yet?"

"No. I haven't even had the nerve to go into her study yet."

"Really? Why not?"

"I don't know. That was always her personal space. She never really liked me going in there."

"Well, that was only because she didn't want you to know about Penelope's steamy romance novels." He smiled. "Can't blame her for trying to protect your innocence." He jotted something else down. "Note to self: Get Daphne the passwords for Dee's computer."

"Thanks."

"More questions?"

As she was looking at her list, the waitress returned with their entrées, which Daphne had to admit looked and smelled delicious. She forked into the tender white fish, then took a sample bite. "Oh, my." She shook her head. "That is really yummy."

He chuckled. "Better than the beef barley soup and a green salad?"

"Oh yeah." She forked another bite. And for another couple of minutes the table grew quiet as they enjoyed their meals.

"It's nice to see you're open to trying new things."

"Yes, I suppose I've lived in a rut of sorts. I need to remind myself that I'm not still there." She grinned. "Driving the Corvette is a pretty good reminder."

"I'll bet." He nodded.

"Okay, now I have a tricky question. I asked you about it before, but you were a little vague. It's about my dad. I feel like he has a right to know that Aunt Dee was really his mother. It seems unfair that I know and he doesn't. I understand that she wanted to protect him, but I really think he'll understand. I mean, he'll be shocked. But I think he'll want to know. Is it okay if I tell him?"

"It's entirely up to you."

"Really?"

"Absolutely. And I agree. I think he deserves to know she was his mother. However, I have to draw the line there."

"What do you mean?"

"You can't disclose anything about *Dear Daphne* or Penelope Poindexter. We have to respect Dee's last wishes for anonymity regarding those two things. You do understand, don't you?"

"Yes. That's not a problem. I don't even *want* Dad to know about those things. I doubt he would understand the Penelope books, and I don't want anyone to know that I'm taking over the column. I can understand why Aunt Dee didn't either. That's a lot of responsibility—giving advice out like that. What do I know about love and all those things?"

"Apparently Dee thought you could handle it. And think about it, what did she know? A spinster aunt? And yet she left behind some of the best advice ever."

"I know. I've always been a faithful reader of her column." She set down her fork. "And you know what? I'm glad I never knew it was Aunt Dee writing it. That would've ruined everything for me."

"So she knew what she was doing to keep it secret?"

"I think so."

She went over her other questions, which were fairly minor, and his answers were not surprising. And finally their lunch came to an end and he insisted on paying the bill, explaining that he always covered his clients' lunches. "A tax deduction," he said lightly.

But the word she heard was *client*. He did think of her as a client. And that meant he understood the distance that would have to remain between them. Oddly enough that was both a relief and a disappointment. But mostly a relief. She had enough to sort through without trying to weigh someone's motives. Really, it would be best if he continued to play the role of counselor and big brother. Just not the Big Brother from Orwell's *1984*—that was creepy.

As planned, she stopped by Bernie's Blooms on the way home. She parked in front and went inside with the excuse of purchasing flowers, which was ridiculous considering that Aunt Dee's yard was full of blooming things. But as soon as she entered the shop, she realized it was much more than just a traditional florist shop. Filled with all sorts of lovely household items, from candles to vases to clocks to kitchen towels . . . and more.

"May I help you?" a young woman asked as Daphne was happily browsing in the candle section.

"Oh no, I'm just enjoying all these delicious-smelling scents."

"Yes, those are soy candles. Very popular."

"Is Olivia around?" Daphne finally selected a candle that smelled like citrus and pine.

"Yes. She's working in back. Do you want me to get her?"

"If she's not too busy."

"I'll go see."

Daphne continued to browse but jumped and nearly dropped the candle when Olivia let out a happy squeal from behind her. "Oh, you came to see me!" Olivia hugged her tightly. "I was just thinking about you and how we need to get together again." Olivia held her at arm's length and looked. "My, don't you look fancy. Heels and pearls. Where are you off to, City Girl?"

"I was just meeting with my attorney," Daphne said. "We had lunch at The Zeppelin and I thought I should dress up a bit." She frowned. "Although I'm not really sure what people wear around here." She looked at Olivia's faded jeans and plaid shirt.

"Appleton's a pretty casual town."

"And I didn't bring much with me from New York. Although I'm afraid what I wear in the city isn't really going to work here. I guess I should do some shopping. Do you have any recommendations?"

"Well, I'll tell you where not to go. Remember Frederica's?"

"Yes. We used to shop there all the—"

"Forget about that. They only have old-lady clothes now."

"Oh."

"And Sharpe's has gone downhill too. Hey, my day off is Friday. If you like, I could take you around to the good spots."

"Sure. I'd love that."

Just then Olivia peered out the window to where the Corvette was parked. "On second thought, you can take us around in your swanky car. Maybe we can do lunch too. Just like old times."

"Sure. And I'd like to find some shops with house things too." She held up the candle. "Touches like this. I want to spruce up Aunt Dee's house a little. Make it feel more like my style, you know?" Even as she said this she wondered, what was her style? Would she even recognize it if she saw it?

"Sounds like fun. Count me in. Now, if you'll excuse me I have to get some arrangements finished. Seems like everyone's having a birthday or anniversary today."

"Yes. Don't let me keep you. But I'll see you on Friday."

They agreed on the time and then Daphne made her purchase. As she carried the bag out to her car, she felt a rush of hopeful optimism. Having Olivia as a friend again was an unexpected delight. Having her as a shopping partner would be just plain old fun.

Chapter 11

Before going home, Daphne decided to check out the shop next to Bernie's Blooms. It was called The Apple Basket and to her pleasant surprise, it was actually a small grocery store that specialized in fresh produce, whole foods, organic dairy products, fresh fish, and lots of other goodies.

She picked up a wicker basket and began to hunt and gather. Her plan was to invite Dad to dinner and to cook in Aunt Dee's kitchen tonight. A cozy private setting seemed preferable to a busy restaurant for telling him the startling truth about Aunt Dee. Dad was usually so even-keeled, but she had no idea how he would react to discovering that his "older sister" was actually his mother.

By the time she made it to the cashier, she had a bag of jasmine rice, a fine-looking pair of salmon fillets, ingredients for salad, asparagus, a box of strawberries, organic ice cream, and a number of other things.

"Looks like someone's in for a good meal tonight," the young man said as he carefully set the last of her groceries in the canvas shopping bag he'd encouraged her to purchase.

"Yes. My dad." She handed him her debit card.

"Lucky dad."

"He loves salmon. I just hope I don't ruin it. I haven't done much cooking lately."

So as he ran her card, he gave her some tips on preparing salmon.

"This is a great store," she told him. "I'll probably become a regular here. At least until my garden starts producing. Although I'll still need milk and eggs and things I can't grow on my own."

"That's great you're planting a garden." He gave her the receipt, then peered curiously at her. "So . . . are you new in town?"

She shrugged. "Not really. I grew up here. But I've been living in New York for the past twelve years."

"And you're moving back home now?"

She nodded, reaching for her bag.

"Good for you." Now he came around the counter and stretched out his hand. "I'm Truman Walters and I own this store. Welcome back to Appleton."

"Thanks." She shook his hand. "I'm Daphne Ballinger." She tilted her head to one side. "But I have to admit you seem a bit young to own a business. Kudos to you."

He laughed. "Yeah. I get that all the time. Some people assume I'm still in high school and I'm just a part-time employee. I'm sure I'll appreciate that a little more someday. But I'm actually twenty-nine pushing thirty." He pushed a strand of shaggy blond hair from his forehead and, standing taller, proudly adjusted his green grocer's apron.

"So how long have you had this store?"

"Just a couple of years. And believe me it hasn't been easy. Most of the locals are used to those big one-stop superstores. You know, where you wheel an enormous metal cart around and pick up your tennis shoes, disposable diapers, and bananas all in one fell swoop."

She laughed. "Not where I lived in New York." She patted the canvas bag. "When you have to walk and use the subway, you learn to travel light."

"And smart." He nodded. "I just hope the rest of town catches on soon. Before I go out of business."

"Really? Is business that slow?"

"I sure hope not. Especially since my folks were skeptical about this business venture right from the start. My dad gave me one year before I went under." He brightened. "But I've lasted for more than two."

"Good for you." She smiled. "And today you gained a new customer."

Now another woman was bringing her basket to the counter so Daphne told Truman good-bye, and feeling that she'd made another friend, she carried her groceries out to her car. Appleton continued to surprise her.

As she drove home, she wondered about Truman. Starting his own business while still in his twenties was impressive. But then he seemed energetic, bright, and cheerful. Hopefully he would succeed at it. She wondered if he was single but instantly reprimanded herself. The boy was five years younger than she—wouldn't that make her a cougar?

Of course, that reminded her of Beverly and Robert. Daphne reflected back to when the three of them had been fellow employees and good friends. In fact, it was Daphne who'd originally befriended Robert when he'd come to work for the paper straight out of college. He had seemed "safe" to her since he was six years younger—kind of like a little brother. She and Beverly had taken the young man under their wing, and then it progressed to enjoying his company for impromptu "dates." Especially if they were exploring the city and felt more comfortable having a guy along. It was a nice arrangement.

Which was why Daphne had felt slightly blindsided when Beverly announced that she and Robert were taking their relationship to the next level. Especially since Beverly was two years older than Daphne, which made her eight years older than Robert. But according to Beverly, age was just a number where true love was concerned. Without telling anyone, not even Daphne, the couple had flown out to Vegas one Friday after work, tied the knot, and been back at the paper on Monday. Daphne had been hurt but, as usual, she had concealed her true feelings.

Naturally, and despite their attempts to include her, everything changed between the three of them after that. Daphne felt she was odd girl out. And although Beverly still claimed to be her best friend, the distance between them grew a tiny bit wider each year. And now with Beverly expecting and Daphne relocating, it would become an abyss. Daphne was glad that Beverly and Robert were happy and she wished them both the very best. And it was a relief to know she would not be lost without them.

As she pulled into the garage, she remembered Beverly's defense for being a "cougar" as Amelia had teasingly called her. "Men age faster than women," Beverly had pointed out. "They wear out sooner. They die younger. So what's wrong with finding a guy who can keep up with you?"

As she unlocked the door, Daphne decided that if Beverly could be happily married to a man eight years her junior, Daphne could show interest in a guy who was nearly thirty. Of course, no sooner was the thought in her consciousness than she knew she was being perfectly ridiculous. Seriously, was she going to start plotting marriage with every single man she met? For Pete's sake, she didn't even know if Truman was single or interested in dating or in marriage.

"Don't turn into a man-crazy fool," she told herself as she went into the kitchen, and set her bag on the table. "Good grief. You should at least pace yourself."

She put her groceries away, then called Dad, leaving her dinner invitation on his voice mail. "I haven't really cooked for a while," she warned him, "but I'll give it my best shot."

Knowing her culinary skills were rusty, she decided to organize herself by washing all the salad things, and then realizing it was nearly four, she decided to just go ahead and make the salad. As she tore lettuce and peeled cucumbers and sliced tomatoes and chopped green peppers, she remembered how many times she had gone through these exact same steps as a girl.

Aunt Dee had taught her to make a simple green salad when she was six, just a year after her mom died. "You're the woman of the house now," Aunt Dee had said as she tied a yellow-and-white gingham child-sized apron on her. "It's time you learned to cook."

The summer when Daphne was seven, she learned to make both boiled and scrambled eggs, macaroni and cheese (from a box), and several other easy things like tuna salad sandwiches, and how to boil hot dogs. And over the years, Aunt Dee had taught her more and more. By the time she was ten, Daphne did all the cooking for Dad and her. And although some of her experiments turned out to be catastrophes, Dad never once complained. He'd simply call out for pizza or grab some take-out Chinese, and occasionally the two of them would end up sitting in a fast-food restaurant at eight o'clock.

However, Daphne wanted tonight's dinner to be perfection. And she put all her energy into being certain that happened. She wanted everything to be ready at the same time so when Dad walked in at six, it would all be just right. And hopefully he wouldn't be late.

Dad arrived at Aunt Dee's like clockwork. "Something smells mighty good in here," he said as he came into the kitchen and gave her a kiss on the cheek. "I've been looking forward to this all afternoon."

"Go ahead and sit." She pointed to the kitchen table, which she'd set prettily with Aunt Dee's Desert Rose Franciscan-ware dishes. "Would you like some strawberry lemonade?" She'd stocked the fridge with fresh lemonade for when Mick should stop by again.

"That sounds delicious." Dad removed his sports jacket and hung it on the hook by the back door. "To what do I owe this pleasure?" He sat down. "You cooking for me like this? I had planned to take you out tonight."

"Oh . . . I just wanted to." She set their salads on the table and sat across from him.

"Shall I say a blessing like we used to?"

"Please, do."

"Dear Lord, thank you for your bountiful gifts, help us to be truly grateful, and bless the lovely hands that prepared this delicious-looking meal. Amen."

"Amen." She laid the pink plaid napkin in her lap and picked up her fork. She told him all about dining with Olivia and Jeff and Ricardo. And about how the garden was coming along nicely, and how she and Olivia planned to go shopping on Friday, and how much she'd enjoyed The Apple Basket today.

"Do you shop there too?" she asked him.

"You know, I'm ashamed to admit I haven't been inside that store."

"Oh, you should check it out, Dad. The foods they carry are so much healthier. Organic. No chemicals or hormones. And Truman, that's the owner, is very knowledgeable about food preparation. He gave me the idea for how to cook this salmon."

He nodded. "And it's excellent. Okay, I'm convinced. I'll have to go to The Apple Basket. And I'll mention it to Karen too."

For some reason she bristled at the mention of Karen. But, as usual, she tried not to show it. "So tell me about you and Karen," she said carefully. "Is it more serious than I thought?"

He made what seemed like a slightly embarrassed smile. "Well, I do enjoy Karen's company. We have fun together. But I'm just not sure."

"Not sure?"

He nodded. "I don't know that Karen is as interested in me as I am in her."

"Oh . . ."

He gazed at Daphne. "You're younger than me and you're probably more up on these things. How does a person know if another person is equally interested?"

His question made her think of *Dear Daphne* and she was certain she'd read letters similar to that in the column. She tried to imagine what kind of answer Aunt Dee would have given, or the answer Daphne would write—when the time came to write. Pressing her lips tightly together, she thought hard.

"Well, I think the eyes have it," she finally said.

"The ayes?" He looked confused.

She pointed to her own eyes. "The *eyes*. Think about it, Dad. Do Karen's eyes light up when she looks at you?"

"Hmmm . . ." His mouth twisted to one side.

"Besides that, I think you can probably tell by her enthusiasm. Does she sound happy when you call her?"

"I suppose so . . . unless she's with a customer. Then she keeps it short."

"That's understandable. But does she seem as happy to see you as you are to see her?"

Dad's brow creased as if deep in thought.

"Have you been paying attention to all the little things?"

"Not particularly. Although now that I think about, Karen always seems happy to see me. And I do think her eyes light up. Or it might be that my eyes are lighting up enough for both of us." He laughed, then shook his head. "I honestly never thought that at my age I'd be this interested in a woman again."

"I know you never dated anyone when I lived at home."

"No, I just didn't feel that was right somehow. It seemed that our life was already full—it was busy enough with just the two of us."

"And you didn't date anyone after I left for college?" She didn't want to mention that had been sixteen years ago.

"I did make some feeble attempts to get back into the dating game. I even joined a singles group at the church for a spell—but I was so outnumbered by women that it was a little overwhelming. Besides, I felt like a confirmed bachelor by then. And I already had my guy friends to play cards and golf and watch ball games with. Most of them acted like they envied my freedom and independence. And I suppose I enjoyed that notoriety some. But the truth was, there just weren't any single women around, I mean, ones that made me feel . . . well, the way Karen does." He let out a little sigh.

"Then for your sake, I hope Karen feels the same as you, Dad." And even though she didn't feel particularly fond of Karen, or maybe Daphne was just suspicious, she meant it. If Dad was truly in love with Karen, she hoped Karen felt the same. She really didn't want to see Karen break his heart. She couldn't even imagine her dear old dad with a broken heart. And if Karen hurt him at all, well, Daphne would have to control herself from throttling the woman.

"Speaking of romance, you mentioned having had dinner with Ricardo." Dad's eyes twinkled with interest. "But you didn't really say how that went."

"It was a nice evening." She nonchalantly explained how it was completely impromptu and how Ricardo kindly gifted them with the meal. "And the dessert—his Appleton pie—was scrumptious."

"Yes, I've had it too. More times than I care to admit. But that's not what I meant. I meant how did you and my good friend Ricardo get along?"

She rolled her eyes. "Still playing matchmaker, are we?"

He feigned an innocent look. "Can't a father care about his daughter's love life?"

"Love life?" She laughed.

"Ricardo is a genuinely good man, Daphne. Why wouldn't I want to nudge you in that direction?"

"I'll admit he's a good guy. And I did get to hear the story of how he'd been engaged to Bernadette." She sighed. "That was very sad."

Dad nodded. "That was one of the things that connected me to Ricardo. We both knew what it felt like to lose a loved one."

"But don't you think that would make it hard on me? I mean, if I was interested in Ricardo in that way? Bernadette was such a lovely person. Those would be some pretty big shoes to fill."

"You're a lovely person too, Daphne."

"Thanks, Dad. But you are just slightly biased." She laughed.

"Remember that Ricardo and Bernadette weren't actually married. Besides that, it's been several years since she passed. I think Ricardo must be ready for a new romance now. Why else would he join you for dinner like that?"

"You could be right, I mean that he's interested in romance. I don't know if you've noticed or not, but he's hired a very pretty waitress named Kellie. And she seems fairly intent on getting romantically involved with him. I'm not the only one to think so either."

Dad looked alarmed. "Oh no, Daphne, I think you're wrong. I've seen Kellie. And she's really not Ricardo's type."

"What makes you so sure?"

"I don't know. Just a feeling."

"Well, I wouldn't bet on it, Dad." She stood and began clearing the table. "I thought we might want to have dessert and coffee later."

"Yes." He leaned back and patted his midsection. "Let's give this time to digest. And again, I have to say it. Everything was delicious, Daphne. You still know how to cook."

"Well, I hardly ever cooked a real meal in New York. So I had to really focus to get this one right."

"You got it just right." As she put some things away, Dad talked about moving into the condo. "I'm really looking forward to setting the place up just how I like it."

"You mean the house wasn't how you liked it?"

"Well, I never really changed much . . . you know . . . it was pretty much how your mom left it."

She nodded. "Yeah, I know."

"I think it's time I moved on."

She forced a smile. "So are you going to make your condo into a swanky bachelor pad?"

Dad laughed. "No, I don't think so. But I might get a leather sofa."

"Good for you." She linked with his arm as she led the way to the front room. She was preparing herself for what she planned to tell him, but she wanted to be sure he was seated comfortably before she began. She had rehearsed her spiel in her head, but as she sat down it felt as if her words and thoughts had been scattered by the wind. As Lucy hopped up into her lap, Daphne took in a deep breath and, stroking the cat's orange fur, decided to simply begin.

"I met with Jake McPheeters again today," she said slowly and deliberately.

"Was there more to go over regarding the will?"

"Sort of. Jake had told me some things on Monday, things that I'd still been trying to sort out. Some, uh, rather surprising things."

"In regard to Aunt Dee's estate?"

"Not exactly. More about Aunt Dee herself."

"Really?" Now Ethel jumped onto Dad's lap and he absently petted her. "What sort of things?"

"Well, it kind of concerns you, Dad." Daphne bit her lip. "I'm not even sure where or how to begin."

Dad looked intently at her and she had his complete and undivided attention. "Go ahead."

"Well . . . it seems that Aunt Dee is not really my aunt."

"What?" He frowned. "Well, of course she's your aunt, Daphne. She's been your aunt for your entire—"

"And Aunt Dee is not really your sister, Dad."

"What?" His tone grew even more impatient. "That's completely ridiculous. Where on earth does Jake McPheeters get off telling you—"

"Calm down, Dad." She took in another deep breath. "As you know, Aunt Dee started college back in 1938 when—"

"Yes, yes, I know about all that. Although it was highly unusual. Most women didn't further their education back then, and besides that, it was still the Great Depression. Even so, what's that got to do with this strange claim that we're not related to Dee?"

"I didn't say we're *not* related, Dad. If you'd just let me finish."

"Sorry." He leaned back, stroking Ethel a bit vigorously. "Go ahead, I'm very curious to hear this—even if it is poppycock."

"So anyway Aunt Dee went to college, but after a while, well the truth of the matter is, Aunt Dee became pregnant and—"

"What?" He stood now, causing poor Ethel to leap down to the floor for safety. "What in tarnation are you saying, Daphne? Aunt Dee never—"

"Dad." She pointed a warning finger. "Do you want to hear this or not?"

He huffed and puffed, then sat back down, crossing his arms in front of his chest. "Yes, yes, go on. I just can't believe you're saying such things about your dear old aunt, who's only been laid to rest a few days."

"I'm sorry. As I was saying, Aunt Dee became pregnant and she had a baby boy the following September in 1941 and—"

"September? 1941?" He stood again. "Why, that's when I was born."

"I know, Dad. Aunt Dee was not really your sister, she was your mother."

A look of stunned realization flashed through his eyes as his hand slapped over his mouth and he sunk back down onto the sofa.

"I'm sorry to break it to you like this. I had planned all these careful ways to tell you. But it seems there really isn't a good way to say something like this." She gently pushed Lucy off her lap and went to sit by her dad. "Are you okay?"

Staring blankly across the room, he slowly shook his head. "Dee wasn't my sister? She was my mother?"

"It actually explains a lot," she said quietly. "Aunt Dee loved you so much. And me too. She always gave us a lot more attention than the rest of the family. I thought it was because Mom died. But now I realize it's because she was really your mother. My grandmother."

"Dee was not my sister. She was my mother," he repeated again, obviously trying to absorb this.

"That's right." She put a hand on his shoulder. "How does that make you feel?"

"Stunned."

"I know how you feel. I was stunned too. I'm sure that, back then, it seemed the right thing for her to do. She wasn't married. She probably felt that having her parents raise you as their son was the kindest way for you to grow up."

He just nodded. "I sometimes wondered that my parents were rather old. I know I was considered a change-of-life baby. But I never guessed Dee was my mother. Never in a million years."

"She took great care to see that you didn't. I'm sure she wanted to protect you."

"I'll bet that's why she moved back home after college," he said slowly, as if soaking it in. "Being so young, I took her presence in my life for granted at the time. But later on I remember hearing how she was such a great author, and we all knew she was making such good money writing all those textbooks and manuals. People said she could've lived anywhere. But she chose to remain in little old Appleton."

"To be near you."

"And you too," he pointed out. "Dee was always there when I needed her too. She attended just about every single event I ever participated in—even more so than my parents . . . rather, my grand-parents." He scratched his head. "That'll take some getting used to."

"I know. I still think of her as Aunt Dee. Not Grandma."

"Maybe it doesn't matter what we call her."

"I don't think so. As long as we still love her. You do, don't you, Dad?"

"Oh yes." He nodded eagerly. "Maybe even more now. When I think of what she sacrificed for me . . . I never knew."

"Do you think that's why she never married?"

"I have no idea. But this was obviously a secret she took to the grave." Dad looked at her. "Why did Jake tell you about it now?"

"Because of the inheritance, I think. It sort of helps to explain why no one else in the family was in her will."

"Are you going to tell the others about this?"

She shrugged. "What do you think?"

"Well, I feel bad that the relatives are acting like it's unfair she excluded them. If they knew you were her only granddaughter, they might be more understanding." He rubbed his chin. "But at the same time I'd like to protect Dee's image. Especially considering how well she concealed this for all those years. It seems respectful to keep a lid on this—for her sake."

"I know."

"So, if you don't mind having your relatives treating you poorly for a while—because I'm sure they'll get past it in time—I would just as soon let sleeping dogs lie."

"So would I." She was willing to bury it down there with all the other secrets she was holding for Aunt Dee. Oh, sure, her life might've been easier if the relatives understood the situation better. But she could do this—for Dad and Aunt Dee.

Chapter 12

As much as Daphne longed for a confidante, especially after Beverly had cut their last conversation short then never called back, she knew she couldn't burden Olivia with her numerous secrets. For one thing, it'd been years since they'd been close friends. Besides that, well, she just couldn't. Daphne was not in the habit of sharing—and old habits really did die hard.

However, she did enjoy Olivia's cheerful companionship as they shopped at a couple of stores in Appleton and later drove over to nearby Fairview to check out a recently built outdoor mall. "Can you imagine how much fun we would've had shopping here as teens?" Olivia asked as they walked around The Fairview Shoppes.

"I can't believe how much has changed since I moved away," Daphne said as Olivia led her through one of her favorite boutiques, piling an interesting assortment of clothing into Daphne's arms before she led her back to the changing area.

"I would never wear something like this in New York," Daphne confessed as she emerged from the dressing room wearing a

Bohemian-looking skirt and lacy top Olivia had insisted was perfect for an author to wear.

"You don't like it?"

Daphne studied the bright-colored skirt. "No, I actually do like it, but it's such a departure from my usual serious clothes."

Olivia chuckled. "Yes, that describes what I've seen you wearing. *Very serious*. At first I thought it was only because your aunt died. But then I realized it's just how you dress. I mean, I'm not criticizing. It's a very classic and dignified look and it probably fits your job. But it doesn't seem very easy going, you know? Not very creative."

"I have two basic modes of dress in New York. My business go-to-work outfits and my slacker weekend wear, ratty clothes that I do not want to be seen in."

"What about fun clothes?" Olivia asked. "Like for nights on the town? I figured New Yorkers usually dressed to the nines, went out clubbing or to shows, basically having all kinds of fun."

"I think Sarah Jessica Parker helped to create that illusion."

"Illusion—you're saying that's an illusion?" Olivia looked disappointed. "But come on, Daphne, what'd you wear on dates? Certainly not your no-nonsense black suit."

Daphne frowned. Perhaps this was a secret she could safely divulge, even if it did reveal more than she was quite comfortable with regarding her unimpressive personal life. Really, why should Olivia be surprised?

"The truth is, I rarely dated." Daphne went back into the over-sized changing room, ready to try on something else. But to her surprise, Olivia, with a number of accessories in hand, had followed her in. Now they both stood in front of the big mirror, but Olivia's expression was decidedly skeptical.

"Seriously, that is not at all how I imagined your life." Olivia held up a pendant, then shook her head as if dismissing it.

"But you've known me for years. I was never what you'd call a social butterfly."

"Yeah, but that was long ago—maybe you were kind of like a shy caterpillar back then, but you blossomed into this gorgeous butterfly. Honestly, I'd have expected men would've been beating a path to your door back in New York."

Daphne laughed. "Thanks for the compliment, but I can assure you there are a lot of gorgeous women in New York. I didn't stand out one bit."

"I find that hard to believe." Olivia eyes narrowed slightly. "Seriously, are you telling me you *never* dated at all?"

"Well, sure, I dated for a while. I'd only been in New York a couple of years when I got into this fairly serious relationship."

"Aha." Olivia nodded. "I knew it."

"But it turned out to be an unhealthy sort of relationship. One that hurt me . . . pretty deeply. And it's taken a long time to recover." Assuming she was recovered. Most of the time she thought she was, but sometimes she still felt frustrated at her overly cautious reaction to men. She was always second-guessing their intentions . . . and herself.

"Oh." Olivia held another necklace up to the lacy top. "But you remember what they say about falling off the horse?"

Daphne shrugged. "Yes. I know. But for some reason, I got stuck in a rut."

Olivia held up the third necklace and frowned. "I always figured you'd be the one to get married and settle down first."

"Why?"

"You were such a homebody. You loved cooking and cleaning and all that homemaking stuff."

"That's because it was expected of me. I mean after my mom died." Daphne tried the wide belt the salesgirl had recommended and cinched it tightly around her waist.

"No, no, loosen it up," Olivia told her. "Like this." She let the belt out so it slid down more comfortably. "Much better."

"Yes." Daphne nodded as she looked at the strange image in the mirror. "I actually kind of like this."

"Enough to wear it sometime?" Olivia tilted her head to one side. "Or will you hide it away in your closet?"

Daphne grinned. "After all these years, you still know me."

Olivia laughed. "Yeah, you were always a bit of a stick in the mud."

Daphne frowned. "A stick in the mud?"

"I'm sorry. That was a little harsh. I just mean you were always the careful one. You never partied with the rest of us. You never skipped school. Not even on senior skip day."

"I heard that we couldn't graduate if we skipped." Daphne sighed. "But that didn't seem to bother anyone else. Everyone graduated just fine."

"So did you ever feel like you were missing out?"

"A little." Daphne considered how much she wanted to divulge. She was so accustomed to keeping things to herself. But realizing how many of Aunt Dee's secrets she couldn't disclose, maybe it was about time to be more open about other parts of her life.

"I always felt this need to be extra careful," she explained as she fiddled with the neck of the cream-colored lacy top. "Because after my mom died, my dad used to say I was all he had. He'd say things like I needed to take good care of myself—for him. So it kind of got ingrained in me, like I needed to be really cautious. Does that make sense? Like I've been stuck."

"Yeah. I do get that." Olivia slipped the beaded necklace over Daphne's head, then stepped back. "Now that is perfect."

"Thanks."

"And I think you should get this outfit. Maybe it'll help you to get unstuck."

Daphne couldn't argue with that and soon purchased the whole thing, including the belt and necklace. She made numerous other purchases too and, finally laden down with a number of other bags—containing jeans and cargo pants and T-shirts and other casual yet stylish pieces of clothing—they decided to take a break at Starbucks. After they were seated with coffees and scones, Olivia brought up the topic of Daphne's cautious way of living again.

"So now I understand why you've been so careful in the past. But do you ever worry that you might continue standing on the sidelines while life passes you by?"

Daphne nodded as she set down her coffee mug. "Just recently, and even before my aunt died, I was giving my boring little life some serious thought. And then after I got here, I felt this sudden urgency to shake things up. I wasn't even sure how. And I had no idea that Aunt Dee was going to be so, uh, so generous. But it felt like an invitation to change."

"I know. Not only that gorgeous house but her fabulous car too. You're one lucky girl, Daphne." She smiled. "Your aunt must've really loved you."

Daphne just nodded, suppressing the urge to blurt out that Dee was actually her grandmother or to mention the strings attached to her aunt's generosity. But she couldn't. "Anyway, it was like I was ready. I *wanted* to make this change. I was ready to give up my job and New York. I feel like I'm finally ready to take some real chances."

"Writing a novel sounds like taking a chance."

"Yes . . . putting my words out there for everyone to see—and without the safety net of a newspaper beneath me. I guess I should prepare myself for some rejection. And I've never been very fond of rejection."

"Who is?"

There was a comfortable pause while they both sipped their coffees. "Thanks for coming with me today." Daphne wanted to say more than that but wasn't quite sure how to. "It means a lot to know I've still got friends in Appleton."

"It means a lot to me that you're moving back. I'm looking forward to spending more time together. And I hope you'll let me help you with some of the updating you plan to do on your house. I can just see you incorporating some shabby chic into it. And there's this great little shop called Sister Suzy that I'm dying to show you. She's like a shabby-chic diva. And her shop has a little bit of everything in it."

"Sounds like fun."

"I mean if I can't spend my own money—because Jeff and I are saving for a down payment right now—I'm always eager to spend someone else's. And Pottery Barn is right next to Sister Suzy, and there are a couple other home stores down on that end of the mall."

Daphne considered how much she'd already spent today. "Well, I might have to content myself with just looking for now." She made a sheepish smile. "Sorry, but I can't give up all my cautious ways in just one day. Besides, I still have things in New York. Although I think I'll try to get rid of most of it."

"I think it's smart to just look at first anyway," Olivia told her. "That way you figure out what you like and avoid making impulse buys. Then you make a plan and you stick to it."

"Right. And I should get some paint colors too. Aunt Dee already picked out exterior paint, which I want to use, but I have no idea of where to begin for the interior paint colors. Maybe I should just paint it all off-white."

Olivia shook her head. "That would be so stark, you'd want to repaint it. Why waste the time and money?"

"Maybe I should just leave it as is." Daphne was thinking about how quickly a year could pass. Maybe it was foolish to make changes to the house.

"But if it needs doing," Olivia said, "why not enjoy it? You can put your mark on it and make it your own. And if you want any help with colors, you know I'd be happy to give an opinion. I love working with color combinations."

"Thanks. I can tell by looking at your shop that you have a good eye for it."

"Well, some of that was Bernadette's doing. She had a really good eye. But I've made some good changes too . . . even if I do say so myself. And if you need the name of a painter, we've got a neighbor who's a painting contractor and he's rock-solid reliable." Her brows arched. "And come to think of it, he's recently become single."

Daphne laughed. "Honestly, it feels like everyone is working on getting me married."

"Sorry. I always hated it when people did that to me, and I promised myself I'd never be like that. But something happens when you get married. You suddenly think that everyone else should be as happy as you are."

"Well, it's nice you're happy . . ."

"Anyway, now that I think about it, Willie's probably too old for you anyway. I think he's close to fifty. I mean, he's young for his age, but that's quite an age gap." Olivia broke off a piece of scone. "So tell me, who else is trying to get you married off?"

Again, Daphne had to watch her words. "Mostly my dad. I think he's worried he'll never be a grandfather."

"Who's he matching you up with?"

Daphne sighed. "Ricardo Martoni. For some reason Dad's got the crazy notion that we'd be perfect for each other."

"You could do worse." Olivia looked slightly offended.

"Oh yeah, I know that for sure. Ricardo is a great guy."

"But you're just not into him?" Olivia frowned.

"I'm not saying that at all. It's just that Dad's been pushing him at me. And when I heard about Bernadette and Ricardo . . . well, I wondered if he's even over her yet."

"I don't know. He hasn't really dated since then."

"And as you pointed out the other night, that waitress seems to have her eye on him."

"Kellie is so not his type."

"That's what my dad insinuated too. But you never know. She's pretty and she seems genuinely interested in him. If nothing else, Kellie could end up being his rebound girl. Or whatever you call that—you know, the one who helps him to get back into the dating world." Suddenly Daphne wondered if that's what she needed too. A rebound guy? And if so, who would he be? Or was that just plain silly?

"You might be on to something. Ricardo has seemed kind of frozen since losing Bernadette. Maybe someone like Kellie would nudge him back into the wonderful world of dating." She laughed. "And then he could see that she's totally wrong for him and go looking for someone more suitable." Olivia looked at Daphne. "Maybe even someone like you."

She smiled. "I'm not going to categorize you with my match-making dad for that. Instead, I take it as a compliment. I'm honored you think I'm worthy of Ricardo."

They visited for a while longer, then went window-shopping at the stores Olivia had mentioned but finally decided that until Olivia chose paint colors, it would be pointless to make a single purchase. So they cut the shopping excursion short and went to a paint store instead. There, Olivia helped Daphne select a wide variety of colors she thought would be suitable for the Queen Anne Victorian. And they even took home some paint samples that Daphne could actually try on the walls.

"But remember that's making a commitment," Olivia reminded her as they drove home. "Once you start plastering different colors throughout the house, you will have to paint."

Olivia came into the house with Daphne and together they carried the paint chips from room to room, trying to imagine how they'd look and which ones were best. And they even tried some of the paint samples. By the end of the day, they had decided on a soft dove gray shade for the front room and foyer and stairway, a buttery yellow for the dining room, and a soft apple green for the kitchen. All the painted wooden trim would remain white but freshened up with a rich coat of milky white. The downstairs bathroom would be a warm peach to brighten it up. And Daphne's bedroom would be a pale robin's egg blue. However, both Aunt Dee's bedroom and the den would remain the same for the time being. Daphne was not ready to change those spaces yet.

"This is so exciting," she said as she walked Olivia out to where her bicycle was parked in front. "Thanks so much for helping."

"Hey, I enjoyed it.

"Well, I never could've picked out those colors by myself. And you made it seem so easy. I don't even know how you did that so fast."

"It was kind of like making a bouquet. I just picked shades that looked compatible, like they'd be happy together. It makes me look forward to when Jeff and I find the right house to buy." She glanced down Huckleberry Lane. "I wish it could be something in this neighborhood, but these homes hardly ever go on the market. If you hear of a neighbor who's even thinking of selling, you better let me know right away."

"You've got my word." Daphne almost added that if Olivia could wait a year, this house might be available, but she bit her tongue.

"And don't forget to call Willie," Olivia reminded her as she hopped on the pink flower delivery bike. "And if I see him first, I'll put in a good word for you. Because I know this is his busy season."

Daphne went inside and looked up Willie Troutman Painting in the Yellow Pages and called. But getting his voice mail, she could only leave a message. And now she was so eager about the paint colors that by the time she hung up, she knew she'd given him way too much information. But it was too late. Hopefully he wouldn't chalk her up as a nutcase and refuse to return her call. But she was relieved when he called later that evening, and to her surprise he quickly agreed to the entire project.

"Without even seeing the house?" Suddenly she felt suspicious. "Do you have any idea how big it is? Or how old it is? Or what kind of condition it might be in?"

"Don't worry, I've seen the house before. Your aunt—and please forgive my manners because I forgot to offer you my condolences. But your aunt already had me out there last winter. I had her scheduled for early June."

"And you can still do it?"

"Fortunately for you, I haven't changed my schedule yet, but I was about to. Your aunt was a real sweet lady, and that house will be a nice change of pace for me and my crew. Lately we've been doing new construction. So anyway, if you don't mind, we'll be out the beginning of next week just like I'd originally planned."

"Oh, I have to be in New York next week."

"Lucky for you. That way you won't have to be around while we're working. I suggest we do the interior while you're gone."

She looked at the kitchen table where all the paint chips were spread out like a small rainbow. "I have all the colors picked out."

He promised to stop by in the morning, and as Daphne hung up the phone, she felt like Aunt Dee was smiling down on her. As if she'd had this all planned out long ago, as if she had known all along that Daphne would see that it got done. As if she'd always felt confident in Daphne's ability to handle everything.

Of course, Daphne knew that she wasn't really handling everything. Not yet anyway. She still hadn't gone into her aunt's study. It was hard enough being in her bedroom, but her study was even more intimidating.

When she returned to Appleton, she would prepare herself to go into Aunt Dee's study, and she would force her feet into Daphne Delacorte's shoes, and she would do her best to write an acceptable advice column. If that were even possible. In the meantime, she preferred not to think about it.

The next morning, Willie Troutman showed up shortly after Mick arrived with some raspberry plants and a few other things. Daphne had just greeted Mick and told him she had lemonade when Willie's paint van pulled into the driveway. A lean, lanky man wearing white overalls climbed out and looked around.

"Doing some home improvements, are you?" Mick asked with interest.

"My aunt had planned to have the house painted this summer." Daphne waved to Willie. "And it needs doing."

"Right." Mick nodded. "It's good that you're keeping the place up. Now if you'll excuse me, I'll just get these plants into the ground before the sun gets too high."

She went out to greet Willie, thanking him for coming. "I'm sure glad you called when you did," he said as he warmly shook her hand. "Otherwise, you'd be on my waiting list by now." He pulled a ball cap over his thin and graying hair and grinned. He appeared to be in his fifties or maybe older. And he seemed nice in a fatherly way.

"Well, I owe Olivia a big thank-you. She's the one who pointed me in your direction. I had no idea my aunt had already booked you."

She took him through the house, showing him which rooms she wanted in which colors and he neatly penned it all down in a little notebook. "And I want the same colors my aunt selected for the outside." She handed him the exterior paint chips she'd found. "They seem like good choices to me."

"So Dee left this all to you?" Willie peered at her, then around the front room. "The whole kit and caboodle? And you plan to stay here and live here?"

"For the time being."

"The time being?" Willie eyed her curiously.

"Well, who knows what's around the next corner?" She shrugged. "I might decide I don't like it."

He glanced around. "I suppose this house is a pretty big house for just one person. And I do know how that goes . . ." A sad look passed over his face. "But your aunt seemed to enjoy living here. Hopefully you will too. Maybe even more so with the fresh paint on the walls."

"I'm sure that will help."

He held up his little notebook. "I'll put this all into a contract for you to sign. Can I fax it back to you later today?"

She frowned. "I'm not sure. I don't even know if there's a fax here."

"Oh, sure there is. I faxed the last contract to Dee. I'll bet she's got a fax machine in her study."

Daphne looked over to the closed door. "Well, I guess I should check to make sure." She hesitantly opened the door and peered into the dimly lit room.

"See, there it is." He walked past her to point at a fax machine sitting on the end of a big walnut credenza. Then he looked around. The walls in here looked the same as they had when she was a girl, a dark dingy shade of mauve.

"You sure you don't want this room painted too?" He gazed at her. "Seems a little gloomy, if you ask me."

Daphne tried to imagine herself writing the *Dear Daphne* column in this depressing space. "You're right. It is gloomy." She looked at the paint colors in his hands. "Which one do you think would be best for here? Or maybe I should get a completely different color."

"Well, if it was me, I might go with that soft gray, but then I'm a guy. Anyway, it would lighten up the room, but it'd still look like an office."

"All right." She nodded. "That's what we'll do."

"And you sure you don't want to touch the downstairs bedroom? It'll be a lot easier to do it when the crew's here instead of waiting until later."

She firmly shook her head. "No. For now I want to leave it as is. If I have anything done, I think I'll consider another wallpaper."

"Yeah, that's a good idea. Keep the old-fashioned feel of the room." He grinned. "Just so you know, I can do papering too. If you ever decide you want it done." He shook her hand again. "Now, if I don't see you before you leave for New York, you have a great time. And know that your house is in good hands. Just make sure you go over the contract, sign it, and get it back to me before you go."

"Oh, I should give you a key," she said suddenly. "And I have a neighbor who's agreed to keep an eye on the cats for me while I'm gone. Hopefully they won't be a problem for your crew. And the cats like being outside on these sunny days."

"Don't worry about the cats. My crew is used to working around pets."

"Then I guess it's settled." She thanked him and went over to tell Mrs. Terwilliger about the plan for painters to be here while she went to New York.

Fortunately, her neighbor didn't seem overly concerned about having painters next door, and she generously promised to keep an even closer eye on Lucy and Ethel. Daphne could hardly believe it, but she felt strangely protective of those two felines. Would they miss her as much as she suspected she would miss them?

Chapter 13

As soon as Willie left, Daphne called Jake and left a message on his voice mail. She explained about securing the painter and the contract he was preparing for her. "So I guess that means I'll need a check from you—rather, from the trust. I mean, I do have enough in my savings to cover the expense, but since it's not officially my house, well, I'm hoping the trust will pay for the improvements. Like we discussed. And since I'm heading to New York on Monday, maybe you can just take care of it directly with the painter. Perhaps I can drop a copy of the contract at your law office today or tomorrow. Thank you." As she hung up the phone, she heard someone behind her and jumped to see Mick was standing in the kitchen.

"Sorry to startle you. But you mentioned lemonade and I was feeling a bit parched and no one answered when I knocked and seeing the back door was open . . ."

"Yes, sure. I'll get you some." She found a glass and filled it with ice. How much had he heard just now—and what exactly had she said to Jake? She poured the lemonade, reminding herself that she needed to be careful. She handed Mick the glass, but she could tell he was pondering something as he took a long sip.

"I don't like to eavesdrop," he began slowly, "but I couldn't help overhearing you say that this isn't your house. So I'm curious, if it's not your house, I'd like to know whose house it is? Just who am I working for anyway?"

"Oh, that." She waved her hand toward the phone as if it was directly responsible for the confusion. "You don't need to concern yourself over it."

"Except that I thought I was working for *you*. And now it sounds like maybe I'm not. On top of that, you're going back to New York?" He frowned. "What's going on here, Daphne?"

"You misunderstood what I said, Mick." She poured herself a partial glass of lemonade. "I have to go to New York to pack my things up. For the move here. When I came for the funeral, I had no idea Aunt Dee was leaving me her house."

"So she *did* leave you her house?" He tightened his gaze on her. "Or are you just managing the property until it can be sold to the highest bidder? I'd really like to know."

Again she felt trapped between the proverbial rock and the hard place. "I realize it's a little confusing," she said with uncertainty. "For now the house is as good as mine. And I will treat it with the dignity and respect it deserves while it's in my care. And I want to see you continue your work in the garden, Mick. I love what you're doing."

"But?"

"But . . . and I'll be grateful if you can keep this to yourself . . . *please*?"

He held up a hand. "I give you my word."

"Thank you. But here's the kicker: I won't know until a full year passes whether or not I get to keep the house. Do you understand what I'm saying?"

He looked confused. "Not completely. It sounds a bit jumbled."

"I know . . . it doesn't make sense to me either. But that's how it stands. And the truth is, that no one besides the lawyer and me—and now you—are aware of this. Even my dad doesn't know, and I prefer to keep it that way because I don't want to worry him."

"So I assume that means there are some conditions attached to your inheritance?"

With lips pressed firmly together, she just nodded, determined not to say another word about this. Hopefully she could really trust him.

"So . . . I might be putting in this garden for you, but someone else might own this place a year from now?"

"That's correct." She frowned. "But I hope that won't happen. And I hope this uncertainty won't make you stop working here. Because I really want this garden and I'm pretty clueless how to achieve it myself. Although I suppose I can hire someone else . . ."

"I appreciate you being honest with me. As you know I invest myself into my customers and their gardens. And I don't like being taken advantage of. It might sound silly to some people, but these gardens are like my own creations. Similar to how a painter or sculptor might feel. It's like a little bit of my heart and soul goes into each creation."

"Which is why they are so lovely."

He finished his lemonade and set the empty glass in the sink with a clink. "Well, as long as everything you said is true and you're coming back from New York—hey, when are you coming back?"

"I leave on Monday and return the following Saturday. And the painters will be working while I'm gone. But they shouldn't be in your hair since they'll start with the inside first. The exterior won't get painted until I'm back."

Mick rolled his eyes. "I just hope your painters don't trample all over the flower beds and shrubbery. Some are notorious plant haters. And the rose arbor is just coming on nice now."

"I'll make a note, asking them to be extra careful."

"I'd appreciate that. And say, before you leave for New York, is there any chance I can get you to come out to the nursery and make some selections for the garden?"

"Sure. You name the time."

"How about after I get the rest of those plants tucked in since I'm heading back there next? You can ride with me if you like. I'll be coming back to town to deliver some fruit trees anyway. Or if you'd rather, you can just follow me."

But she agreed to ride with him and less than an hour later, they were riding in his pickup with the windows down, and he was heading out of town. "My grandparents used to live out this way," she told him as he turned onto a familiar road.

"Yeah, I know."

"You know?" She glanced suspiciously at him. "How can you possibly know that?"

"Because it's where I met Dee."

"What?" She was confused.

"On your grandparents' farm."

"But they've been gone for ages now, and the farm was sold shortly after they passed on."

"Yeah, I reckon that's true. But up until a few years ago, Dee owned the farm property. You didn't know that?"

"No." She stared at him in wonder. "Seriously, you know for a fact that my aunt owned my grandparents' farm, but I didn't know it? And my dad didn't know it?"

"That's right. I know it for a fact because I bought the property from Dee."

Why should this even surprise her? The more she found out about Aunt Dee, the kookier it all seemed to get. The next thing Daphne knew, she'd probably discover that Aunt Dee had been operating a casino in her basement. Which reminded Daphne that she still hadn't gone down there.

"I don't get it," she told Mick. "The way I understood it, the farm was sold. And the inheritance was shared equally among the children."

"That may be so. But Dee owned the deed to the farm. I bought it from her."

Daphne was trying to reconstruct this in her head. Was it possible that Aunt Dee had paid off the farm without the family's knowledge? From what Daphne could see, Aunt Dee could have easily afforded it. But what would she want with an old farm? Especially when she had her beloved old house in town. Or maybe it was simply her way of helping out her relatives—anonymously. So much about Aunt Dee was anonymous. Why should this even surprise Daphne?

"Dee preferred to keep our business dealings quiet for some reason," Mick said. "And that wasn't a problem for me. Especially considering how she gave me a real fair deal on the land."

"So that's where your nursery is located?" Daphne was still wrapping her head around this. "On Grandma and Grandpa's old farm?"

"Yeah. And it's a great piece of property too."

"I know." She nodded. "I always thought it had great potential. But it was too much for my grandparents to keep up. My grandpa didn't really have any experience with farming. I think he'd owned some kind of business before moving here. But I used to imagine it as a real farm. You know with crops and animals and the works."

"I think Dee had hoped that someone in your family would want to live there someday. Perhaps even you."

"But she never told any of us about it."

"Yeah. I reckon that's a bit odd. But then she was a character."

"I'll say."

As they got closer to the old farm, Daphne could not believe her eyes. "Look what you've done to the place," she said quietly as he drove under an entrance with the words *Garden Guy* hanging over it. On either side of the gravel road grew lush-looking rows of green vegetation. And farther on were all kinds of trees and shrubs. There were several large greenhouses situated back by the old barn. And the old barn looked charming with its dark red paint and white trim. "Everything looks so beautiful."

"Thank you. Did you think it would be ugly?"

"I—uh—well, I just didn't know. The last time I was out here . . . well, it was so run-down." She studied the brick house, which looked better than she recalled with what appeared to be a new roof and clean white trim and a shiny black door. The front yard, which used to be just dirt, was nicely landscaped too. Complete with a pond and fountain near the front door. "How do you manage to do all this? By yourself?"

"Oh, I'm not by myself. I have my people." He nodded to a young man with a wheelbarrow. "See there's one of my guys there. I've got about ten high school kids working for me this summer. And besides that, I've got six full-time employees as well and I might hire a couple more. I just hope I can keep them all during the winter. You never know which way the economy is going."

As she got out of the truck, she was so stunned by the transformation of the previously run-down farm that she felt literally speechless. Simply walking with him and taking it all in, she could only shake her head in wonder. Even though she'd thought this place could've been more, she never imagined anything like this. It seemed nothing short of miraculous.

"I wish my dad could see this," she finally said as he led her over a little wooden footbridge that crossed a corner of a large pond. The surface of the water was filled with blooming water lilies, and large multicolored fish darted about between the cheerfully spouting fountains.

"Bring him out here anytime."

"I'd love to."

He took her over to look at some varieties of strawberries now, insisting she sample them and explaining they would soon be sending out runners and he felt her garden should have some. But as usual, she didn't really know which variety was best.

"Why don't you just tell me what I want. They all taste sweet to me."

He laughed. "That's what I figured you'd say."

She peered curiously at him. "Why did you really bring me out here?"

"Honestly?"

She nodded. "Tell the truth."

He grinned. "Probably just to show off?"

She laughed. "Well, you deserve to show off." She waved her hands. "Just look at this place. It's amazing. Totally amazing."

"I was hoping you'd like it. Especially since it had been in your family. Dee liked coming out here from time to time. And I always liked showing her around. It seemed she was part of it, you know. Kind of like a silent partner."

"Was she really silent?"

"No. You know how your aunt liked to express herself. But when she expressed herself out here, I was glad to listen. She appreciated what I did with the place."

"I'll bet she did. So, do you mind if I look in the house?" Daphne asked hopefully.

His cheerful countenance paled. "Oh, I don't know about that."

"Please. For old times' sake?"

"It's just that it doesn't match up to what's out here. It's been a bit neglected, if you know what I mean."

"Don't worry. I don't care about that. I just want to see it again. I haven't been here since I was about six or seven . . . after Grandma died."

"Well, I don't usually let customers go inside, but seeing how it was in your family, I reckon it's all right. Just don't judge a man by his housekeeping."

"I won't."

"So fine. While you're snooping around inside, I'll load up the trees I need to take into town."

As she walked up to the brick house, Daphne felt like she'd slipped into a time warp. She paused on the porch, standing in front of the front door as she suddenly remembered a time long ago—something she'd all but forgotten. She'd come out here with her mother, and it had been warm and sunny and much like today. She and her mother had gone out to the barn to look at some kittens.

Daphne had instantly fallen in love with a tiny black-and-white kitty, begging to take it home. But as she recalled the kittens were still too small to leave the mama cat. However, Daphne had been so shattered to leave the kitten behind that she cried, perhaps she'd even thrown a tantrum. Not long after that day, her mother became sick . . . and they never did get the kitten.

Daphne felt a stab of old childhood guilt as she let herself into the old farmhouse. Why had she acted like such a spoiled brat that day? For all she knew, her poor mother was already getting sick, but too young to understand, Daphne had thrown a selfish fit. Oh, she knew it was irrational to judge the actions of a frustrated five-year-old, but it felt painful to remember it just the same.

Trying to push the uncomfortable memory away, she went through the living room and into the kitchen. Mick hadn't exaggerated about his lack of housekeeping skills. The place was a mess. Trying to look past muddy boots and discarded items of clothing, she glanced at the kitchen with its cluttered countertops and sink piled high with dirty dishes. She quickly made her way through the house. And resisting the urge to start picking things up and putting it back to order, she hurried outside.

She tried to put both the untidy house and messy memory behind her and distracted herself by going through the gardens and admiring the ponds. Then, noticing that Mick and a couple of his guys had finished loading the small trees, she went over to the truck. But as she got closer, she realized that one of the workers was actually a young woman. And a pretty one too.

Wearing short denim shorts, she was sitting on the tailgate of the truck, kicking a dusty pair of cowboy boots back and forth in what seemed an effort to show off a pair of long tanned legs. Unless it was just Daphne's imagination. The leggy girl had on a straw cowboy hat and a snug-fitting white T-shirt, and she could've easily passed for Daisy Mae's twin sister if she'd had some fluffy blond hair. But this girl's hair was jet black, running halfway down her back, in a long sleek braid.

"But I already told the Hammonds that you'd come with me," she seemed to be making some kind of appeal to Mick. "Please, don't make me look like a liar."

"Sorry." He secured a rope holding the trees snugly against the cab.

"Come on, Mick, you know you want to go."

"I told you I already have plans for Saturday." He tied the rope off, tucking the ends in.

"You're blowing off the Hammonds for stupid old poker." She made a pout. "You can do that anytime. The Hammonds' barbecue is only once a year. And I told them I'd bring you again."

"You should've checked with me before accepting the invitation." Noticing Daphne now, he smiled in her direction and politely introduced her to Julianne Preston.

Daphne politely greeted Julianne, making some small talk about the nursery and the weather as she tried to determine her age. Best guess was early twenties, but it was based more on Julianne's immaturity than her appearance. Daphne supposed she could be anywhere from twenty-five to Daphne's age, maybe older.

"Mick is being so stubborn," Julianne told her. "He says he'd rather play dumb old poker with his buddies than go to a really great party with me."

Not caring to be pulled into the middle, Daphne just shrugged. "I guess he has his reasons."

"That's right." Mick firmly nodded. "I do."

Julianne stared at Daphne now. "So . . . did you find what you were looking for out here?" But Daphne suspected there was more to this question than a business inquiry.

Mick explained to Julianne that the farm had once been in Daphne's family. Then he reached over and took her hand. "Now, if you don't mind removing yourself from my tailgate, we'd like to be on our way."

Julianne hopped down, dusting off her backside as he slammed the tailgate shut. "See you later, Mickie." She barely glanced at Daphne. "Nice meeting you, Doreen."

"Daphne," Mick said as he opened the door for her.

"Nice meeting you too, Julianne. Have a good day."

"Julianne's not usually in such a snit," Mick explained after he started the pickup. "She can actually be rather charming when she puts her mind to it."

"Unless you have poker night?"

He chuckled. "Why is it that all women seem to hate poker?"

"Not all women."

"What?" He looked surprised. "Don't tell me that the prim and proper Daphne Ballinger is a closeted poker player."

"No, not actually. But my dad enjoys poker. And he played regularly when I was growing up. Once a month he'd host poker night at our house and I would make all the refreshments. It was fun. I always looked forward to the guys coming over."

"Your father is a lucky man." He turned back onto the road. "So tell me the truth, were you shocked and dismayed when you saw how I defiled your grandparents' home? Are you completely disappointed in my slovenly style of living?"

"Not at all. It's obvious that you invest all your energy into your business. You spend so much time on your plants and your nursery and other people's gardens. It's no wonder your house is a wreck."

"A wreck?" He pretended offense. "My house is a wreck?"

She laughed. "Yeah, that was putting it mildly."

"Right. I suppose it's a bit shoddier than when you saw it last. But if you looked beneath all the piles and clutter, you might've noticed that I replaced carpets and floors and a few other things as well."

"To be honest, I didn't notice."

He frowned. "That bad, eh?"

"Why don't you hire a housekeeper to come out a time or two a week?" She chuckled. "Tell her to bring a shovel and a hazmat suit to start with."

"Very funny. See what comes of me trying to be nice, letting you into my private domain. The thanks I get."

"I'm sorry." She smiled at him. "Thank you for bringing me out to visit. I never would've believed it if I hadn't seen it with my own eyes."

"You mean my dodgy housekeeping?"

"No, I mean your beautiful landscaped gardens. My grandpa would be pleased. I think he had dreams of doing something more with the place, but he was already getting old when they moved there. And he had some health problems. I don't think he was able to do as much as he hoped. He died when I was really little. After that, it was hard for Grandma to keep it up and she didn't last much longer anyway."

"Dee told me she'd been leasing it for all those years after her parents passed. I reckon some of the earlier tenants kept it up some, but the last ones let it get pretty run-down and nasty. Which is why she gave me such a good deal. And I was glad to get land that hadn't been overly used in recent years. Made it that much easier to get the soil built up again."

"I'm glad the old farm got into your hands," she said. "I can tell it's a happy place now."

They continued visiting all the way into town, and as he dropped her off at the house, she realized Mick was good company and quite likeable. She wondered why she'd been slightly put off by him when they'd first met. Maybe it was just being caught in her nightie and the way he'd acted like she'd done it on purpose. Or maybe she simply hadn't given him a fair chance. As she walked back to see the garden, which looked even better now than it had the previous week, she realized that the Garden Guy was worth considering. However, she was curious about his relationship with Julianne. Something about the familiarity in their conversation, the bantering back and forth, and the territorial way Julianne acted—it all raised a flag. She suspected it was Julianne's subtle warning that she and Mick were more than just coworkers or casual friends. And it bugged Daphne that she cared. Once again, she found herself communicating with Dear Daphne in her head.

> *Dear Daphne,*
> *There's a man I find attractive and enjoy spending time with. And unless it's my imagination, this guy has been flirting with me. However, I just discovered there's another woman in his life—a very beautiful woman—and she is acting as if this man belongs to her. Should I back off from getting involved with him—or should I just ignore the other woman and go for it?*
> *Anxious in Appleton*

As she picked some sprigs of mint, she constructed Dear Daphne's answer.

> *Dear Anxious,*
> *Unless this man is engaged or married to this woman or unless he's given you reason to believe he's in love with this other woman, I would say that it's open season. But before you go hunting, you'd better make sure of your own feelings. You don't want to pursue a man just because you think someone else wants him. Get to know him and determine whether or not he's someone you want to be in a serious relationship with.*
> *Daphne*

Chapter 14

Daphne was surprised at how reluctant she felt while boarding the jet that would take her back to New York. Despite knowing she would only be there a week, just long enough to pack her things and tie up loose ends and say some good-byes, she felt like it was a step backward. To her amazement, everything in her longed to remain in Appleton.

However, as she buckled her seat belt, Daphne reminded herself, she would be visiting tomorrow night with Beverly and Robert. Really, that would be nice. Of course, she had yet to tell Beverly about her plan to relocate, and although she didn't expect a brokenhearted reaction, she was not looking forward to it. She was also not looking forward to going through her small but tightly packed bedroom and deciding what to do with her accumulation of stuff. Was there really anything she wanted there? Just thinking of it felt overwhelming.

As the plane took off, Daphne tried to remember the pointers Olivia had given her when they'd met at Red River for coffee yesterday. Daphne had confessed her frustration over the idea of returning to the Brooklyn apartment to sort out her life and junk. "I only have a few days to go through twelve years' worth of accumulation—mostly clothes and junk."

"The secret to streamlining your closet and home is really simple," Olivia explained in her usual methodical way.

"How do you know what to keep and what to toss? I pick up an object or piece of clothing and I begin to imagine that I really need it when I know I don't. And then I can't get rid of it." Daphne cringed to think of the storage crates in her room. She didn't even know what they contained. Did she really want to pay to ship them to Appleton?

"There are three easy-to-remember rules," Olivia told her.

Of course, Daphne couldn't even recall one of them now, but then she spied the edge of the coffee company napkin in her purse pocket, remembering that she'd written Olivia's organizational tips down. She pulled it out and studied the three rules.

1. Is it useful—have I used it in the past year?

2. Is it eye pleasing—do I like how it looks?

3. Does it feel good—is it comfortable?

As she stuffed the napkin back down in her purse, she thought it sounded too easy, but she hoped it would at least be helpful. Looking out the window, she remembered how she'd felt that last time she'd flown—how she'd gotten gloomy by reminiscing about how Ryan broke her heart. Now he seemed like a distant memory. Yet if anyone had told her a few weeks ago that she'd be feeling romantic interest in a guy, she would've been doubtful. And if someone had told her she'd be feeling interested in several guys, she would never have believed it.

Of course, she suspected that most of the "eligible" bachelors she'd experienced an interest in might not be truly eligible . . . and more likely, they probably wouldn't be interested in her beyond a business sense. Because really, that was how most of them were connected to her—rather to her deceased aunt. Jake McPheeters had been her aunt's attorney. Mick Foster had been her aunt's yard man. Even Willie Troutman had been contracted as her aunt's painter. That left Ricardo Martoni, but he had been her aunt's neighbor. And the green grocer Truman Walters, well, he might not have a connection to her aunt . . . but he was rather young.

Even so, it amused her to go over her short list of men as she flew. It was entertaining to imagine what it would feel like to fall in love again and interesting to wonder if any of these five guys might be "the one." Or was she simply trying too hard? Was she just grasping at every bachelor who crossed her path? How pathetic was that? She didn't even want to think about what Dear Daphne would tell her.

Daphne's first night back in the Brooklyn apartment was not so different than previous nights there. She unlocked the door to a quiet apartment where Oliver the cat was still locked in the bathroom. Feeling some feline empathy, probably from the relationship she'd been enjoying with Lucy and Ethel, Daphne opened the door. "Want to come out? Or do you like it in there?"

The big gray cat eyed her curiously as he sauntered out. Almost like he was saying, "Where have you been?"

She reached down to scratch his head. "I guess you're not such a bad guy. We just never hit it off, did we?" He rubbed against her leg as if to confirm this. "And now I'm moving away. Leaving you for a couple of girls."

Daphne went to her room and set her carry-on down. Everything looked exactly as she'd left it. With all the crates and stuffed closet, she had her work cut out for her. But she just wasn't ready to attack it yet. So she poked around the apartment, trying to understand what had enticed her to stay here for twelve years. Except that she'd been stuck.

As usual, Greta came home late from work. "Oh, I forgot you were coming back today." She kicked off her shoes and set her brief-case on the table by the door. "Did you have a good flight?"

"Uneventful." Daphne set down the magazine she'd been read-ing. "Have you rented my room yet?"

"I've got a gal who wants to move in as soon as you're out."

"That will be on Saturday."

"Great." Now Greta frowned. "Well, not great that you're leav-ing, Daphne."

"That's okay. I understand."

"Quite honestly, as roommates go, you've been one of the very best. And you know me, I don't hand out praise lightly."

"Well, thank you." Daphne didn't know what to say.

"And you probably already guessed that Shelby's out with John Junior." Greta flipped through some junk mail, tossing it back down on the table. "She's certain he's about to pop the question, but I told her not to hold her breath."

They visited awhile but, like always, it wasn't a friendly warm conversation. It was more of an exchange of information about New York, the weather, Greta's job status, and whether or not Oliver had been fed.

"Sorry, I didn't even think of that," Daphne admitted.

"I'll feed him." Greta slowly stood. "And then I have some work to do."

Taking the hint, Daphne excused herself to her room, and

turning on the little TV, she tuned into HGTV. But this time as she watched, instead of being lulled into a vegetative state, she was excited to think that a real house and garden waiting for her back in Appleton—a house and a garden and two cats—needed her.

The next day, she rolled up her sleeves and attempted to start the process of sorting her room. But instead of making decisions based on the three simple rules, she kept getting stuck. And being a procrastinator, it didn't help to know she had several days to figure it all out. And that only allowed her the luxury of taking too long to examine every little thing. At the end of the day, she had packed one crate to ship home, with one small pile to give away, and even less in the trash.

She was relieved to stop and clean up for dinner. Beverly had called earlier, saying that she and Robert had decided to fix dinner in their apartment instead of going out like they'd previously said. Daphne was a little surprised and slightly disappointed since she'd actually been looking forward to a good restaurant meal, but she figured it had to do with the expectant couple's need to nest.

She discovered shortly after arriving at their apartment that it had more to do with the expectant couple's finances. "Robert made an offer on a house," Beverly announced happily. "And it was accepted yesterday. So we have to pinch our pennies."

Robert opened a bottle of sparkling apple cider to celebrate, and Beverly showed her photos of a little, unimpressive-looking house. "I feel so bad telling you this as soon as you get home," Beverly apologized. "But I knew you'd be happy for us. And I'm sure you'll come out to visit and see the baby."

Daphne gave her a genuine smile. "I am so happy for you. It's wonderful news—and what a sweet little house. Congratulations!"

"Really?" Beverly almost seemed disappointed. "So you're not bummed to see us go?"

"Actually . . . I have a little announcement of my own." Daphne quickly explained her decision to relocate to Appleton.

"You're leaving New York?" Beverly looked stunned.

"Well, you're leaving New York," Daphne reminded her as she washed the lettuce.

"Not like that. I mean, we can just hop on a train and be back here in a couple of hours. You're really leaving. How can you bear to do that, Daphne? Won't you miss the theater, the restaurants, the museums, the culture, everything? I can't believe you're settling for your hometown. That doesn't seem like you." Beverly peered curiously at her. "Is it because of us? Because we're expecting . . . and moving from the city?"

Daphne tried not to be offended by this assumption. She wondered if pregnancy might lead to narcissism. "Being back there reminded me of how much I love Appleton. And the town has changed and grown a lot." She described some of the new businesses and how she loved being in the charming little town. "And it helps that my aunt left me her house. And I've been running into old friends and making new ones. And honestly, it's just where I want to be."

Beverly looked uncertain as she stirred the spaghetti sauce. "That's cool. If you really like it that much."

"What's the house like?" Robert asked as he sliced a tomato. "The one your aunt left you."

Still feeling a bit defensive, Daphne went into full detail about the house, even explaining how the painters were there right now and how Olivia helped her to pick colors. Daphne even put down her knife and ran to her purse, getting the set of samples that Olivia had insisted she should keep handy in case she needed to make any shopping decisions, as well as her phone that had some photos in it. With enthusiasm she showed them, explaining her plans to make the home feel more like her own.

The kitchen grew quiet as the three of them continued with food preparations. And so Daphne filled in the space, rambling on about Mick the Australian Garden Guy who'd discovered her sunbathing in her nightie and how he resembled Matthew McConaughey. "And the garden he's making for me is incredible. And he took me to see his nursery last week, which was actually built on a farm that belonged to my grandparents."

"Cool." Beverly put pasta into the boiling water. "What will you do for a living?"

"That's the best part." Daphne was shredding lettuce into the bowl. "I'm going to start writing a novel."

"Really?" Beverly sounded a little cynical. "A novel?"

"I don't want to rain on your parade, Daphne." Robert's brow was creased as he chopped radishes. "But an old house like you described could be pretty expensive to maintain. And then there are property taxes and insurance and all sorts of hidden expenses. And what about your health insurance—when you're self-employed you have to think about these things? Seriously, have you really thought this move through?"

"And writing a novel?" Beverly frowned as she stirred the pasta. "Wouldn't it be more prudent to do some freelance magazine articles instead? You know, like I've been doing? At least that would bring in a little income. Not enough to support yourself, but at least it would be something more dependable than selling a novel."

Daphne felt irritated by their assumptions. As if they really perceived her as their pathetic, incapable, needy, foolish friend. Was that how she'd come across all these years?

"Expecting a baby and purchasing our first home has been a reality check for us," Robert continued in a paternal tone. "Having to verify our income and project into the future—it's made us realize our need to become more fiscally responsible."

"And that's good you're doing that. But my situation is a little different." She set the bowl of shredded salad lettuce in front of Robert. "For one thing, I'm single and not expecting." She laughed. "That alone makes my life much less expensive. But besides leaving me the house, my aunt has been very generous in her will. And well, her estate was a lot larger than anyone imagined."

Hoping to lighten the serious atmosphere, she told them about the Corvette with low miles and how much fun she'd been having driving it around with the top down, even showing them a photo of the car on her phone.

"You're kidding," Robert sounded slightly envious now. "A 1955 Corvette that's hardly been driven? That's unbelievable."

"So as you can see, there's not really that much to be concerned about." She smiled at both of them. "In fact, for the first time in my life, I think I'm learning how to have fun. I guess it's about time, huh?"

Holding a wooden spoon loosely in her hand, Beverly stared at Daphne with a hard-to-read expression. And then, to Daphne's surprise and horror, Beverly burst into sobs, and without saying a word, she ran from the kitchen to the bedroom, slamming the door behind her.

Robert cleared his throat. "Uh, Beverly's been having some mood swings lately. It has to do with hormones and the pregnancy. But it should be getting better soon. The second trimester is—"

"Excuse me," Daphne told him. "I'm going to check on her."

"Oh, I wouldn't do that."

But it was too late, she was tapping on the door and then going in. "Beverly," she said gently as she sat next to where Beverly was lying facedown on the bed. "Did I upset you just now? I didn't mean to go on like that. I'm sure it sounded pretty arrogant. I only wanted to put your mind at ease, you know, that I'll be okay in Appleton. I'm sorry if it sounded like I was bragging."

Beverly sat up with a tear-streaked face. "No, you were just happily telling me about your life, Daphne. I'm sorry to get so emotional." She reached for a tissue, blowing her nose. "The truth is, I'm probably jealous. It sounds idyllic. The house, the car, writing your novel. Of course, I'm jealous. But I'm happy for you too. You deserve a break like this." Beverly reached out to hug her. "You've been such a good friend to me—and Robert too—and I know your life's been disappointing. I'm really glad for you." But now she was crying again.

Daphne stroked Beverly's short, dark hair. "You are so blessed. You have Robert. And you two are having your first baby. A baby— can you believe it! That is so exciting. And now you'll have a house to nest in. You have so much to be thankful for. We all do."

Beverly nodded. "We do, don't we?"

"Absolutely. And like your understanding husband just told me, you're feeling hormonal because of the pregnancy. It's natural for you to overreact sometimes."

"Yes, you're right." Beverly stood now. "We should check on dinner. And Robert." She giggled. "The poor man. But you're right, he is understanding. I'm not sure if it's because he's younger or just wired that way. But I've got a lot to be thankful for."

"You really do." Daphne almost added that they both did but stopped herself. She didn't want to set Beverly off again.

For the rest of the evening, Daphne was careful to keep the spotlight of happiness on Beverly and Robert. And she didn't even mind doing so. She was getting some new glimpses now and she sensed that their life was a little more precarious and a bit less perfect than she'd originally thought.

After helping to clean the tiny kitchen, she could see that Beverly was tired and it seemed the perfect reason to excuse herself. Thanking them for the dinner, she prepared to leave.

"I've got a lot of sifting and sorting to do back at my apartment. A friend in Appleton gave me some rules, but it's still a challenge." Daphne looked around the cluttered apartment. "I'd offer some of my stuff to you, but you probably have some sifting and sorting to do yourself. I mean, before you move to your new house."

"Hey, why don't I come over and help you tomorrow?" Beverly suggested. "I don't have much going on this week."

"Really? You'd want to do that?"

"Sure. Maybe I'll find something you're tossing that I could use at the new house."

"That'd be great."

"And it'll allow us to spend some more time together," Beverly told her.

But as Daphne rode the subway home, feeling more like a visitor than a resident, she hoped it wasn't a mistake. What if having Beverly there just slowed the work down? Or what if she fell apart again? Daphne decided it wouldn't really matter. Maybe the important thing was just spending a day with her old friend. Her old friend who was probably not quite as happy as Daphne had assumed.

To Daphne's relief, Beverly was in better spirits the next day and she was actually surprisingly helpful in the sorting process.

"They say a trick to getting rid of stuff is not to actually touch it or hold it in your hands," Beverly had explained early on in the process. "It's a psychological thing. I saw it on a hoarders show."

Beverly would pick up an item and let Daphne look at it from a safe distance as Beverly asked her the three simple questions. And this system was actually working. But at the end of the day, instead of three piles, there were four. The send-home pile, the giveaway pile, the throw-away pile, and the Beverly-and-Robert pile, which had grown steadily.

"I don't know how to thank you," Daphne told Beverly when they were done. "I never could've done this without you."

"You're thanking me with all the cool stuff you're giving me," Beverly said as she continued bundling her pile into bags and boxes.

"I'm also going to pay for the taxi to take you home." Daphne tied off the trash bag she'd just filled. "Will Robert be there to help you get it upstairs?"

"He should be home by then." Beverly sighed.

"Are you tired?" Daphne said suddenly, clearing a spot on the cluttered bed. "Here, sit down. Don't overdo. I keep forgetting that you're pregnant."

"Being pregnant isn't like being sick." Beverly sat down. "You're supposed to stay active, keep doing what you normally do."

"Even so, you rest while I pack the rest of your stuff up for you."

"I'm really going to miss you," Beverly said sadly.

"At least you have Robert."

Beverly sighed again. "Yeah . . ."

Daphne stared at her. "Are you okay? I mean, you and Robert? Is everything all right between you two?"

"Sure. I guess so. It feels like things are changing. Despite always wishing for kids, I can tell I'm dragging my heels a little. And hearing about your life, being free and single and running around in your convertible, has probably depressed me a little." She made an attempt to laugh. "You know, the old grass is greener on the other side."

Daphne laughed. "Do I know? I usually look at you and Robert like that."

"I really am happy for you. Appleton sounds like a perfect change."

"And it won't be long until you and Robert are settling into your new house," Daphne reminded her.

"Yes . . . hopefully."

"I thought it was for certain."

Beverly shrugged. "Robert is trying to be positive about it, but we're still having some problems with the bank . . . for financing. It's hard with my income being freelance. They see us as some kind of risk."

Daphne remembered Robert's fatherly spiel last night, warning her to be careful of her finances. Perhaps he'd been preaching to himself. "Well, hopefully, it'll all work out."

"Hopefully. It's such a nice house. I'd hate to lose it because of the bank. Robert has suggested we get some kind of private financing. Like our parents. Except that they're not exactly rolling in the dough either."

She gazed at Daphne with a look that seemed somewhat expectant . . . or curious. "You mentioned a large inheritance . . . but it's probably not enough to do home loans." She laughed. "And really, I would never ask that of you . . . of a friend."

Daphne set down on a pile of crates, looking earnestly at her friend. "Beverly, if I could loan you the money, I would. I really would. But my inheritance is kind of tied up for a year. My aunt had some conditions in her will. I'm not really supposed to talk about it though."

"Oh?"

"The truth is, I might not even be able to remain in my aunt's house at the end of a year's time. If I don't meet her, uh, her conditions."

"Really?" Beverly seemed slightly encouraged by this. "So after a year, you could be homeless as well as jobless?"

Daphne gave a weak smile. "Actually, I could."

"Oh, I'm sure you'll land on your feet." Beverly stood again, looking at her watch. "I guess I should get the rest of this packed up. Robert will be on his way home by now."

It was close to seven by the time Daphne got Beverly and all her stuff loaded into the taxi. She had just paid the driver and was waving good-bye to her friend when Shelby came walking up.

"Hey, I thought you were home," Shelby said cheerfully as they went up the stairs together. "But you must've gone to bed early last night."

"And you went to work before I was up this morning."

"Lucky you." Shelby opened the door. "I can't wait until I'm a lady of leisure and able to sleep in too."

"So how is it going with John Junior?" Daphne glanced at Shelby's left hand. "Any talk of diamonds yet?"

Shelby giggled as she set her purse down. "Not exactly. But I have hinted to him that the Fourth of July would be a nice day to get engaged on. Then we could be engaged for almost a whole year before we have a June wedding."

"Sounds like a plan." Daphne picked up a garbage bag. "I'm heading down to the Dumpster."

"And I'm heading for the shower and a quick change. John Junior is picking me up at eight."

Daphne just nodded, then continued on outside. Going out at eight on a weeknight was no big deal for New Yorkers, but it suddenly sounded like craziness to her. Clearly, this was a sign she didn't belong here anymore.

Chapter 15

Daphne could hardly believe what a change the new interior paint colors made to the house. At first, she felt slightly shocked and, to be honest, a little upset to think she'd made such a drastic change to Aunt Dee's sweet old house. But the more she walked around, talking to the cats who were happy to see her, and the more she looked at it from all angles and various forms of light, the more she thoroughly loved it. It brought a whole new energy to the old house.

"It feels like it's given the house a brand-new life," she told Olivia as she walked her through the rooms on Sunday evening.

"It's fabulous. Lighter and brighter and yet the colors we picked have a classic old-fashioned appeal that are respectful of the house."

"Yes. The house seems happier." Daphne looked around the cluttered tables and shelves that had been somewhat rearranged by the paint crew. "Except for all this stuff. But after cleaning out my place in New York, using your three simple rules, I think I'm ready to attack this space too."

Olivia glanced around the front room. "And yet I think this might be a different kind of challenge."

"How do you mean?"

"It might be a little like a treasure hunt."

Daphne nodded. She knew she wanted to keep some things. But which ones?

"Because there are definitely some treasures here." Olivia pointed to a group of dusty-looking china figurines cluttering the top of a bookshelf under the window. "For instance these—they feel a little busy and a bit too sweet." She picked up a figurine of a shepherdess. "But this one. Well, it's actually quite nice. And I'm guessing it's old and maybe valuable too. Not that you want to pick things just because they're valuable. But if you grouped this piece just right with some other things, it might be rather attractive."

"I'm not sure I understand." Daphne tilted her head to one side, trying to figure out what she'd do with the figurine.

"Mind if I show you?" Olivia's dark eyes twinkled.

"Please do."

Olivia bustled about the room, picking up this and that, and then clearing a mahogany side table of its fussy crocheted runner and numerous dust-catching unrelated knickknacks, she set a brass lamp, which she'd switched lamp shades on, along with an African violet that she'd placed into a pretty pale blue bowl she'd found in the kitchen, and then she set the shepherdess just so in between.

"Voilà," she proclaimed as she turned on the lamp. "It's simple but elegant."

"Wow, that looks really nice." Daphne stepped closer, examining Olivia's magic. "How did you know how to do it like that?"

"From working at the flower shop. I'm always rearranging things there. It's kind of like playing house. And I'm not saying you need to leave the table like this." She turned the African violet around so the blooms faced out. "It's just to show you."

"No, I want to leave it just like that. It's the best-looking thing in this room."

Daphne glanced around. "I get what you're saying about having treasures here. I'm just not sure I can pick them out."

Olivia stuck around for about an hour, helping to choose what she called the "keepers," which they set on the dining room table. "But don't take my word for it," Olivia said as she was getting ready to go home. "Maybe there are still some pieces that are special to you. Go ahead and set them aside too."

"Good idea. But I wonder what I'll do with the rest of it? Aunt Dee really managed to collect a lot of stuff. I suppose I could just store it."

"Or you could sell it on eBay or consign it in town or a yard sale."

Daphne remembered Jake's warning that she wasn't to profit from her aunt's estate yet. But he had said she could give things away. Maybe after she figured out what she wanted to remain with the house, she could offer the rest to her relatives. Certainly there were those like Martin who would probably turn up their noses, which were already out of joint, but there might be others, like the women, who might enjoy a memento or two from dear old Aunt Dee. And for all Daphne knew, some of these things might be valuable. Perhaps the relatives would find a treasure.

As Willie's paint crew worked on the exterior of the house, Daphne started to sort and sift on the inside. She quickly realized this was a huge undertaking for just one person. If Daphne had accumulated a lot in twelve years, Aunt Dee had managed to accumulate about a hundred times more in her lifetime. Daphne was going to need some help. Especially if she was going to start working on the *Dear Daphne* column as planned by the end of the month. But after she'd taken all of Dee's jewelry to be assessed by The Jewel Box, a place recommended by Olivia, she decided to call her young cousin Mattie.

"Hi, Daphne," Mattie said cheerfully. "How're you doing?"

"Very well, thanks." She was relieved that Mattie wasn't one of the relatives with an ax to grind. "I sorted through Aunt Dee's personal things and I have a nice assortment of costume jewelry and old hats and handbags and scarves and things. I remember how you're a collector and I wondered if you'd be interested in any of them."

"Really?" Mattie's voice was full of enthusiasm. "You'd let me have them? To keep?"

Daphne laughed. "Of course. I think Aunt Dee would be happy for you to have them. And I'm sure you'll take good care of them too."

"Cool. When can I come over?"

"Whenever you like."

"I'm on my way. Hey, is it okay if I bring a friend?"

"Sure. And I'm not sure how busy you are, but I need to hire some part-time help this week. Just to sort and clean and move some things. Probably several days' worth of work. Maybe you know someone who's looking—"

"I'll do it," she said eagerly. "I don't have a summer job yet. Besides babysitting, which I am so over." Mattie promised to be there within the hour and Daphne returned to sorting.

She'd decided to utilize the basement as her holding area. Fortunately, other than cobwebs and dust, it was mostly empty. She wanted to set up sawhorse tables, which Mrs. Terwilliger had offered to loan her after Daphne gave her a tour of the freshly painted house and explained her ideas. The basement would look kind of like a tag sale, except there would be no tags involved since everything would be free to the relatives to pick and choose from. She was calling it a Grab and Go instead. And she hoped to kill two birds with one stone—to thin out her aunt's belongings and win back some of her relatives.

But first she wanted to put the house back in order, which hopefully Mattie would be helpful with. When it looked presentable, she would invite all her relatives to browse in the basement as well as the yard, where she would set out the larger items of furniture she wanted to share. She had no doubts that many of the older pieces were valuable. But she was trying not to let monetary worth cloud her generosity.

Appleton was a small town and already she had crossed paths with various relatives here and there. A few, like Mattie, were pleasant and sweet. Others were polite but cool. And then there were some, like Martin and his wife Diane, who were civil but downright frosty—as if they personally blamed Daphne for the way Aunt Dee had set up her last will and testament.

"Come in," Daphne told Mattie and the bright-eyed blond girl with her.

"This is Jenna McPheeters," Mattie said.

"Oh, you must be Jake's daughter." Daphne shook the girl's hand. "Your dad mentioned that you're starting to collect costume jewelry too."

"Yeah. Mattie's gotten me hooked."

"Everything is in my aunt's old bedroom," she said as she led the way. "I've laid it all out on the dressing table and the bed."

Both girls were suitably impressed with the display. They took turns oohing and aahing over the various pieces and exclaiming over what decade they thought items were from. "Do I really get to keep all of this?" Mattie asked incredulously.

Daphne nodded.

"I'll share some with you," Mattie told Jenna.

As they continued to gush over their bounty, Daphne went to get them some bags to carry it in. When she came back, Mattie asked if Jenna could work for her too. "We decided we want to work for free," she told Daphne. "Just to thank you for all this."

"Oh, I can pay you."

Mattie shook her head. "No. Some of this stuff might be valuable. I mean—" Now she looked worried, as if she expected Daphne to snatch it back.

Daphne just smiled. "I'm sure some of it might be valuable. That's why I think you should have it. You appreciate it for what it is, but you understand its worth."

"So can we work for you in payment?" Jenna asked hopefully.

"I really do need help. But maybe we can talk about reimbursement at the end of the week," Daphne told them.

They agreed. And for starters she walked the girls next door to where they picked up the old sawhorses and plywood from Mrs. Terwilliger. "They belonged to my late husband," Mrs. Terwilliger told them. "But I used them for garage sales from time to time."

Daphne thanked her and before long there were several tables set up in the basement. And thanks to Mattie's energetic incentive and a couple of brooms, the cobwebs and dust were soon cleared to the corners. Then, slowly but steadily, the girls helped Daphne get load after load of things down the steep stairs, where they dusted and cleaned each item and placed it on the tables.

It was five and Daphne proclaimed an end to the day's work, but when she offered to pay them, once again they refused. "But will you come back tomorrow?" she asked. To her relief they agreed.

For the next few days the two hardworking girls helped her to make amazing progress in her plan. Whether it was cleaning or carrying or sorting, they both labored steadily. As they worked, the girls chattered back and forth. Sometimes they talked about the old things they found, trying to figure out the age or the value of an item. Sometimes they talked about boys or clothes. And one time, Daphne overheard them talking about their families. She didn't really mean to eavesdrop, but since she was in the laundry room and they were in the kitchen, it was hard not to hear.

"I think my mom wants to get back with my dad," Jenna was saying. "I heard her talking to my aunt about it."

"That'd be cool," Mattie replied. "I mean, I guess it would. What do you think?"

"I think it'd be awesome."

"Yeah, even though my parents fight a lot, I'm glad they're still together," Mattie said. "If they split up, I don't know what I'd do. I mean, it's like you get caught in the middle."

"Tell me about it."

"My grandparents almost got divorced a few years ago," Mattie confided, and naturally Daphne's ears pricked up at this. Was she talking about Martin and Diane? "I almost wished they would because sometimes my grandpa can be so mean to Grandma."

"Really?" Jenna sounded surprised. "They seem like such nice people."

"Yeah. But I heard Grandma telling my mom that she couldn't afford to get divorced. Can you imagine what that would be like? I mean to be an old woman and stuck in a miserable marriage and feel like you couldn't get a divorce?"

"It'd be rough."

"I think it's because my grandpa's an attorney and Grandma's worried he would have the advantage."

"That's not right. I mean, Dad's an attorney and he was really fair about their divorce."

"Yeah, well, your dad's not like my grandpa."

Suddenly the subject switched to guys and Daphne, feeling guilty for eavesdropping—what else could she call it?—hurried out the back door and into the backyard where a couple of painters were painting the main body color. Pretending to be inspecting their work and relieved to see that they had taken the care to cover the plants near the house with drop cloths, she walked around the house to admire the front where Willie was just starting to work on the trim.

"That's looking really good," she told him.

"You're just who I needed." He stepped back from the house. "I want you to make some decisions. We've got the olive and orange trim colors, but I'm not sure which goes where." He pointed to a column. "I thought that might look nice in the green, but what do you think?"

She studied it and nodded. "I think that would be pretty. And maybe that band above it could be orange."

He agreed, then pointed out several other parts of gingerbread, window trim, and other decorative elements, dabbing each one with the appropriate color of paint as they made their decisions. Finally, although the house now looked a bit splotchy, they seemed to have it worked out. "And if you change your mind, don't worry, it's only paint."

She stepped back and looked over it, imagining how it would look completed. "No, I think it's going to look just perfect."

As she went inside, she was still pondering over the conversation she'd just overhead. It saddened her to think that Martin and Diane had marriage problems, but at the same time it softened her heart toward Diane. Maybe she'd been acting chilly because she was unhappy. Anyway, Daphne would do what she could to be kinder to the older woman.

Perhaps more disturbing, and she felt blindsided by her reaction, was that it sounded like Jake and his wife might be getting back together. She should be delighted to hear of their reconciliation, especially for Jenna's sake, but the truth was, Daphne felt dismayed. She would never have admitted it to anyone, and hardly even to herself, but Jake had held a high position on her "eligible bachelor" list. Now she had to mentally scratch him off. But as she did this, she said a silent prayer, asking God to bless him and his ex-wife and Jenna. She knew it was just plain selfishness to wish for anything else.

By the following week, with the continued help of Mattie and Jenna, Daphne finally felt like her task was nearly complete. As she paid the girls on Tuesday afternoon, convincing them that their efforts had helped her accomplish her goal, they seemed disappointed that their temporary employment was ending.

"If you ever need more help be sure and call us," Mattie said as the girls lingered on the steps of the front porch. The three of them had just put the last of the furniture out there. Not the best way to show off the house's lovely new paint job, which was finished, but it was only a temporary place to store the furnishings she planned to offer her relatives in her Grab and Go on Saturday.

"Don't worry, I will," she assured them. "You girls are at the top of my list."

Now Mattie nudged Jenna, quietly saying, "Go ahead—*ask her.*"

Jenna tossed Mattie a slightly aggravated glance.

"Come on," Mattie urged her. "It's okay."

"Daphne's busy," Jenna told her.

"What is it?" Daphne gently pressed Jenna. "What do you want to ask?"

"Nothing." Jenna just shrugged. "We should probably go."

"Jenna wants to be a writer," Mattie blurted out.

"Oh, that's great, Jenna." Daphne smiled at her.

"And she wants to ask you some writer questions," Mattie continued.

"But I know you're busy," Jenna told her.

Daphne nodded. "I am a little busy just now. Olivia wants me to pick her up at four. We're going to look at some new furnishings for the house. Fill up some of those empty spaces we just made."

Jenna gave Mattie an I-told-you look.

"But you could come by another time," Daphne told Jenna. "I'm not the best writer, but I can try to answer your questions."

"But you worked for *The New York Times*, didn't you?" Jenna asked. "Anyway, that's what my dad told me."

"Yes. I was at *The Times* for twelve years. But I was only a wedding writer."

"But you're writing a novel now, aren't you?"

"Well, I hope to start one . . . when things settle down."

"And your aunt wrote books, didn't she?" Jenna persisted.

Daphne tried not to react, but how much had Jake told his daughter? Worried that they might stumble upon something revealing, she hadn't even let the girls go into Aunt Dee's office. "Yes . . . she was a writer too."

"She wrote textbooks," Mattie filled in.

"So maybe we could get together after I have the Grab and Go," Daphne told Jenna. "Life won't be so hectic then."

"Yeah." Jenna nodded. "That'd be great."

"Do you want us to come on Saturday, to help you with the Grab and Go?" Mattie offered.

"Sure, I'd love some help. I plan to serve a light luncheon in the backyard. Just sandwiches and finger food. But you girls can help with that. And I'm sure there will be lots more to do."

"I told Grandma about what you're going to do," Mattie confessed with some hesitation. "I hope that was okay."

"Sure. I've got the invitations ready to send out." Daphne had been careful not to mention anything about the silent family feud. She didn't want Mattie to feel caught in the middle. "Do you think your grandma will come?"

"Oh, yeah." Mattie nodded. "She'll be here."

"Good. I hope they all come."

"I'm sure they will," Mattie said.

Daphne smiled. "Hopefully we'll have good weather and a pleasant day." She glanced at her watch. "I'm going to head out, girls, to pick up Olivia."

As Daphne got into her car, she felt optimistic. If all went well on Saturday, it would give her a fresh start with her family. Because as much as she loved Appleton and wanted to make it her permanent home, it spoiled everything knowing that some of her relatives really resented her.

Chapter 16

With Olivia's guiding hand, Daphne managed to pick out a number of furnishings, including an incredibly comfortable club chair and ottoman. These were the pieces she would combine with some of Aunt Dee's things, the various items Daphne had decided to hold on to. Her goal, according to Olivia, was to marry the old with the new and give the house an inviting yet stylish look.

"Kind of shabby chic reinvented," Olivia told her as they were picking out some additional accessories at Pottery Barn.

"I don't know how I could've done this without you," Daphne said as they took a dinner break. "And I don't know how I can thank you. I wish you'd let me pay you for your services or something."

Olivia waved her hand. "Forget that nonsense. This is like a girls' night out for me. Besides, Jeff and his brother are watching the NBA finals tonight." She feigned a yawn. "You could just shoot me if I had to stay home and endure that."

"Well, I appreciate your help."

"I appreciate you letting me help." Olivia wiped her mouth with her napkin. "In fact, it's inspiring me to start offering some consulting services to my customers. I'm carrying more and more decor items in the shop, and I'm always giving someone advice. But this is the first time I've done anything this big and I love it."

"And I love how Aunt Dee's house is looking."

"You mean *your* house." Olivia shook a finger at her. "You need to stop calling it your aunt's house, Daphne."

Daphne nodded, but she wished she could divulge the truth. "Yes, but it's hard when you have so many childhood memories. But I'll admit that it doesn't really look like her house anymore."

"Thank goodness." Olivia laughed. "It was just fine for a little old lady's house. But it was so not you."

They shopped for another hour after dinner. Then as Daphne was driving Olivia home, they made plans to meet again on Thursday. "By then all your furniture should be delivered," Olivia said. "And I can help you with the final tweaks. That way everything will be looking good when your relatives come for your wingding on Saturday."

"I'll be so glad when that's behind me."

For that reason, she shouldn't have been too shocked when after nearly two weeks of feverish preparations and after getting in provisions for the luncheon on Saturday, Jake called on Friday morning to warn her that Martin Ballinger was contesting Aunt Dee's will.

"What does that mean?" she asked.

"Not that much, really. I'd expected something like this, which is why the will was written so tightly. I've given Martin a copy of the general will, which clearly specifies you as sole inheritor and should convince him that contesting the will is futile."

"So he won't have to know any of Aunt Dee's secrets?"

"That's right."

She explained about her Grab and Go tomorrow. "Should I call it off?"

"I don't think so. Not yet anyway. I just faxed Martin the will. Let's see how he responds."

"Yes, please, let me know if you hear anything."

"I will. And hey, I wanted to thank you for befriending Jenna. She's really excited about getting to talk to you about writing. It's her dream to be a writer."

"Well, like I told her, I'm a pretty small potato when it comes to writing. Nothing compared to my aunt. Not that she would've been forthcoming regarding her illustrious career."

He chuckled. "That's probably a good thing. I can't really imagine Jenna penning romance novels. Actually, she wants to be a journalist."

Daphne sighed. "That's what I thought I wanted too. Sometimes I want to kick myself for not going after it harder."

"You'll be kind of like a journalist . . . when you take over the column. When do you plan to start that anyway?"

She bit her lip. This was something she was trying not to think about. "My plan was to begin next week. After the Grab and Go. But the truth is, I have barely stepped foot in her study."

"Don't be intimidated," Jake said. "Dee had complete confidence in you."

"I know. I just wish I did."

"All you need is to do your best. And remember Dee only expected you to try. There is nothing in her will that stipulates you must successfully write the column to receive your inheritance."

He cleared his throat. "Because, as you know, that's something else altogether."

"Right." She grimaced.

"So, how's it going in the romance department? If you don't mind my asking."

"Quite honestly, I've been so distracted with the house lately, I haven't really given it much thought." She looked around the front room, which Olivia had helped her to arrange last night. Today it was pure perfection and she couldn't help but smile when she looked at it.

"Well, you'll have to excuse me for asking from time to time. But it's kind of my responsibility to keep tabs on you."

"What a fun job *that* must be," she said sarcastically.

"It has its ups and downs. So, how is the house coming? I know the painting's done, right? Willie just sent me the bill for the finished job. Before I make out the check, I need to know it was completed to your satisfaction."

"He did a beautiful job. Even Mick was impressed."

"Mick?"

"You know, The Garden Guy."

"Yes, I know who Mick Foster is. But why was he impressed?"

"Because Willie's crew didn't trample any of his precious plants."

Jake chuckled. "Oh yeah, that makes sense. Speaking of Mick, I assume he's one of the bachelors you're considering. And just so you know, I'm sure he's one of the guys Dee would've heartily approved."

Was he encouraging her toward Mick? And if so, why did that irritate her? But instead of reacting, she told him about how surprised she'd been to find that Mick had purchased her grandparents' farm. "I can't believe what he's done with the place."

"Dee mentioned how impressed she was too."

They chatted a bit longer and finally Jake told her not to worry about her cousin's obsession with his aunt's estate. "Martin might create a temporary tempest in a teakettle, but once his legal sensibilities kick in, he should realize he'd be fighting a losing battle. And most attorneys don't like to lose."

"I hope you're right." She thanked him for the heads-up regarding Martin and even invited him to stop by the house to check it out if he wanted. She'd intentionally kept their conversation cool and casual . . . professional. But as she hung up, she wondered if a man suddenly seemed more attractive when he was unavailable. And if so, why was that? Was it because it felt like forbidden fruit? Or was it because an unavailable man felt safer? Perhaps it was a combination of both.

Puttering around her pretty house, Daphne decided she was not going to worry about Martin's legal threats. As she did some pre-preparation for tomorrow's luncheon, she did regret that she'd forgotten to put an RSVP on the invitations. What would she do with all this food if no one came? Maybe she could simply host an impromptu open house for her real friends. Now that would be fun.

It was about five in the afternoon, and she was up to her elbows in egg salad, which she planned to make into sandwiches tomorrow, when she heard the doorbell ring. After a quick rinse of her hands, she grabbed a dish towel and hurried to the front door in her bare feet. To her surprise, it was Jake McPheeters and in his hand was a gorgeous bouquet of peonies in varying shades of pink. "For your new and improved house," he said as he handed it to her.

"These are gorgeous." She stepped back. "Thank you. And come in."

"I hope I'm not catching you at a bad time, but you did tell me I could come by and see the place." He nodded with approval as he stepped into the foyer. "Very nice. Very, very nice. I feel like this is a completely different house."

"Not an old lady house anymore." With the peonies still in her hands, she was looking around and trying to decide where to put them.

"Olivia said the table in the foyer." He pointed to the marble-topped table that used to be upstairs. It had taken her and the two girls just to carry the heavy top down. "I assume she means there."

Daphne moved the oversized bowl of bright green Granny Smith apples over to one side, and the grouping of framed old photos to the other, setting the clear vase of peonies in the center, centered with the big mirror hanging above. She stepped back and nodded. "Perfect."

"Olivia said they would be perfect. She did an intervention when I almost went for the tiger lilies, but she guided me toward those instead."

Daphne grinned. "I like tiger lilies."

He laughed. "Maybe next time."

Curious as to what that meant, she apologized for her grubby appearance as she started to show him around. "I was making egg salad for sandwiches. It probably smells like eggs in here now."

"I happen to like egg salad."

"Do you want one? I mean, you probably don't—not this close to dinnertime anyway. But if you do, there's plenty." She knew she sounded ridiculous, stumbling over her words, but it was like she couldn't help it.

"I'll take a rain check." He was looking in the dining room now. "I like this color. Very warm and inviting. And a nice contrast with these dark furnishings."

"I decided to keep the original set. It just seemed to go so well in here. But Olivia insisted on getting the chair seats recovered. I can't believe what a difference that made." She admired the blue-and-white basket-weave fabric and how it set off the blue-and-white Chinese vases on the sideboard. More treasures Olivia had unearthed in Aunt Dee's packed china cabinet.

"Everything looks fresh and clean," he told her. "And full of life."

"That's mostly Olivia's doing." She took him into the kitchen, which was looking a little messy now.

"Mind if I sample?" he asked as he spied the bowl of egg salad.

"Not at all." She handed him a spoon. "Have at it."

"I consider myself a bit of a connoisseur when it comes to egg salad." He dipped in the spoon, took a generous scoop, and popped it into his mouth. With eyes half closed he acted as if he were taste testing for Le Cordon Bleu. "Mmm . . ." He nodded. "I give you two thumbs up."

"Thank you."

He set the spoon in the sink. "And I like this shade of green in here. Very energetic."

She continued the tour, explaining how she was waiting to do Aunt Dee's bedroom later. "And the study . . ." She sighed. "Well, it did get a fresh coat of paint, but everything in there is pretty much as she left it. I'll start going through it next week."

When the tour ended, Jake didn't seem eager to leave. So she invited him to sit in the kitchen while she finished up. As he sat at the table, another set she'd decided not to replace, he explained that he had not heard back from Martin yet.

"I'm of the opinion that no news is good news where he's concerned. I suspect he's realizing that it's foolish to contest the will."

"I hope you're right."

They visited a bit more and then he stood to go. "I shouldn't take up your time. I'm sure you have a lot to do to get ready for your relatives tomorrow."

She shrugged as she walked him through the front room. "I think I've got it covered. And your daughter and Mattie are coming to help in the morning."

"So I hear." He paused in the foyer. "So it's a Friday night in Appleton. I'm guessing you already have dinner plans."

Okay, this caught her completely off guard. Was he asking her out?

"Sorry. I probably shouldn't have asked."

She tilted her head to one side. "What do you mean exactly?"

"Well, I've wondered about this. I do represent your aunt's estate. In essence you are kind of like my client and I never date clients. Although you're not exactly my client since you didn't actually employ me." He gave her a lopsided grin. "It's more like you got stuck with me. Anyway, I've been concerned about the need to keep my relationship with you strictly professional."

She felt her cheeks flush. "So you are asking me out on a date?" she said, instantly regretting her assumption.

"I guess you could say that. Although I'll admit it was kind of a backhanded invitation. And I wouldn't blame you if you turned me down flat."

She bit her lip, trying to think of a gracious response. "Well, I'm flattered, Jake. But I, uh, I'm curious. What about your relationship with your wife—I mean your ex-wife?"

"What?" He looked confused.

"Aren't you getting back together with her?"

He looked blindsided. "Getting back with Gwen?"

She just nodded.

"Where did you hear that?"

Now she shrugged.

He looked perplexed. "I honestly don't know where you got that idea, but as far as I know, it's not happening. Gwen has made it clear that she's moved on with her life."

"Oh . . ." Daphne knew she couldn't divulge her source. Not only would it be unfair to Mattie, it would reveal that Daphne had been eavesdropping. "But sometimes divorced couples reconcile. I mean, it can happen. How long have you been divorced anyway, if you don't mind my asking?"

"It'll be eight years in August." His countenance seemed grim as he studied her. And she felt certain he regretted asking her to dinner now.

"Well . . . I . . . uh . . ." She didn't know what to say. Could this get anymore awkward?

"I should probably be going."

"Thanks for the flowers," she said meekly.

"Thanks for the tour." He offered a businesslike smile. "You've done a great job on the house. And good luck with your relatives tomorrow."

She thanked him again, waving stupidly as he hurried out the door and down the porch steps. She felt like such a fool as she returned to the kitchen. Why had she brought that up? What business was it of hers? Except that he'd been asking her out. And how could she go out with a man knowing that his ex-wife wanted to get back together with him? And it wasn't as if she could explain that. Not without sounding like a complete fool. Oh, that was right, she'd already sounded like a complete fool.

As she cleaned the kitchen, she attempted to dissect and discern her conflicting emotions toward Jake, but it only made her feel more confused. What would Dear Daphne tell her?

> *Dear Daphne,*
>
> *A man I respect and am good friends with asked me to go out with him, and I was all ready to say yes when I remembered a conversation I'd overheard recently. You see, this man is divorced, and according to what I heard, there's a possibility he will be getting back together with his ex-wife. Going out with him makes me feel like I'd be ruining their chance of reconciling—or like I was going out with a married man. And it made me feel disgusted with myself and slightly angry at him. It was as if I liked him better before he asked me out. What should I do?*
>
> *Agonizing in Appleton*

As she finished up in the kitchen, she pondered over how Dear Daphne might answer her letter.

> *Dear Agonizing,*
>
> *First of all, I must question your methods of collecting information about a man you said you respected—were you eavesdropping? But never mind that, it sounds as if you have answered your own question. If going out with him would make you feel miserable, why would you bother with it? I suggest you continue being this man's friend. It sounds as if he can use one.*
>
> *Daphne*

As Daphne went to check on the cats, she decided that she'd felt more attracted to Jake when he seemed unavailable. And it had nothing to do with the old forbidden-fruit theory. It was simply because it felt safer. An unavailable man meant there was no risk involved. And really, wasn't that how she'd purposely lived most of her life? Aside from the mistake she made with Ryan. She'd lived cautiously, carefully, prudently—and totally risk free. Her guarantee that her heart would never be broken again. Going out with Jake was too risky.

Chapter 17

It was nearly a month since Aunt Dee's funeral, and once again her relations were traipsing through her home. However, it no longer looked like Aunt Dee's house. And several of the older relatives did not approve, and they didn't seem to care who heard them complaining.

"What has she done?" Diane said to her daughter shortly after they entered the house.

"Mother," Jocelyn used a warning tone.

"Welcome," Daphne called out as she left the kitchen where she'd been coaching Jenna and Mattie. "Most of the others are outside." She joined them in the front room. "In the backyard."

"Yes." Diane was taking it all in. "You've changed everything."

Daphne smiled. "Yes. A friend helped me."

"But why?"

Daphne shrugged. "Why not?"

"It looks very nice," Jocelyn told her. "Don't mind Mom. She still loves her 1980's style house. Everything is cabbage roses."

"I like cabbage roses," Diane said indignantly. "And I used to like Aunt Dee's house. Now I'm not so sure."

"Well, it doesn't matter whether or not you like it," Jocelyn pointed out. "Since it belongs to Daphne now."

Even though Jocelyn seemed to be defending Daphne, she thought she heard a slight edge to her voice. As if she wondered why it hadn't been left to her instead.

"So anyway," Daphne led them through the kitchen, "if you'd like to join the others outside, we've put some lunch things out there. And the gardens look lovely."

"Oh my!" Diane gasped, pointing to the apple green kitchen walls. "How can you stand that dreadful color, Daphne?"

Daphne shrugged again. "I find it lively and cheerful."

"Poor Aunt Dee must be turning in her grave."

"Mother!" Jocelyn shook her head. "Come on."

"So . . . Martin's not coming?" Daphne asked cautiously.

"Oh, he'll be here," Diane assured her. "He's bringing a truck."

Daphne just nodded. "After lunch, I plan to explain how this will work. I want to keep it fair so everyone gets a chance to get what's important to them."

As Daphne led them outside, Diane began inquiring about particular pieces of furniture, making it known that she had some specific items in mind. "I'd prefer to tell everyone how it'll work at the same time," Daphne said. "But please, help yourself to some food."

Daphne returned to the house feeling the need to brace herself for whatever was coming—and it seemed certain a storm was brewing. She ran upstairs and barricaded herself in her peaceful bedroom and attempted to quiet her mind. Before she left, she said a quick prayer, asking God to grant healing to her fractured family. However, she suspected that was the same as asking for a miracle.

When she returned to the backyard, she could tell that some of her relatives, like Diane and her sister-in-law Marlene, were very suspicious of Daphne. But Daphne tried to act oblivious, going around and visiting with everyone as if nothing was wrong.

"You're doing just fine," Dad assured her as she refilled his cup with iced tea. "I expect before the day is done, you'll have them eating out of your hand."

"Or eating me for dessert."

He chuckled. "Don't worry. I've got your back."

She smiled, knowing he meant it. Dad would not let them take her down. Not without a fight. After Martin arrived, a full hour late, and after he grimly refused the food as if she'd laced it with cyanide, and after it seemed everyone else was done eating, Daphne announced it was time for everyone to "listen up."

"I want to give you the details of the Grab and Go now," she said as they quieted down. "And although I called it a Grab and Go, I hope no one gets in too much of a hurry. And I hope everyone will find something really special to remind them of our lovely Aunt Dee."

"Yeah, now that it's all picked over," a male voice mumbled loud enough for her to hear him.

Daphne wasn't sure who said it, but she decided not to ignore it. "I know that some of you don't approve of the way Aunt Dee made her will. To be honest, I was as shocked as you all were to find out she made me sole inheritor. But it was Aunt Dee's choice to do as she pleased with her estate. And I hope you'll respect her right to do that."

"We might respect it better if we knew why she did it," Diane said loudly.

"It's because Daphne was named after her," Marlene said. "If my mom had named me Daphne, I'd probably have inherited it."

"Well, it still seems unfair," Marlene's daughter Lori said. Lori was almost the same age as Daphne, but they'd never been very close. "I used to come over here several times a month to visit Aunt Dee." She pointed at Daphne. "But you never did. After you moved to New York, you hardly ever came back."

"Daphne's job was demanding," Dad told her. "Besides that has nothing to do with why Dee left her the estate."

"Then why did she?" Martin demanded. "I've read over the will and I can't find one reason why Dee would leave everything to Daphne."

And suddenly everyone started speaking up and then they started arguing. Some seemed supportive of Aunt Dee's right to do as she wished. Others, like Martin, refused to accept it. Daphne was trying to settle them down, but the more she raised her voice, the louder they seemed to become until she finally became concerned for her neighbors. If this kept up, she wouldn't blame them for calling the police.

"That's enough!" Dad yelled. "Everyone settle down right now."

Fortunately, that seemed to work and the yard grew quiet.

"Daphne didn't invite you over to fight. And Dee would be ashamed of how some of you are acting."

"How else would she expect us to act?" Martin said. "Dee overlooked her entire family—her loved ones who've been by her side all these years—and instead chose her prodigal niece, the girl who ran off to New York City, to bestow her worldly goods upon. Why wouldn't we take offense?"

"Are you saying Dee didn't have the right to give Daphne her estate?"

"I'm saying I question whether or not Dee really did that." Martin pointed a finger at Dad. "I question whether or not that was really Dee's will."

"*What?*" Dad's face reddened. "What are you insinuating?"

"That something smells fishy and I intend to get to the bottom of it."

"Dad!" Jocelyn shook her finger at her father. "You've gone too far now."

"Not far enough," he told her. "I happen to know that Dee was a very wealthy woman. Far wealthier than any of you can even imagine. Except for the two of you." He pointed at Dad and Daphne. "I've almost got the whole thing figured out."

"Figured out?" Suddenly Daphne was worried. Was he going to expose Dee for writing sleazy romance novels or being the creator of *Dear Daphne*?

"Your game," Martin told her. "Rather your dad's game. I suspect that even you don't know all the details yet."

"What details?" Daphne asked him.

"Never mind right now. I came here today to put a stop to your little giveaway party, Daphne."

"But I—"

"You have no right to give away things that may not rightfully belong to you, young lady. And if you insist, I will see that everything is loaded into the moving truck parked down the street and put into storage."

"Grandpa!" Mattie shook a fist. "Why are you being such a Grinch?"

His face softened. "For you, sweetie. It's wrong that your cousin is taking everything when Dee's will was clearly bogus. I plan to set it straight, once and for all, for everyone. I knew Dee as well as anyone here. And she never would've done something so selfish and divisive. This is the work of three selfish people. Don and Daphne and their lawyer, Jake McPheeters, have manufactured a false will."

Everyone began to murmur again and Daphne felt tears coming, but she was determined not to cry. It was hard enough hearing such nasty accusations against her and Dad and Jake, but having everyone, including Jake's daughter Jenna, witnessing this ugly scene and seeing their confused expressions. Well, it was so wrong!

"That is enough!" Dad shouted. Again the crowd quieted and Dad looked at Daphne as if to ask her something. She simply shrugged, wiping a renegade tear from her cheek before anyone noticed. Anything he could do to smooth this over was fine with her.

"I didn't want to have to say this," Dad said. "Out of respect for Dee, I planned to keep silent. But because of Martin's foolish accusations here today, I feel I must defend Dee now." He took in a deep breath. "Dee chose to give her entire estate to Daphne for one reason and one reason only. Daphne is Dee's only grandchild."

Daphne's jaw dropped, and she could see by her relatives' expressions that some were shocked and others were simply skeptical.

"You expect us to believe that?" Martin demanded. "We all know you're Dee's brother. How can Daphne be—?"

"Dee was my mother," Dad proclaimed. "And I am proud to say so. She was a wonderful woman and she brought more joy to my life, and to Daphne's, than I even felt we deserved. I never realized she was my mother until she passed on. Then the facts came to light. However, I wanted to protect her image by keeping it between

Daphne and me." He pointed to Martin. "*You* forced me to divulge it." Now Dad told everyone the same details she had told him a couple of weeks ago, explaining the circumstances and why Dee felt it was best to take this secret to her grave.

Dad looked up at the sky. "I hope you'll forgive me," he said quietly.

"Of course she will, Dad." Daphne went over to stand by him, putting an arm around him. "So now you all know the truth. I hope you don't think less of Aunt Dee." She sighed. "Even though I know she was my grandmother, I still think of her as Aunt Dee. And if anyone here is still interested in taking something of hers home, I would like to explain how the Grab and Go is supposed to work."

Everyone seemed to be listening politely—even Martin—as Daphne explained. "My helpers Jenna and Mattie are passing around envelopes, one for each of you. On the front of the envelope is your name and your ID number. Inside the envelope you will see that you have stickers, which also have your ID numbers. But beside the ID numbers are letters. *A, B, C* . . . and so forth. When it's time for the Grab and Go to begin, you will be free to roam the front yard and porch, where you saw the larger items, and put a sticker on whatever it is you want. And there are also a lot of smaller items down in the basement to choose from.

"But you need to know that an item can have more than one sticker on it, but you also need to know that *A* stickers have the highest value and they will triumph over *B* stickers. And *B* stickers over *C* stickers. So take care with how you use them." She asked if anyone had questions, and when it seemed they all understood how it worked, she announced that it was time to start. "We will let the bidding run for an hour. And then you can bring your purchases, either the items or the tags if it's a large piece, to the dining room where the cashiers will check you out. Now, let the games begin. Just keep it civilized, please," she yelled as some of the younger ones took off running. "And really there's no hurry."

Martin and Dad were the only ones left standing in the yard with her. Both men had their envelopes in hand, and both were looking down at the ground. She wasn't surprised that Dad was in no hurry to Grab and Go since she'd already given him the items he wanted from Dee, but she was curious as to whether or not Martin would participate.

"Aren't you going to go get some things?" she asked them.

Martin gave Daphne an uneasy look. "You still want me around here? After all I just said and did?"

She went forward to him. "I'm sure you were simply looking out for what you thought were the best interests for your children. Just like Aunt Dee, my grandmother, was looking out for her own."

"I never would've guessed she was your mother," he said to Dad. "But after you explained everything, well, it made sense. It all made sense." He shook his head. "I hope you two can forgive me."

They assured him they did.

"I know I've been accused of putting my foot in my mouth—more times than I care to admit—but I'm pretty sure I shoved in both feet this time. I'm sorry."

Daphne patted him on the back. "Why don't you go see if there's anything you like. Maybe you and Diane should work together to make sure you don't use your most valuable stickers on the same things."

He tapped the side of his head. "I like your thinking."

Dad chuckled after Martin left. "Well, this didn't exactly turn out like you'd hoped. But who knows, maybe it was better this way. You think?"

She just nodded.

By the end of the Grab and Go, it seemed that everyone had gotten at least one or two, if not numerous, items that they really wanted. The cashiers in the dining room, Jenna and Daphne and Mattie, were kept busy for the next hour making sure that everyone had been treated fairly. But to Daphne's delight, after the last of them left, nearly everything had been cleared out. What few things remained, she decided to stow in the basement for the time being.

"What will you do with these?" Jenna asked after they took the last load down.

Daphne shrugged. "Nothing for now." She noticed Jenna looking longingly at a box covered with shells. It didn't really seem like anything special, probably something Aunt Dee had picked up in her travels. "Would you like anything down here?" Daphne asked Jenna.

"Really?" Jenna's eyes lit up.

"Absolutely. Both you girls, feel free to take anything you like from down here. Consider it your tip for your help today." She reached into her apron pocket and pulled out two more envelopes. "And here is your pay." She patted them on the backs. "Thanks. And don't forget to turn off the lights down here when you're done." She let out a tired sigh as she went upstairs. "I am going to take a shower and put my feet up now."

Walking through the calm and serene house, now peacefully vacated from her boisterous relatives, Daphne felt a deep sense of satisfaction. She paused by Aunt Dee's bedroom door, and momentarily resting her hand on the glass knob, she experienced an unexpected rush of gratitude.

"Thank you, Grandmother," she whispered. In the same instant, she remembered what Aunt Dee used to say to her. Four simple words of praise she would use after Daphne successfully completed a project. It could be for a cleaned bedroom, a good drawing, learning to sew on a button, baking cookies, or writing a poem. Aunt Dee would beam down at her and say: *"Well done, dear girl!"*

As she went up the stairs, those pleasant words echoed through Daphne's soul once again.

Chapter 18

Daphne gave herself until Monday morning to go into Aunt Dee's study. She wasn't even sure why facing this room caused such trepidation. Perhaps it was just a remnant of her childhood experience when she'd accepted that this space was off-limits.

She'd grown up respecting that this was Aunt Dee's workplace, a no-nonsense room where her aunt toiled over very serious textbooks and academic manuals and other "boring" things. And when Aunt Dee was working, it was Daphne's job to occupy herself. To that end, Aunt Dee always made certain the house was stocked with crayons and craft materials, puzzles and books, as well as a full VHS selection of every Disney movie ever made.

She pushed open the door to her aunt's study and was relieved to see the morning sunshine peeking through the slats of the dark wood blinds. The first thing she would do, after moving Aunt Dee's computer to a safe spot, was take down those gloomy blinds and allow the sunlight to pour into this space. It took nearly an hour to get those stubborn dusty blinds down, and another to clean the windows. But seeing the dove gray room now washed in light gave Daphne hope.

After that, she gave the room a thorough cleaning, removing all the bric-a-brac and pictures and clutter until all surfaces were bare and the dark wood gleamed. She also thinned down the bookshelves, crating the books she felt she'd have no use for and making room for her own books. Although she was determined to get rid of most of her aunt's things, she did save a few special items, including some old framed photos of her aunt and Dad and Daphne, as well as her aunt's old black Underwood typewriter.

Surveying the room, Daphne reconsidered her earlier decision to have all the heavy wooden office furniture painted white or else removed. Seeing it like this, clean and clear and washed in light, she realized it was actually rather handsome—it had the look of a writerly room. Was *writerly* actually a word?

Finally she decided to roll up the dark Oriental carpet to reveal the wood floor beneath. Then she took out the office chair as well. Although it was in good shape and not a bad style, it felt too personal to reuse. The chair, like her aunt, was ready for retirement. Then she spent another hour carefully going up and down the steep basement stairs as she transported all these things down there for the time being.

After a shower to remove the dust and grit she'd accumulated in the clean-out, she stood in front of the cleared-out office and looked on in satisfaction. The room had been truly transformed. Now all she needed was a new office chair and perhaps a lighter, brighter rug to soften it up. And maybe a table lamp and a few other things. Her first instinct was to call Olivia and ask her advice. But Daphne stopped herself. Olivia had coached Daphne enough that she felt she could handle this.

By the end of the day, Daphne, with the assistance of Dad and his pickup, had her new office completely set up. And she would no longer call it a study but an office.

"It looks good," Dad said as Daphne turned on the desk light for effect.

"Thanks. I think I can work in here now."

"You don't feel like you're in a fishbowl with all those bare windows?"

She shrugged. "I suppose if it were dark outside, I might. But I'll just live with it for a while and see."

"So, you're ready to start writing that great American novel now?"

Daphne had almost forgotten that Dad didn't know her real reason for wanting to transform this space. But, of course, he was still in the dark about *Dear Daphne.*

"Not quite ready," she confessed. "I still need to go through the drawers and cabinets and storage spaces."

"What will you do with all of it?"

"For now I'll crate it and store it in the basement."

He nodded. "I'm glad you're not throwing everything away. Someday we might want to go through Dee's old things and find out more about the books she wrote."

Daphne just smiled. "Yes, maybe we will . . . someday."

Dad excused himself, explaining it was bridge night at the country club and that Karen was waiting for him to pick her up. Daphne thanked him again and even told him to say hello to Karen for her. Okay, it wasn't much, but at least she was trying. And she really didn't want Dad to think she didn't like his girlfriend. If Karen was his girlfriend.

Daphne slid her new office chair under the desk, running her hands over the soft bone-colored leather. Elegant but useful. And the new rug, a graphic design of pale gray and aqua and off-white seemed the perfect touch. Feeling pleased with her progress, Daphne decided to treat herself to dinner at Midge's Diner.

It was one of those perfect June evenings as she walked to town. She felt strong and happy and life felt good. Tomorrow she would turn on her aunt's computer and officially begin writing the advice column. At least, that was what she was telling herself. The little girl inside questioned this. Who was Daphne to give romantic advice to anyone? However, she was consoled to consider Aunt Dee—what had made her such an expert?

"How many?" Kellie politely asked Daphne.

"Just me." She smiled.

Kellie looked around the crowded diner. "Do you mind eating at the counter?"

"I suppose that's okay." Daphne really didn't want to eat at the counter, but it would be selfish to tie up a booth. However, if Kellie offered a booth, she would gladly accept.

"Take any spot you want at the counter," Kellie said pleasantly.

Daphne took a stool at the end and, trying not to feel conspicuous, scanned the menu. Now she wished she'd stayed home. And she still had some leftovers from Saturday too. Tempted to say she changed her mind, she closed the menu and started to stand.

"Hey, Daphne," Ricardo said in a friendly tone as he emerged from the kitchen.

She smiled. "Hey, Ricardo. What's cooking?"

He came over and leaned against the counter in front of her. "I just finished throwing some smoked salmon chowder soup together."

"Ooh, that sounds good."

He glanced at the empty seat beside her. "Eating alone tonight?"

She nodded.

He grinned. "Well, I admire a woman who can eat alone."

She let out a sheepish smile. "You want the truth?"

His dark brows arched. "Sure."

"I was about to leave because I felt conspicuous eating alone at the counter. Is that pathetic or what?"

He laughed, then pointed to a vacant booth. "Would you be more comfortable over there?"

"I hate wasting a whole booth on just one—"

He grabbed up her menu and glass of water. "Come on, Daphne."

Kellie watched as Ricardo escorted Daphne to the booth, and the expression on her face showed she wasn't pleased. Still, this was Ricardo's restaurant—couldn't he sit customers wherever he liked?

"How's that?" He set down the water and handed her the menu again.

"Much better. Although I still feel guilty for tying up this space when you're busy like this."

He slid in across from her. "Would you feel better if I joined you?"

Her cheeks warmed. "Oh, you don't have to do that, Ricardo, just to make me feel better."

He chuckled. "I'm doing it because it makes me feel better. I'm hungry and you're good company. Do you mind?"

"Not at all."

"Great. I'm going to have a bowl of my smoked salmon chowder and a green salad. How about you?"

"That sounds great. I mean, I'll have the same. And iced tea too, please."

He went over to tell Kellie, then quickly returned with their beverages. "I haven't seen much of you lately." He sat back down.

So she explained about New York and then cleaning out the house and the Grab and Go and even about setting up her new office space today. "So I guess I'm celebrating tonight."

"My mom told me about all your relatives coming over to your house on Saturday."

"Oh, dear." Daphne grimaced. "I hope she wasn't too disturbed by all the arguing."

"She said it got a little loud." He grinned.

"Loud? At one point I thought I would have to call the police."

"Family feuds can get out of hand."

"But it all turned out just fine," she said.

"So is it true, then?"

"Is what true?"

"That Dee was actually your grandmother?"

She blinked. "How did you hear that?"

"It's a small town, Daphne. And your cousin Marlene is good friends with my mom. She told her. And Mom told me." He smiled. "I thought that was pretty cool news. And it explains why Dee was so generous to you in her will."

She nodded. "I'm actually relieved that the cat's out of the bag. I honestly don't see why Aunt Dee was so concerned. Well, except that life was different back in her day. I suppose people could be cruel.

And like you said, it's a small town. But I was glad it was my dad who exposed her secret. Not me."

Before long their soup and salads came. "Ricardo, this soup is fabulous."

"Thank you. It's one of my favorite recipes."

"Really, it is so good. If you served this in New York's finest restaurants, the food critics would rave about it."

As they ate and visited, Daphne couldn't help but wonder. She knew this wasn't a date, but was it possible that Ricardo really did have some romantic interest in her? But too soon the meal was done and she knew Ricardo was needed in the kitchen.

"Thank you for dining with me," he told her as he stood. "And don't even think of trying to pay because this was on me."

"But—"

"No arguing." He held up his hands.

She stood too. "Okay. But now you have to promise to come see my new-and-improved house. I want to have a little housewarming this week. Will you come?"

"You bet." He nodded.

"I haven't actually picked the night yet. What's your best night?"

His brow creased. "Well, weekends keep me busy here. Thursday is my night off."

"Thursday it is." She nodded. "Let's say seven."

"I'll be there." His dark eyes gleamed and she felt an unexpected warm rush. He was still as handsome as in high school. No, he was even more handsome now.

She told him thanks and good-bye and went home to make a list of the others she would invite, and since it was rather last minute, she decided that before it was too late in the evening, she would just call them. Her plan was to invite friends and neighbors and then everyone, including Willie's paint crew, who had helped with the house. By the time she finished, she had spoken to or left messages for more than twenty people.

The next morning she decided to walk to town and visit The Apple Basket. She remembered seeing a sign there about catering and she hoped Truman might be able to help her. In less than an hour, a simple menu for a small buffet of appetizers and drinks was all worked out.

"And if you like, I have a gal named Katy who works here," Truman told her. "She's a great server for dinners and parties. She wears a neat white shirt and black trousers and acts very professional. I can see if she's available."

"Perfect. And I'd love for you to come as a guest, if you'd like. There might be some people there you know . . . or would like to meet."

He eagerly agreed and after the final details were settled, Daphne went back home, determined to go to work.

It took a while for her to correctly enter the passwords and figure out the storage system for Aunt Dee's computer, but before long, she was opening up e-mails containing letters from what she assumed were real people, although some of the letters were so ridiculous, she felt they must've been phony. But she soon discovered that her aunt had created files for all sorts of letters. They went from *A* to *Z*, including everything from *Addicted to Love* to *Zealously Jealous* and everything in between.

Reading over the old columns, Daphne was surprised at how familiar they felt. Partly because she'd read the column for years. But it was almost as if she could hear her aunt speaking those comforting words of wisdom. And some of the letters Daphne had crafted in her head fit right in. It felt as if her writing voice was similar to Aunt Dee's—and that gave her hope.

Giving herself the freedom to make mistakes and knowing she could throw her first attempts away, she jumped in and began to write responses. But she soon learned two things: (1) Her answers had a tendency to sound too cheeky, and (2) she seemed to lack the genuine connection that had come so naturally to her aunt. Perhaps this was not as easy as she'd assumed.

"How did you do it?" Daphne finally said. Leaning back in the chair, she closed her eyes and attempted to clear her mind, wishing Aunt Dee would send her some kind of message. But nothing came.

Soon she was pacing, going around and around in the office, flailing her arms as she walked in small circles, just like her mind seemed to be circling . . . getting nowhere. Suddenly she wished she hadn't given Aunt Dee's study this makeover. What if something had been lost in the transformation? Something that Daphne would never get back? Daphne changed the direction of her circling, going counterclockwise in an attempt to unwind her mind.

And then she stopped. It was time to start going through her aunt's mysterious-looking cabinets and drawers. Some of them were locked—and those were the ones that interested her the most. She'd already discovered a handsome engraved silver cigarette case that looked like it was from the forties. In it were a number of small keys. It didn't take long to figure out where the keys fit.

As she unlocked one of the cabinet doors, she found it was filled with multiple copies of all the Penelope Poindexter books. She pulled one out, studying the glossy depiction of a beautiful buxom blonde struggling against a swarthy pirate with handsome, rugged looks. So typical. So cliché. Had Aunt Dee truly penned this sort of tripe?

Taking the book to her chair, she sat down and began to read *Gabriella's Bounty*. She prepared herself to laugh at her aunt's bodice-ripping romp, but instead she found herself quickly tugged into the story. And although she felt simultaneously amused and embarrassed to be entertained by the simple plotline of this fluffy romance book, she continued to read.

Daphne wanted to understand how it was possible that she was starting to care about the young Gabriella Barteau. Pulled in by the beautiful yet naive Gabriella, orphaned as a child and raised by nuns, Daphne felt sorry for her when she was kidnapped by an evil man who believed Gabriella to be an heiress he could exchange for ransom. Then stepped in the dashing Jean Luc Bouchard, captain of a ship full of renegades that everyone assumed were pirates. And on the story went.

Daphne could hardly believe it was nearly two o'clock when she finally closed the book and shook her head. Aunt Dee could really write. To Daphne's relief, the book had not been smutty. Not a bit like she'd expected. In fact, despite being filled with romantic tension, it was fairly chaste and moral. And it had been enjoyable—for an escape read. And who didn't need an escape from time to time?

Daphne sat there studying the suggestive cover and trying to wrap her head around this. Aunt Dee seemed to understand something about life and love—something that Daphne had missed. And something about this fluffy little book had great appeal to Penelope's readers. And yet Daphne couldn't quite put her finger on it. What was it exactly that had made Penelope Poindexter's books so popular?

And then it hit her—just like that. She stood in triumph, nodding in eager realization as a lightbulb seemed to go on inside of her brain. "Of course, that must be it," she proclaimed as she paced around the small space.

Yes, it was all starting make sense. Penelope Poindexter a.k.a. Aunt Dee had compelled her readers to *care* about the characters. While reading this book, Daphne had felt as if she were actually in Gabriella's delicate black velvet slippers as the unfortunate girl was being held captive by the evil Claude Lasser. Daphne had felt the longing in Gabriella's heart as well as the constriction of her corset after she was rescued by the dashing pirate Jean Luc.

Now Daphne returned to the computer and opened the file of letters asking the wise Daphne Delacorte for advice. She clicked on to the top one, and after reading the plea for help, Daphne felt instantly pulled into this young woman's world. To her delighted surprise, she truly cared about *Frustrated in Florida*. And without really thinking or second-guessing herself, she opened a Word doc and began to type an answer. Her fingers flew over the keyboard, similar to when she wrote wedding announcements, and by the time she finished, although her response wasn't perfect, she felt it was pretty good.

Standing up and stretching, she felt slightly light-headed. Or maybe she was just heady from having written her first *Dear Daphne* response. Or more likely, she simply needed nourishment. She hurried to the kitchen and fixed herself a plate of finger food, then rushed back to her office, eager to review her work. As she munched on her lunch, she slowly reread the letter from *Frustrated in Florida* as well as her *Dear Daphne* response.

Dear Daphne,

I'm twenty-nine and moved back in with my mother about a year ago, right after my father died. First I have to say that I love Mom dearly and I mostly respect her. But she is putting some serious brakes on my love life. Every time I go out, she complains about what I'm wearing. And I dress pretty conservatively. She also complains if I stay out too late, although I've never been late for work the next day. She also complains about the guys I go out with. I've learned not to bring them home. Nothing and no one seems good enough for her or her little girl. She's driving me totally nuts. But at the same time, I know she wants me around. She keeps telling me she's worried that I'll move away and she'll be all alone. What should I do?

Frustrated in Florida

Dear Frustrated,

First of all, let me express my sympathy for the loss of your father. I'm sure that must be hard on both you and your mother. You sound like a kind and caring daughter, and I'm sure your mother loves you dearly and is grateful to have had your emotional support during this difficult phase in her life. However, I suspect that the time is coming when, for both your sake and your mother's, you will need to consider moving out and living on your own again. Although your mother seems worried to lose you, she also seems

*to be pushing you away by complaining so much.
If you continue to live under her roof, I suspect her
complaints will drive a wedge between you and her.
Whether your mother can see it or not, she needs some
space to grieve and heal and restart her life again. So
do you. Then you can maintain a healthy and happy
relationship with her from a safe distance.*

Daphne

Feeling it was a good day's work but still a little unsure of herself, she e-mailed it to Jake, admitting it was her first attempt and asking him to give her his honest opinion. She really hoped he would like it, and she felt confident he would be honest.

She was just shutting down the computer when the doorbell rang. Thinking it might be Mick since he liked to pop in unexpectedly, she hurried to the door and swung it widely open. But when she saw the man standing there, smiling hopefully at her, she felt as if the floor beneath her had vanished . . . as if she were suddenly tumbling.

Chapter 19

W hat are you doing here?" she quietly asked in a flat, lifeless tone. It must've been close to eighty degrees on the porch, and yet she felt a chill in the air.

"*Daphne!*" Ryan Holloway's blue eyes sparkled. "It's so great to see you. You look fantastic. Prettier than ever."

"Why are you here?" She folded her arms across her chest and glared at her ex-boyfriend, the man who had broken her heart. And even though it had been nearly ten years since she'd last spoken to him, it suddenly seemed like yesterday.

"Is that how you greet an old friend?" The sparkle left his eyes. "I'm sorry to catch you by surprise like this, Daphne. I thought about calling first, but I was worried you'd hang up on me."

"You got that right." Despite the years, Ryan hadn't changed much. He was still boyishly handsome. Except as she looked more closely, it seemed his sandy hair had grown thinner. Whereas his waistline had not. Dressed neatly in a tan jacket, beige shirt, and brown pants, he reminded her of a cardboard cutout. Flat looking. Or maybe it was just her.

"So you aren't going to ask me in?" He sighed. "I guess I should've known better."

"Yes." She nodded. "You should've."

"You won't, at least, hear me out before you send me packing?"

"Hear you out about what?" she asked cautiously.

He glanced over his shoulder as if he was worried the neighbors were watching. "You really won't let me in?"

She rolled her eyes, then opened the door wider. "Fine. Come in. If you must."

"Thank you for your warm hospitality," he said teasingly as he followed her into the front room. "This is a pretty house."

She pointed to the couch. "Have a seat."

"Thank you." He sat down and looked around. "This really is a pretty house. Both on the outside and the inside. Did it really belong to your spinster aunt?"

She sat in the club chair and frowned as she tried to recall how much she had told him about her past . . . probably everything. "Yes. This was my aunt's house."

"It just doesn't look like a place where an old person would—"

"I've made some changes," she said sharply. "Is that why you're here, Ryan? To discuss home decor ideas?"

"No, of course not." He gave a nervous smile. "Just making small talk and hoping to warm the temperature a little."

"Why don't you get to the point?"

He sat up and leaned forward. "The point is that I'm sorry, Daphne. I'm truly sorry. And I wish, for once and for all, you would let me explain myself."

"I've heard your explanations before, Ryan. They didn't work then. They will not work now. The bottom line is that you led me to believe you were single. But you were married with two sons. That was wrong. And that was the end of it. There is nothing more to be said."

"Yes, there is." He looked intently at her. "I'm not married anymore. Belinda and I are divorced. And more important, I still love you, Daphne. I never quit loving you."

Once again, she felt as if the floor had been pulled out from under her. To steady herself she clung to the arms of the chair and just stared at him.

"I know I don't deserve for you to give me the time of day," he continued. "But you can't blame me for trying. That year spent with you in New York, it was the best year of my life. And I know it was good for you too. And I hate how it ended. My marriage truly was over long before then. I just wish I'd gotten the divorce before I ever met you."

"But you had young children."

He nodded sadly. "My boys, Clark and Jackson, they were the only reason I didn't leave Belinda a long time ago. And they're the reasons I went back and tried my best to make the marriage work. I made Belinda go with me to counseling. And there were a couple of good years when I thought we were going to make it. But then Belinda went back to her old ways . . . and I suppose I went back to mine. We got divorced three years ago. Mutually."

"Oh." She sighed. "Well, I'm sorry about that."

"Don't be sorry. It was for the best. Belinda remarried shortly afterward. And I have to admit he's a good guy. And they're a better match. Even the boys like him . . . well, sort of. But they're teenagers, they don't like much of anything."

Despite her resolve, Daphne felt her heart softening toward him.

"I'd been meaning to go out to New York, ever since the divorce became final. But then I thought I should give it some time. I thought you might respect that more. And then there was the job, and I was trying to stick around for the boys."

"How old are they now?"

"Jackson is eighteen, just graduated high school and will start college this fall. Clark is sixteen and thinks he knows everything."

She had imagined they were teens, but younger somehow.

"I know I've overwhelmed you," he said. "I should probably just go."

She bit her lip, trying to decide what to do. Part of her wished he'd leave and never come back, but another part of her . . . was unsure.

"I mostly wanted to see how you were doing. I flew out to New York last week. Apparently I had just missed you." He shook his head. "Story of my life."

"I was out there to pack things up. I've moved back here permanently."

"I know. I talked to Fiona at *The Times*. She filled me in and gave me your address. I hope you don't mind."

She shrugged.

"Mostly I want to know if you're doing okay, Daphne. Are you happy? I know I messed up badly in New York. But I never meant to hurt you. You were the last person in the world I wanted to hurt. I hope you can believe that."

She looked down at her lap. Why was he doing this? Why was he here?

"I always thought I was going to get it all sorted out," he continued, "and that one day you were going to marry me and we would live happily ever after. But I suppose I was living in a delusion back then. I can see now that I was immature and selfish. I can admit to wanting you so badly that I was willing to do anything to keep you. I knew if I confessed to you that I was married, it would be over. So I just allowed it to keep going. I wanted to keep it going for as long as I could . . ." His voice faded like he was giving up on her.

She looked back up to see his head hanging down and his hands clasped together. So unlike the vibrant guy she remembered, the one who was always on top of the world. This looked like a defeated man, and despite herself, she felt sympathy. "Well, if it's any consolation, I have forgiven you. Sometimes I even pray for you and your family."

He looked up hopefully. "Really? You do that?"

She just nodded.

"That means so much to me, Daphne. If the only thing I can accomplish with this visit is to secure your forgiveness, it's completely worth it."

"So that's why you came?"

He nodded.

"Then you have it, Ryan. And I wish you the best for the rest of your life."

He gave her a half smile. "I don't think you mean that."

"I do mean it."

"No . . . if you meant that—if you really wished me the best— you would be saying you wished we could be together." He gave her a sad smile. "But I know that's not what you mean." He stood up slowly. "I'm sorry to have interrupted your day."

She stood too, uncertain of how to act. "It's okay. I was done with work anyway."

"Work?" He looked curious. "What kind of work are you doing?"

"Writing."

"That's great. What are you writing?"

"Oh, this and that. I hope to start a novel soon."

"Lucky you." He shook his head. "I've got a novel started, but I never seem to find the time to finish it."

Just like that they were talking about writing—in the same way they used to do. Feeling off guard and slightly guilty for her earlier hostility toward him, she knew she should show him a smidgen of hospitality—before she sent him packing. So she invited him into the kitchen for something to drink. Then something odd happened. They sat across from each other at the little kitchen table and, companionably sipping iced tea, they talked and talked and talked.

"Oh, Daphne." He gazed intently at her. "Do you know how much I've missed this? How much I've missed you? Missed us?"

She swallowed hard.

"What I would give to have this back?"

"I, uh, I don't know." She glanced over at the clock. "My, it's late. I had no idea."

He looked at his own watch. "How about if I take you to dinner?" he asked hopefully. "For old times' sake. And then I promise I'll go and never darken your doorstep again. Okay?"

Her stomach rumbled and she reluctantly agreed. "I guess that'd be okay."

She went upstairs to freshen up, and before long he was driving her through town in a nondescript rental car. She decided The Zeppelin was the safest bet. Being that it was late, she hoped to avoid running into anyone she knew. She wasn't even sure why that mattered. Perhaps it was because Ryan was from what she considered a dark part of her past, something she preferred to remain hidden.

Their conversation continued on throughout dinner, and by the time he was driving her home, Daphne felt relaxed and very nearly happy. Of course, that in itself was disturbing. "Please, don't walk me to the door," she said as he started to get out of the car. "This wasn't a date and I don't want to remember it as one."

He nodded somberly. "All right. I can respect that."

"Thanks." She released a timid smile.

He put his hand on her arm as she was getting out. "It's just so amazing to see you again. Almost as if nothing has changed."

She bit her lip as she pulled away. "But a lot has changed."

"You haven't changed, Daphne. You're still sweet and good and wonderful."

She knew she was softening, but was determined to remain strong. "I can't believe I'm saying this, but it was good to see you today, Ryan. And I do wish you well."

His face lit up. "Do you know, this was the best day I've had in years . . . maybe since New York. Thank you for allowing me to crash your life like this, Daphne."

She tipped her head, then waved and shut the door. Hurrying up toward the house, she never looked back. But after the door was closed and locked, she broke down into inexplicable tears.

As Daphne went through the house turning off the lights, locking the doors, making sure the cats' water bowl was freshened, she continued to cry. As she went upstairs, she was still crying. Were these tears of relief? Tears of regret? Or what? She honestly did not know. But she let herself cry until her tears subsided . . . and then she fell asleep.

To her relief, she didn't feel like crying in the morning. But she did feel a little wrung out. Even so, she forced herself to go to work on the column. To her delight, Jake had e-mailed her back, saying that he thought she'd done a great job on her first column and encouraging her to go for it.

Feeling bolstered by his praise, she jumped right in, and by four o'clock, she had written three more *Dear Daphne* responses, all of which she e-mailed to Jake. Thankfully, the column only ran biweekly, and if every piece she'd written was acceptable, that would've been a whole week's worth of work in just two days.

As she puttered around that evening, she couldn't help but notice how big and quiet the house seemed. Was it because last night Ryan had been here, filling up the space with conversation and laughter? As she made herself a can of soup for dinner, she wondered about Aunt Dee . . . and all the nights she must've spent alone here. Hadn't she been lonely too? Perhaps that was why she had been so insistent that Daphne should marry.

On Thursday morning, Daphne was busily getting the house ready for the housewarming, but it was Mick who pointed out that her front porch wasn't very inviting. "We could put some potted plants here." He pointed to either side of the steps. "But you still need some chairs up there."

She nodded. "You're right. I don't know why I didn't think of that before." She peered at the barren-looking porch. "Do you think wicker would look nice?"

"Don't know why not. But I reckon you can't get many chairs into that little car of yours. Maybe you should talk me into taking you in my truck." He grinned. "You buy me lunch and I'll be your helper for the afternoon."

"It's a deal!"

After lunch at the diner, they went out to the nursery where he helped her pick out some large pots and plants for the porch. "Can I give you a hand?" Julianne asked as they were loading the plants onto the nursery wagon.

"Sure," Mick told her. "Can you get these transferred into those two pots over there?" He pointed to the ones they'd selected. "Daphne needs them today."

As Julianne was wheeling away the cart, Mick invited Daphne to go with him to the barn. "I'm just starting something new in there. It's not really open to customers yet, but I'll let you have a sneak preview, if you'd like."

"Sure. I haven't been in the barn since I was little." She tried not to remember the kittens.

"I thought this would expand my landscaping business," he said as he slid the door open. "To offer a small selection of outdoor furnishings." He led her inside where some tables and chairs and umbrellas were strewn about. "As you can see, it's not set up yet. But we hope to get it nicely arranged with plants and whatnot." He waved his hand. "I don't have any real wicker, but I've got some of the new vinyl pieces that look like wicker and are nearly indestructible. Plus they're made from recycled materials."

"I'd love to see them."

She had picked out several chairs, including a rocker and several side tables. "This will be a good start," she told him as they both picked up a chair and carried it out to his truck. By the time they got all the pieces loaded, Julianne was wheeling back the freshly potted plants and they looked fabulous.

"Those are beautiful," Daphne told Julianne.

Julianne beamed. "I added a few extras, to fluff out the pots. I hope you don't mind."

"Not at all." Daphne thanked her. "And since you've been so helpful, I'd like to invite you to my housewarming tonight. I know it's late notice, but—"

"I'd love to come," Julianne assured her. "Maybe I can get Mick to give me a lift." She gently elbowed him. "Since my scooter's not that safe at night."

He nodded with a hard-to-read expression. "Sure, I'm happy to."

To Daphne's relief it was only three by the time she and Mick started unloading the outdoor furniture and potted plants. If she stayed on task, she would still have sufficient time to complete her housewarming to-do list. She was just reaching for an end table when a certain nondescript rental car pulled up in front of her house. Just the same, she tried not to act surprised or even irritated when Ryan came over to see what they were doing.

"Need a hand with that?" he offered as he took the table from her.

She quickly introduced the men, but as Ryan helped them to unload and arrange the items on the porch, Mick tossed her a curious glance. After they'd finished transforming the empty porch to a space that was both attractive and inviting, she asked if they wanted to test it out while she got them all some cold drinks. Returning with iced tea and lemonade, she set the tray on a table, then sat down in the rocker and sighed.

"This is nice," she proclaimed as she rocked and sipped. "Thank you, Mick, for all your help." She glanced at Ryan who seemed to be waiting. "And thank you too."

"So Ryan tells me you and he go way back," Mick said to Daphne.

"That's right," Ryan said before she could answer. "Daphne and I met at *The Times*, right after I went to work there. We dated about a year. Isn't that right, Daphne?"

She took a slow sip, then nodded. "Sounds about right. But it was a long time ago. Our paths haven't crossed since then. And it's been more than ten years."

"So what brings you to Appleton now?" Mick asked Ryan.

Ryan winked at her. "Daphne here."

"Let me get this straight. You come to Appleton to see a girl you dated more'n a decade ago?" Mick sounded slightly suspicious now.

"Hey, I thought it was about time." Ryan turned to Daphne with longing in his eyes. "It'd been way too long. But I already told you all about that last night."

Daphne stifled the urge to pour her iced tea over Ryan's head.

"Aha," Mick said triumphantly. "So you admit it, then. You're trying to reignite the old flame, are you?"

"Would you blame me, if I was?" Ryan's eyes were still locked on Daphne.

"Speaking of flames, it's getting entirely too warm out here for me." She stood suddenly. "Now if you'll excuse me, I still have a lot to do to get ready for tonight."

"*Tonight?*" Ryan asked eagerly.

"Never mind." Daphne quietly told him. Then hoping to distract him, she thanked Mick again, perhaps even gushing a little. "Thanks to your help, this porch looks better than ever. And I think I'd like to get another potted plant or two." She waved as she went inside. "Later."

Despite her attempt to maintain a polite front, she was glad to escape both of them. Ryan's assumptions were just plain aggravating. But Mick encouraging him like that, well, that was too much!

Besides, she didn't have time to sit making small talk with them. There was much to do before the housewarming tonight. She wanted to thoroughly clean the kitchen and get the dining room set up for serving as well as make sure the downstairs bath was guest ready. And after that, she still needed to shower and dress and do something with her wildly curling hair. She didn't have time for these juvenile games.

Chapter 20

To Daphne's irritation, Ryan not only crashed her housewarming, he arrived twenty minutes early—while she was still taming her curly hair.

"I hope you don't mind." He handed her a bouquet of red roses.

Very subtle, she thought as she took them.

"But you were so busy this afternoon. And Mick extended the invitation to me. Nice guy, that Mick."

Daphne was dumbstruck as she looked around the house, trying to decide what to do with the flamboyant bouquet. "Olivia said to put them on the marble-topped table," he told her.

"Did she really?" Daphne narrowed her eyes.

He grinned. "Nice gal, that Olivia. Although she did try to talk me out of the roses." He frowned. "Not sure why."

Daphne removed the vase of peonies, which were actually looking a bit faded now, plunking the vase of roses in its place. Okay, it did look elegant there on the marble table. But a bit overly formal. Not to mention presumptuous.

"If you'll excuse me, I need to finish getting ready," she said stiffly. Carrying the peonies upstairs, she set them on her bureau and smiled at the results. Very pretty. Then she looked at her wild mop of hair, which she had been attempting to straighten out. Not so pretty. As she wrestled with the smoothing iron, the same question rolled around and around in her head. *What is he doing here?*

It was nearly seven when she went downstairs, where Ryan was relaxing in the club chair in the front room, his feet on the ottoman like he thought he was king of the castle.

"Excuse me," she said as she hurried past. "I need to speak to the caterer. Just make yourself at home." She hoped he wouldn't miss the irony there.

But Ryan not only made himself at home, he decided to make himself into the host as he proceeded to answer the door for her, greeting her guests and introducing himself before she could get to them. First he let in Dad and Karen, which would require some explaining on her part as she watched Dad looking curiously at her, wondering what was up with his daughter. Karen, unaware of the awkwardness, simply chatted congenially with Ryan.

Next came Jake and Jenna and Mattie, and once again Ryan beat her to the door. Daphne barely made it to the foyer in time to see that Jake seemed very interested in Ryan as he inquired his whereabouts and job status. However, Jake handed the gorgeous bouquet of tiger lilies directly to her.

"These are lovely," she told him. "I love tiger lilies."

He grinned. "I remember you saying you liked tiger lilies."

She greeted the girls, and then glancing at Ryan who was still chatting with Jake, she removed the arrangement of roses he'd brought, placing the tiger lilies in the prominent foyer table position.

"Say, girls," she handed the roses to Mattie, "you know your way around. How about if you find another spot for these? Maybe the bathroom or my office."

They hurried off and she remained in the foyer, listening as Ryan revealed to Jake that he was the old boyfriend. "We go way back. We first met more than ten years ago."

"That's right," she added. "So it was pretty shocking to see him after all this time."

Jake nodded. "Welcome to Appleton."

"And welcome to Daphne's new digs," Ryan said back.

Now Jake glanced at her and she suspected by his expression, he was jumping to conclusions. He probably assumed she'd invited Ryan here in the hopes of securing her inheritance with a husband. She would have to straighten him out later.

The next guests to arrive were Olivia and Jeff. Again Ryan made himself handy by opening the door and greeting Olivia like an old friend, even though he'd only just met her this afternoon. He also invested a fair amount of energy buddying up to Jeff. It was irritating to see how easily he was worming his way into her world. But even more aggravating was that a small part of her liked it. Had she learned nothing these past ten years?

"Hey there, Mick," Ryan cheerfully greeted Mick as he let him and Julianne into the house. "How's it going, *mate*?" Daphne cringed to hear his bad attempt at an Aussie accent, but Mick took it in stride, joking right back at him and introducing him to Julianne, who looked stunning in a red-and-white sundress with her jet black hair pouring over her shoulders.

"Just make yourselves at home," Ryan told the two of them. "There's some good eats in the dining room." He put his arm around Daphne now. "This girl really knows how to put together a party."

Maybe that was when Daphne gave up. Really, what was the point of trying to stop Ryan from taking over? It was like attempting to hold back the tide. He seemed determined to run her housewarming, her friends, and maybe her life. Why not just let him?

Except that she didn't want to. Frustrated to the point that she was afraid she would explode on him, she pressed her lips tightly together as she extracted herself from his embrace. Then pretending she was needed by the caterer, she excused herself. Certainly with Ryan playing host, no one would miss her. In the solitude of the cheerful kitchen, she wiped down an already clean countertop and silently fumed.

"Why aren't you out there with your guests?" Truman curiously asked as he set a nearly empty veggie platter on the counter and began refilling it. "The food is all under control. And Katy is handling everything quite nicely. You really should be out there enjoying your guests, Daphne. That's why you hired help, remember?"

She gave him a guilty smile. "You're absolutely right. I should be out there." She waited for him to finish with the platter, then linked arms with him. "Would you care to join me in meeting my friends and neighbors, Mr. Walters?"

He nodded. "You bet."

She could see that Ryan was not pleased to see her on Truman's arm like this. But she decided to use this opportunity to introduce Truman to the guests he hadn't met while he'd been helping Katy in the kitchen. As she led him around from guest to guest, she sang the praises of his store and catering business. "Truman is responsible for our food tonight," she told Mrs. Terwilliger and the Millers from across the street. "It's all set up in the dining room. Please, go on in and help yourselves."

She didn't release Truman's arm until the doorbell rang. "Excuse me," she said as she hurried to the front door, thankfully beating Ryan for a change.

"Happy housewarming." Ricardo grinned as he handed her an oversized pottery pie dish, wrapped in a blue-and-white gingham towel. It looked and smelled like his famous Appleton pie inside.

"Is this what I think it is?" she asked.

He nodded. "I wasn't sure what to bring to a housewarming. But it was still warm and I thought why not?"

"This is perfection. But I'm not sure I want to share it. It would be yummy for breakfast tomorrow."

He laughed. "Do as you like with it. If you share it tonight, I'll bring you another one tomorrow."

As more people arrived and the party grew livelier, Daphne tried to relax. Overreacting would only make matters worse. Putting on her best game face, she visited with her guests and showed them her house, attempting to utilize them to create more distance between herself and Ryan. But as the evening wore on, he became even more determined to usurp the role of her attentive companion. Whether he was bringing her a drink or talking about something they'd done in New York, he seemed intent on convincing the world at large that she belonged to him.

However, something unusual happened as a result. The more he cozied up to her, the more she flirted—yes, she actually flirted—with every other eligible bachelor in the house. It was shameless and foolish, and she knew she'd regret it later, but she just couldn't stop herself. Somehow she had to send a clear message to Ryan, and everyone else here, that she and Ryan were *not* a couple.

"You did such a fantastic job on this house," she was telling Willie, gushing in front of Ryan about how Willie had transformed the house into a showplace with his fine painting skills. "I never knew there was such an art to house painting."

"I'd call it more of a craft," Willie said humbly. "But thank you." He nudged her off to the side. "Can I show you something?"

"Sure." She gave him a big grin, as if they were about to go and have some secret tryst. Never mind that he was nearly her dad's age.

He led her back out to the foyer and pointed up. "I just noticed it, but didn't want to say anything."

"What?" She looked up.

"I missed that crown molding up there." He shook his head. "Not sure how it happened, but I want to finish it for you."

"You know, I probably never would've noticed it."

"Oh, sure you would've. If the light was just right. Anyway, I can't make it over for a week or so. Hope that will be okay. Or I can send one of my guys over and—"

"No hurry." She patted him on the back, fully aware that Ryan was watching her. "Thanks for even noticing it."

Now Olivia joined them. "I want to see what you did to the office. Without my help."

"Yes, I hope you'll approve." She excused herself from Willie.

"So what's up with Ryan and you?" Olivia asked as soon as the two of them were alone in the office.

"I wish I knew." Daphne shook her head.

"He's the one who broke your heart, right?"

"Is it that obvious?" Daphne ran her hand over the desktop.

Olivia shrugged. "Well, you'd told me about the guy from New York. And from what I can see, it looks like he's still in love with you."

"He claims that he is." Daphne sighed.

"How do you feel about him?"

Daphne considered this—how did she feel? "I'm not totally sure. At first I felt angry that he showed up like this. I felt like I hated him and wanted to kick him out of my house and my life."

"That seems pretty natural. After all, he did break your heart."

"But it's like he's softening me up now—and that's irritating too."

Olivia looked skeptical. "I don't think a person can be softened up unless she wants to be."

"You could be right. But it's only a small part of me that's soften-ing. The rest of me feels hard and cold toward him. Just seeing him here tonight . . ." She lowered her voice. "Seeing him acting like he owns the place, owns me. Well, that sort of makes me mad."

Olivia nodded. "I'm not surprised."

"Hello?" Jake stuck his head into the office. "Private party?"

"No, of course not." Olivia waved him in. "Just some girl talk."

"Which is over now," Daphne assured him.

"Jenna told me I should see what you've done to your office," Jake explained as he and Jenna joined them.

"It was so cool to see where you actually write," Jenna told Daphne with wide eyes. "Very inspiring."

"That's right." Daphne remembered. "You wanted to talk to me about writing. We should set up a time to do that."

"How about Saturday?" Jenna asked hopefully.

"That sounds perfect." Daphne nodded. "It's a date."

"I'm going to go help Katy now," Jenna said as she went for the door. "Mattie and I promised to help her with cleanup."

"You've got an awfully sweet girl there," Daphne told Jake.

He grinned happily. "Thanks. I think so too."

"She and Mattie were great help to me in sorting out this house. I never could've accomplished as much as I did without them."

"This house looks better than ever," he told her. "You've made some great changes here and throughout the house, Daphne. Everything looks so much brighter and happier."

"Thanks to Olivia's help." She smiled at her friend, feeling relieved that Jake seemed to approve. She'd been worried that since he was managing the estate, he might complain about all the extra expenditures.

Jake was walking around now, checking out the office. "And this space is much better too. It always seemed rather dark and gloomy in here before. But Dee said her eyes were so old that she needed the dimness in order to write."

"I might need to put up curtains or something for privacy some-day," Daphne admitted. "But for now I like the openness. And it's pretty looking out on the yard."

"Maybe you could put up sheers," Olivia suggested.

"Good idea." Daphne ran her hand over the smooth desktop, noticing that the girls had placed the red roses in here. They actually looked somewhat elegant on the sleek dark wood.

"I got your e-mail," Jake told Daphne. "I really like what you wrote."

Olivia's brows arched with interest, but she said nothing.

"I sent Jake a sample of my writing." Daphne felt worried that Olivia might assume they were sending secret love letters or some-thing equally scandalous. "For, uh, some critique. He's my first reader."

"You started your novel already?" Olivia asked.

"I've started writing. I'm not really sure that you'd call it a novel . . . per se."

"But at least it's a beginning." Olivia patted her on the back. "Good for you."

Daphne exchanged glances with Jake, but he just nodded. "Yes, good for you. I think you're off to a brilliant start. I can't wait to see more."

They returned to the living room where most people were congregated, but now Daphne's dad took her aside, claiming he wanted to see Dee's old bedroom. Once they were in the room with the door closed, he began to grill her.

"I know that's the same Ryan who broke your heart in New York. What I'd like to know is what is he doing here?"

"I'm not sure."

"Did you invite him to visit here in Appleton?"

"No, not at all. And I didn't even invite him to the housewarming tonight. That was Mick's doing."

"But Ryan is acting like he—well, like you and him, well, you know, like you're a couple or something." Dad was clearly flustered. "Do you want me to throw him out on his ear?"

Daphne laughed. "No, Dad. Not just yet anyway."

"Well, I am relieved that you're not interested in that buffoon."

"Buffoon?"

He shrugged. "He seems a little full of himself. Right now he's out there bragging to some of the guys, going on about all the sports stars he knows and how he travels all over the country and goes to all the pro ball games. As if he's intent on impressing everyone."

She put an arm around him. "Well, I'm glad he hasn't impressed you."

"So, you're really not interested in him?"

"The truth is, a tiny part of me is still interested, Dad. But trust me, the rest of me is so totally over him."

"I could throw him out," he said again. "I could do it politely."

She grinned. "If I want him thrown out, you'll be the first to know."

The night wore on and the hour grew later, and soon people began thanking Daphne for her hospitality and excusing themselves to go home. But Ryan, it seemed, was determined to stay on until the last guest had left. Feeling she was fighting a losing battle, she tried to simply grin and bear it. But as she told people good night, with Ryan by her side, she could see the questions in her friends' faces. They all wanted to know what was up with her and Ryan.

Dad and Karen were the last ones, besides Ryan, to go. And she could tell Dad was uneasy to leave her here alone with the "buffoon." But she hugged them both, whispering in Dad's ear not to worry, that she would handle it. And then it was only Ryan and Daphne in the house. Well, and the cats, which she hurried to let out of the spare room upstairs. She actually hoped that Ryan would be gone when they came back down. But there he was waiting expectantly at the foot of the stairs.

"Well, you lasted to the very end," she told him with narrowed eyes. "Does that mean you've won this round of the game?"

"Game?" He looked at her with innocent blue eyes. "You think this is a game?"

"What is it, then?"

"It's me trying to show you how much I care about you. I want you to know that I'm ready to stick around. And that I'll do whatever it takes to win you back."

"Win me back? See, that sounds like a game to me."

"I'm sorry. I don't mean it to sound like a game." He stepped closer to her, looking intently into her eyes. "I love you, Daphne. I never stopped loving you."

"Stop it right now!" She held up her hands, palms toward him. "Please, stop talking like that and leave, Ryan. Please, go home. I am exhausted and I cannot do this tonight."

He nodded, but there was a hurt look in his eyes. "I understand. I'm coming on too strong. I'm sorry." He stepped back. "I'm going now. Good night, Daphne." He tipped his head, and just like that, he left.

Once again, she felt like crying. But this time she refused to let the tears fall. Instead, she threw herself into cleaning up. She put all her energy into putting the house back into perfect order. By the time she fell into bed, it was past two in the morning, and completely exhausted, she went immediately to sleep.

Chapter 21

The next morning, she slept in later than usual. It was nearly nine when she crawled out of bed and pulled on a rumpled jogging suit and went downstairs to feed the cats. But as she returned to the kitchen, she noticed that nondescript rental car, which was becoming way too familiar, pulling in front of the house. Ryan, now dressed casually in cargo shorts and a T-shirt, ambled up to the front door, carrying a coffee tray and a paper bag. Despite the urge to pretend like she wasn't home, the thought of coffee and whatever was in the bag was appealing.

"What do you want?" she demanded as she opened the door.

"Good morning, sunshine. I thought you'd be all worn out today. And I remembered how we used to do this in New York. I went to the Red River Coffee Company and got your favorite breakfast bagel and a nice big latte."

"Thank you," she said meekly as she let him into the house. "But don't think you can bagel your way into my heart, Ryan Holloway." She led the way into the kitchen and sat at the table. As he found plates for the bagels, she peeled the lid off her coffee and attempted to think of a polite way to hold on to her unexpected breakfast and send the delivery boy packing.

But as they sat there, eating their tasty breakfast bagels and drinking their coffee, he continued to chatter cheerfully and it was hard not to be pulled in by his charm. After all, Ryan truly was likeable. People had always described him as personable and charismatic. And really, he hadn't changed in that department. Plus, because of his job and his travels, he was interesting to listen to. Sure, he was a little full of himself at times. But she'd been fully aware of that character flaw ten years ago. Ironically, it was one of the things she'd been attracted to. Perhaps because it was so different from the way she was wired. Where she was always doubting her abilities or second-guessing her choices, Ryan plowed ahead, self-assured and confident.

Was she wrong to be so set against him now? Was she just being childish? Or was she attempting to punish him, holding him off at arm's length, penalizing him for his wrongdoings? Seriously, wasn't this what she'd always hoped for? That Ryan would come crawling back to her, apologizing, announcing that he was divorced and free to marry, proclaiming his undying love, and promising to never hurt her again? Hadn't that been her dream? Why was she so resistant now?

And what about the conditions of her aunt's will? Already a whole month had passed, and besides Ryan, she was no nearer to a serious relationship. Although she'd had some moments that seemed promising, she had yet to go out on an actual date. And some of the guys she was attracted to were not as available as she wished. Jake had his ex-wife to figure out. Mick appeared to have some kind of relationship with Julianne. Even Ricardo had Kellie eagerly waiting in the wings.

The next eleven months would probably fly by fast. What if, at the end of this strange road, she found herself unmarried? What if, just one year from now, she was completely alone and penniless and homeless? What if she was forced to start all over again? Did she have it in her? And really, what would be wrong with living a comfortable life in this beautiful house with someone who adored her as much as Ryan seemed to?

"What are you thinking about?" Ryan asked gently.

"What?" She blinked, bringing herself back into the present.

"You have such a faraway look in your eyes. A very pretty faraway look . . . so where were you anyway?"

She shrugged and looked down at her coffee. "I don't know. I think I'm still just waking up. Waiting for the caffeine to kick in."

He reached across the table, taking her hand in his. "Daphne, I don't know what I have to do to prove that I love you. What I need to do to undo the damage I did in New York. But I am determined to do whatever it takes. Because this time, I refuse to give up. Not without a fight anyway."

She was speechless. She turned away from him and, looking out the window, noticed Mick's truck was parked in the driveway. He waved to her as he opened his tailgate, but she could tell by his expression that he had seen her and Ryan sitting here together—and she could tell that he was curious. But really, what difference did it make? Mick had his own life . . . his own romance. Why should he concern himself with her?

She pulled her hand away from Ryan. "I'm sorry, but I'm just not ready for this." She stood. "So much has been happening lately. I'm still getting used to living here in Appleton. Trying to get my feet beneath me. And I'm still slightly in shock to see you, Ryan. Can you understand that?"

He nodded. "Absolutely. I was worried that I might overwhelm you. But you know me. I jump in with both feet and consider the consequences later."

"Yes . . . I remember."

"So here's what I'll do, Daphne. I'll give you your space. And I'll give you some time to think about it. I mean, to consider how you feel about me. But I'm not going to give you a long time because I suspect you know your answer now." He was standing too, looking intently into her eyes again. "You know what we had together. I'm sure you can imagine how much better it could be this time. Doing it the right way."

"Doing what the right way?" She frowned at him. What was he really saying? Or did she even want to know?

He reached for her hand. "What I'm trying to say, Daphne Ballinger, is that I want to marry you. I want us to spend the rest of our lives together."

She just stared blankly at him. Was he really standing there proposing to her? And here she was unshowered, wearing grubby warm-ups, hair sticking out all over—had she even brushed her teeth? What was wrong with him?

"I don't want you to answer me yet. I want you to take your time and really think about it. I want you to remember how good we were together . . . how we were best friends and how much fun we had in New York." He squeezed her hand. "I'm challenging you to dig deep inside of yourself, Daphne. Be honest about what you want for your life. Neither of us is getting any younger, you know."

She felt like she was having an out-of-body experience. Was Ryan Holloway really standing here in her kitchen asking her to marry him? It was just too weird.

"And one week from today I'll come back here and you can tell me your decision." He leaned in closer now. And cupping her chin in his hand, he kissed her. Gently, but with an unmistakable intensity. Then he let her go, and without saying another word, he turned and walked out of her house.

She just stood there in the kitchen, too stunned to even think straight. What had just happened? Was that really a proposal? And if it was genuine, how did she feel about it?

As she showered and tamed her hair and brushed her teeth, she attempted to replay Ryan's unexpected speech. Had he really said they weren't getting any younger? That was not terribly romantic, was it? The whole thing just seemed presumptuous and slightly arrogant. How dare he waltz into her world and attempt to sweep her off her feet!

With her hair still damp, she went outside, hoping to dry it in the sunlight as she enjoyed some fresh air and cleared her head. Curious as to what Mick was up to, she went around to the garden, but he wasn't there. Had he left already? She went on back around to see that his truck was still in the driveway.

"I'm over here," he called out from the porch. "You said you wanted some more potted plants for the porch. Come and see."

She walked on around and was pleased to see three pots of flowers and greenery. "Julianne made these yesterday and I thought they'd look perfect."

"They're gorgeous. Julianne has the right touch." She watched him closely for a reaction but he simply nodded.

"She's definitely got a good eye for mixing colors and blooms."

After several tries, they decided the best locations for the new plants. Daphne stood back admiring them. "Very, very nice." She smiled at Mick. "Thank you!"

"No problem." He leaned against a column, crossing his arms over his chest. "So what's up with you and Ryan?"

She let out an exasperated sigh.

"He looked fairly intent this morning."

Now she was worried—did Mick assume Ryan had spent the night? "He caught me by surprise when he showed up with breakfast. But you're right, he was pretty intent."

Mick chuckled. "Not that I was spying on you. But I couldn't help but notice you two."

She shrugged. "I have nothing to hide."

"And you're good with that? I mean, Ryan being so intent . . . showing up uninvited with breakfast?"

She frowned. "Not really."

He just nodded.

"But as you may have noticed, Ryan is a rather pushy sort of guy."

"Yeah. I noticed. I reckon the question is whether or not you like being pushed. Somehow you don't strike me as the type who likes being pressured. But maybe I'm wrong."

"No." She shook her head. "You're not wrong. I don't like being pushed or pressured."

"So what are you going to do about it, then?"

She shrugged. "I'm not really sure." She studied him, wondering why he was so interested. "It's confusing, you know, thinking you were once in love with someone—and that you'd never get over him—and suddenly there he is and you just don't know." She bit her lip, wishing she hadn't said so much. "Sorry, I'm sure you're busy and

I don't need to unload on you." She forced a smile. "Thanks for the flowers. And as usual, you can send the bill to Jake." She hoped Jake wouldn't mind. But he'd told her that everything that was for the house and stayed with the house could be charged to her aunt's estate.

"I actually understand," Mick said quietly.

"Understand what?"

"I know how it feels to have loved someone and been hurt."

"Really?" She was surprised he was being this open.

"And I don't know what I'd do if she showed up in my life today." He frowned. "I'd probably be suspicious."

"Suspicious?"

He nodded. "Yeah. I'd probably start asking myself why, after all these years, was she suddenly interested in me? Had she fallen on hard times? Did she see me as her meal ticket?" He shrugged. "But I suppose I am by nature a somewhat suspicious sort of bloke."

"Or maybe you're just smart." Did she need to be more suspicious of Ryan?

"I'm no expert on relationships, Daphne. But sometimes I have a good sense about people. Your aunt thought I did."

"So what is your sense of Ryan?"

Mick's mouth twisted to one side, as if he was considering his words. "Quite honestly . . . I don't trust him."

"Oh?"

"And I think you deserve better."

She didn't know what to say.

"But if I just stepped over the line, I hope you'll excuse my bad manners." He grinned. "And if you decide that Ryan is your dream bloke, well, I wish you both the best and I'll be happy to dance at your wedding."

"He did ask me to marry him," she confessed.

"I reckoned he did."

"He gave me a week to think it over."

Mick laughed. "A whole week, did he? Well, now that was generous of him." He checked his watch. "I've got to head out now. Again, if I said anything out of line, I hope you'll forgive me."

"Don't worry. I actually appreciate your advice. Thanks."

Sitting in the rocker on the porch, she petted Lucy and watched as The Garden Guy truck drove down the street. Admiring the attractive pots, she wondered just how serious Julianne and Mick really were. Seeing them together last night—and they were a striking pair—she had felt that there might be more to their relationship than she had originally supposed. But hearing Mick advising her so thoughtfully this morning . . . well, it made her wonder. Still, Mick had enjoyed a sweet relationship with Aunt Dee. It was quite likely he was just being kind to Daphne as well.

She went into her office and turned on the computer and opened a Word doc. She began to write a letter to Daphne Delacorte.

> *Dear Daphne,*
>
> *The man I thought I loved came back into my life this week. After ten long years of trying to get over him for breaking my heart (by pretending he was single when he was actually married with two children), this guy has reentered my world, proclaiming his undying devotion and proposing marriage to me. But because of the past, I feel uncertain. What should I do?*
>
> *Apprehensive in Appleton*

Now she sat there looking at the letter and wondering how Daphne Delacorte would answer it. Of course, she had no idea. And maybe she didn't really want to know. At least not yet. After all she had seven whole days to mull over the strange proposal. Why rush things? Besides, she had planned to go bicycle shopping today.

She'd decided after seeing how much Olivia rode her bike, that it would be sensible to have a bike. She would put a basket on it and use it for nearby errands, which would protect the mileage on the Corvette. Plus it would provide Daphne with some good exercise. To that end, she walked to town and into The Bike Shop and, after an hour of browsing and a couple of test rides, decided on a retro-style cruiser in aqua blue. Before she left, she had also purchased a basket, helmet, and bike lock.

Feeling pleased with herself, she rode her bike directly to Bernie's Blooms and showed it to Olivia.

"Way to go, girl." Olivia gave her a high five. "Welcome to the slow-paced world of flatlanders."

"Flatlanders?"

"That's what some people call these one-geared bikes that are only good for flat roads. Flatlanders." She laughed. "Believe me, I learned that lesson the hard way when I tried to ride Miss Daisy up Bonner Hill." She patted the pink bike parked in front of the store.

"You named your bike Miss Daisy?"

"Actually, that was Bernadette's doing. She named her."

"I guess I should think of a name for my bike too. And I should let you get back to work now." Daphne wished Olivia had time to talk but didn't want to ask.

"Anything wrong?" Olivia asked. "You seem a little down."

Daphne shrugged. "Just mulling something over."

"What?"

Daphne let out a long sigh.

"Hey, it's time for my lunch break. Want to ride our bikes over to the Dairy Queen like we used to do as kids?"

"Sure." Daphne nodded eagerly. And suddenly they were free-wheeling it down Main Street, just like they used to do when they were girls, growing up in this small town. It was amazing to feel the wind whistling past her, almost like she was flying. This was free-dom—and she loved it.

Chapter 22

About ten minutes later, they were seated at the heavy cement picnic tables outside of Dairy Queen, all ready to pig out on their cheeseburger baskets. Daphne, who normally avoided fast food like the plague, hoped her new bike would assist in burning off all these carbs and fat.

"Now, tell me everything," Olivia insisted as she stuck a straw in her chocolate shake.

So Daphne filled her in on Ryan's unexpected proposal over bagels and coffee this morning. "I think I'm still in shock."

"That's so sweet." Olivia grinned. "I've never heard of a proposal like that. Very original. And very memorable, don't you think?"

"But I was wearing dirty warm-ups and my hair was a mess and I honestly don't think I'd even brushed my teeth yet."

"Eeuw." She wrinkled her nose. "That's not the kind of thing you want to remember."

"Tell me about it. I couldn't have felt more unromantic. Seriously, how could he do it like that?"

Olivia tilted her head to one side with a thoughtful look. "Maybe we're looking at this all wrong. Come to think of it, the way he did it might be extremely romantic. I mean, if a man loves you so much that he can see past your bed head and bad breath and baggy warm-ups, maybe that means he really, truly loves you—for better or for worse. You know?"

Daphne considered this. "I suppose that might be true."

"So what did you say to him? Yay or nay?"

"He gave me a week to think about it."

"*Think* about it?" Olivia looked confused. "Seriously, you need to think about it?"

"Well, it was all so sudden. I was totally unprepared. I didn't know how to react."

"But you've known him for years. It seems like you'd know."

Daphne explained a bit more about her years of heartache. "So I honestly thought I was over him. I *wanted* to be over him."

"But you're not over him?"

"I . . . uh . . . I'm not sure."

"Well, he certainly seemed obsessed with you last night," Olivia continued. "It was like he didn't want to let you out of his sight."

"Believe me, I know." Daphne didn't like to remember how claustrophobic she'd felt with him shadowing her like that.

"It was kind of sweet."

"Maybe . . ." She wanted to add that it was kind of creepy too.

"Jeff really liked Ryan."

"Really?" Daphne picked up her cheeseburger.

"Oh yeah. I mean they were talking sports. And Ryan was tell-ing him about a time he'd spent a whole day with LeBron James. Jeff loves Lebron and he was like all ears. Seriously, I even accused Jeff of having a man-crush. Because after we got home, all he could talk about was Ryan."

Daphne laughed.

"So what are you going to do?"

"Do?"

"With your one-week deadline. Are you going to make him wait the whole seven days, or will you have mercy on him and answer him sooner?"

"I honestly don't know."

"If you had to answer him today—what would you say?"

As she chewed, Daphne considered her aunt's will. "I'm not sure," she mumbled.

"But you must know. I mean, how can you not know? Either you want to marry him or you don't. Right?"

Daphne took in a deep breath. "It seems like I should know. I wish I knew. If he'd asked me ten years ago, I would've known how to answer."

"You'd have said yes?"

Daphne nodded.

"Except that he was married then."

"Right. Just one small detail he'd forgotten to mention."

"Here's a question. If you do decide to marry him, where would you guys live?" Olivia peeled a pickle off her burger.

Daphne blinked. "Well, here, of course."

"Is that what Ryan said?"

"We didn't actually talk about it."

"Maybe you should." Olivia squirted out more ketchup. "And you can tell Ryan for me, and for Jeff too, that we'll vote for you to live here."

The lunch hour passed too quickly. And although they talked about the proposal, examining it from every angle and going over it with what seemed a fine-tooth comb, by the time they parted ways and Daphne was riding her new bike home, she felt no closer to an answer than she had been in the kitchen this morning. If anything, she felt even more confused. For the most part, Olivia seemed supportive of Ryan.

She had sounded eager to see Daphne married. She was already planning the wedding and making suggestions for the honeymoon, and she was even making plans for the couples to go on vacations together next year. And although Daphne appreciated Olivia's enthusiasm on some levels—and having her friend's help in planning a wedding sounded fun—Daphne still felt very wary. And confused.

But interwoven in her confusing emotions was the ever-constant pressure of her aunt's will. Although Daphne had never considered herself a "material girl," she was thoroughly enjoying Aunt Dee's house and car and all that went with it. She did not want to lose it. As shallow as it seemed, she did not want to pass up this opportunity with Ryan if it would secure her future here in Appleton.

Besides, she had been head over heels in love with him before. And she had definitely felt some electricity when he'd kissed her this morning. Perhaps the time had come to completely ignore her usual careful ways.

As she got ready for bed that night, she remembered how carefree and happy she'd felt on the bicycle earlier. Perhaps that was what was waiting for her—complete abandon and freedom—as soon as she let go of her inhibitions and agreed to marry Ryan.

Before she went to sleep, she asked God to lead her in this important decision, but as she was drifting off, she thought her mind was completely made up. She was certain that she was going to say yes. Most definitely—*yes!*

By the next day, she was just as certain she was going to say no. Most definitely—*no!* What could she possibly have been thinking last night? What kind of desperate and pathetic person was she? Had she really been willing to leap into Ryan Holloway's arms simply to inherit her aunt's estate? As she measured coffee into the filter, she knew she would rather live out her days being poor and alone than to settle for the likes of Ryan.

As she waited for the coffee to brew, she knew she would never have considered it *settling* ten years ago. Back then, she would've felt like she'd won the prize pumpkin if Ryan had proposed to her. She would've triumphantly taken him home and shown him off to everyone. Indeed, that was what she'd always wanted to do—but she'd never gotten the chance.

As she poured her coffee, she wondered if she had truly stopped loving him. Or was she simply deluding herself? Was love something that you could turn off and on like the coffeemaker? Or was she still so hurt by him that she couldn't get past it? As she took her coffee out to the front porch, she really didn't know.

Sitting in the rocker, she pondered this. Was she so accustomed to shutting down her feelings, or to concealing them, that she no longer knew how she felt? Was it possible to stifle yourself so much that you completely lost touch with your genuine emotions? If so, had she done it? And if she'd done it, was there some way to undo it? Maybe she needed to go see a shrink. Or write another letter to *Dear Daphne*. She formulated a letter in her head.

Dear Daphne,

    I am afraid I have been so wounded by love that
I have completely shut myself down to experiencing
true love again. I'm worried that even though
I'm only thirty-four, I may never be able to love
sincerely—from my whole heart. It feels as if my heart
was permanently ruined all those years ago. Please,
tell me if there is any hope for me. Or will I be forced
to remain shutdown and single for the rest of my days?
    Hopeless on Huckleberry Lane

Daphne was caught off guard when a silver BMW pulled into her driveway, and then, to her surprise, Jenna hopped out of the passenger side carrying an oversized bag. That's when Daphne remembered her promise to spend time with the young author today. As she stood to greet her, a petite woman with short wispy blond hair got out of the other side, peering curiously at Daphne.

"Hello," the stylishly dressed woman called out in a breathless sort of voice as she approached Daphne. "I'm Gwen, Jenna's mom. It's so generous of you to talk to Jenna about her writing. I'd stick around, but I have an appointment that I'm already running late for." She checked the sleek platinum watch that looked too big for her slender wrist. "Please, forgive me for dropping her off and dashing away."

"No problem." Daphne smiled. "I've enjoyed spending time with your daughter and it was nice to meet you."

"And I'll pick you up before noon," Gwen told Jenna.

Then she turned away, and as quickly as she'd come, she was gone. Daphne was a little surprised. Somehow she had figured Jake's wife would be different than the soft-spoken pretty woman she'd just met. Or maybe she'd just hoped she would be someone a little more dislikeable. Gwen seemed perfectly sweet. Kind of like cotton candy.

"Your mom is pretty," Daphne said as they went inside, then instantly wished she hadn't because it seemed such a lame sort of comment.

"Uh-huh." Jenna just nodded.

"So, did you bring your writing with you?"

Jenna held up her bag. "It's in here."

"Great. Why don't we take it to my office?"

They got a chair from the dining room and soon they were settled in her office, where with Daphne's encouragement, Jenna pulled out her laptop and began to read a short story she'd recently created. She'd written it in the perspective of an abandoned cat, which was actually quite interesting.

"That was wonderful," Daphne told her after she finished.

"Really?" Jenna asked hopefully. "You honestly liked it? You're not just being nice?"

"I honestly liked it, Jenna. It's very good."

Jenna let out a happy sigh.

"I love that you wrote from the cat's point of view. You made me really believe that the cat was telling the story. That was very clever."

"Do you know how I can improve it? I want to get it as good as possible to enter in a short-story contest for high school kids. The deadline is next week."

"Well . . ." Daphne rolled her chair over to look over Jenna's shoulder. "There might be some things you could tighten. And I think you might've gotten mixed up on some of your verb tenses. You hopped from past to present a few times."

Together they went over it, fixing and tweaking until Daphne felt it was as good as it could possibly be. "I don't consider myself a short-story expert," Daphne told her. "But if I was judging the contest, I'd be impressed with this."

Jenna looked at the clock on Daphne's bookshelf. "Is that right?" she asked with a worried expression.

Daphne looked up, surprised to see that it was nearly one. "Yes, it's right."

Jenna hurried to save her work and close her laptop, then shoved it into her bag. "I need to call Mom." She pulled out her phone. "I'm supposed to babysit for my aunt this afternoon. Mom was going to take me." Jenna hurried out of the office, and Daphne could hear her talking, but it sounded like she was leaving a message and then another. Finally she came back with a worried look. "My aunt would come get me, but she'd just put the kids down for a nap and—"

"Why don't I give you a ride?"

Jenna gratefully accepted and soon they were on their way to the other side of town. As Daphne drove, Jenna explained that her aunt lost her husband last fall. "Uncle Jason had served in Iraq but came home with really bad PTSD. No one likes to talk about it, but my dad told me that he took his own life. And Aunt Bonnie just got this part-time job this summer, so I'm trying to help with the babysitting. Because she's really tight financially, you know."

"That's generous of you." Daphne sometimes heard people complaining about teenagers, saying how they were all so entitled and spoiled. But Jenna and Mattie seemed to have escaped that stereotype.

It turned out that Aunt Carrie lived in the same neighborhood Daphne had grown up in, and after dropping Jenna at a ranch house very similar to Daphne's childhood home, she decided to go by and

pay her dad a visit. But when she got to his house, she saw a prominent open-house sign with red and blue balloons planted right next
to the for-sale sign. Suddenly she felt disoriented, as if this house no
longer belonged to Dad. Spotting Karen's bright yellow Mustang in
the driveway and some lookers inside, Daphne drove on past. Dad
was probably playing golf today. Or maybe he was already getting
settled into his new condo at Green Trees. She would see him later.

At home, she spied what looked like Jake's car in front of her
house. She pulled into the driveway and went around to find Jake
knocking on the front door with an urgent expression.

"Hello?" she called out as she walked up to the porch. "Can I
help you?"

"Oh, there you are, Daphne. I'm here to get Jenna and we need
to hurry—"

"I just dropped her off at her aunt's house."

"Oh, good." He nodded with a relieved look. "Thank you for
doing that. I got Jenna's message and then my sister called too. I came
as quickly as I could."

"She thought her mom was picking her up at noon," Daphne
said cautiously.

"Yes, I know. Gwen was supposed to pick her up. But Gwen,
being Gwen, probably got distracted with her own life." He shook his
head. "Happens all the time."

"Oh . . ." She didn't know what to say.

"Sorry." He made a sheepish smile. "I didn't mean to burden you
with my personal problems."

She tilted her head to one side. "You have personal problems?"
she asked in a slightly teasing tone. "You always seem so together to
me. I wouldn't think you'd have any problems."

He laughed. "Right. I'm divorced and I have a teenaged girl. I have absolutely no problems whatsoever."

She smiled. "It does make you seem more human."

He frowned. "You think I'm not human?"

"No, no . . . that didn't come out right." Just then she noticed a car slowly approaching, but as it got closer, she realized it looked like the same silver BMW that had dropped Jenna earlier. "Is that Gwen?"

He turned to look as she parked in the driveway. "Yep. That's her."

Looking flustered and worried, Gwen hurried up to the porch. "Where's Jenna?"

"Daphne took her to Carrie's," Jake calmly told her. "Hopefully she wasn't too late since it's Carrie's first month on the job."

Gwen glowered at him. "Your sister should find a regular baby-sitter instead of relying on Jenna all the time. It's not fair."

"Carrie doesn't rely on Jenna all the time. Besides, Jenna likes helping her with the kids."

"Carrie takes unfair advantage of Jenna's generosity," Gwen snapped back at him.

"Carrie's had a rough year," he said quietly. "Jenna realizes that."

Although Daphne already felt invisible and completely unnecessary to this awkward conversation, she was quietly backing up and hoping to slip unnoticed into the house, in order to give these two their privacy as they hashed out their differences on her front porch.

"Carrie takes advantage of me too," Gwen continued hotly. "I'm the one who has to chauffeur Jenna back and forth, catering to Bonnie's every beck and call."

"Don't forget that I give Jenna rides too. I came here today for Jenna."

Daphne had her hand on the doorknob and was about to open it.

"Anyway, thank *you,* Daphne," Gwen said loudly. "Forgive us for making a scene in your front yard."

Daphne released an uneasy smile. "No problem."

Then without saying another word, Gwen turned and marched back to her car. She noisily started it, then backed out so quickly she spit gravel beneath her wheels.

"I'm sorry about that."

"Why was she so angry?" Daphne watched as the silver car streaked down Huckleberry Lane. She hoped no children were playing in the street.

"That's Gwen." He held up his hands. "Sometimes she's so sweet that sugar wouldn't melt in her mouth and other times, like you just witnessed, the claws come out and it's best to just lay low."

"Does she have a chemical imbalance?" Daphne knew it was none of her business. Except that Gwen had just thrown a hissy fit right in front of her.

"She sees a psychologist. But so far the only thing they've come up with is that Gwen's got a lot of hostility from her childhood." Jake had such a sad expression that Daphne felt sorry for him.

"If it's any consolation, you seem even more human to me now."

He flashed a half smile.

Now she decided to show him some hospitality. "I'm thirsty. Would you like some iced tea or lemonade or something?"

"I'd love some iced tea," he said.

"Make yourself comfy and I'll be right back." As she went inside, she wondered why she'd brought up her silly comment about seeming human again. She knew what she'd meant by it, but it sounded wrong.

She returned with their iced teas and sat in the chair opposite him.

"So, you were saying before we were interrupted by that unfortunate scene that you didn't think I was human. . . . Why was that?"

"I didn't say you weren't human." She took a slow sip. "At least that's not what I meant. But I suppose because of the role you play with Aunt Dee's estate, I tend to see you as this slightly rigid authority figure. You know, sort of like how you regard the principal when you're in grade school."

"But why would you see me like that?"

"Because you have all the power. It's like you get to make the rules and you tell me what to do and—"

"Wait a minute." He held up one hand. "That's not fair. It was Dee who made the rules. Not me. I just have to enforce them."

"So instead of a principal, you're more like a policeman then, the enforcer?"

A slow smile crept onto his face. "Okay, I guess I can see how it might feel like that to you."

"It's just that it's so hard for me to forget the condition that seems to be hanging over me. It's like this time clock is ticking, ticking, ticking." She shook her head. "Already more than a month has passed. And I haven't made any progress."

"No progress?" He looked doubtful. "How exactly do you describe progress, Daphne?"

She shrugged. "I haven't been asked out on a single date. Small as that seems, it would feel like progress."

"Hey, you've got a lot of available men flocking about you."

"That depends on how you define available."

"If a man is single, I'd say that makes him available. And don't forget I even tried to ask you on a date."

She had nearly forgotten that awkward moment. And now it was back again, staring her straight in the face. "Yes . . . that's right."

"Although I'll admit it was a rather halfhearted attempt on my part. But that was just because I'm uneasy about dating a client." He took a sip of tea. "And then there was that concern you had about my ex, whom you've now had the pleasure of meeting."

She took another sip, wishing he'd change the subject.

Instead he set down his glass and peered curiously at her. "Although I'm still a little confused. What was up with that anyway? What made you think Gwen and I were getting back together?"

"Oh, I'd heard something. Something that made me think you and Gwen might give your marriage another try."

"I swear, Daphne, that is not happening. You just saw my ex. Do you honestly believe we have a future?"

"I don't know. But it's possible she's just hurt and lashing out like that to hurt you back."

He just shook his head.

"Besides I really do believe that a marriage commitment should be a forever thing. Like until death we do part."

Feeling uncomfortable, she decided to change course slightly. "Although I'm well aware that I'm no expert on love and marriage. I should probably keep my opinions to myself."

"Don't be so sure. You sounded like an expert in the *Dear Daphne* column you sent me." He grinned. "I didn't want to gush the other night, but I was really impressed."

"Thanks. Maybe Aunt Dee is helping me somehow." She didn't want to admit to having read a Penelope Poindexter book or how that seemed to ignite her writing. They sat quietly for a couple of minutes, with only the sound of birds chirping and children's voices in a yard down the street.

"So back to me being the enforcer . . . the cruel timekeeper," Jake spoke slowly, "ticking away the months, weeks, days until you tie the knot and inherit Dee's estate."

"Something like that."

"I'm the man behind the scheme that threatens to ruin your life." He shook his head. "That's too bad."

"Sorry." She ran her finger down the condensation on the tall glass. "It's just that it's a lot of pressure, you know?"

"I did try to convince Dee to do it differently."

"Why didn't she listen?"

"She was Daphne Delacorte. She thought she knew what was best for you and your love life."

"How was that possible? What made her an expert on me?"

"Life . . . experience."

Daphne didn't get this. "But she was a spinster."

"Maybe I didn't tell you that your dad's father—your grandfather—he was the love of Dee's life."

"Then why didn't they just get married and live happily ever after?"

"Because she never told him she was pregnant. She believed he loved her and she wanted him to propose to her out of true love—not because she was expecting his child."

"Oh . . . and he didn't?"

Jake shook his head. "He broke her heart when he didn't. But she was too proud to tell him the truth, that she was having his baby. Instead, she broke off contact with him. She had the baby and, well, you know the rest of that story. But after she returned to college she discovered it was too late."

"Too late?"

"For her and her true love. Because by then he was engaged to one of her friends."

"Oh, poor Aunt Dee. I never knew that."

"She spent a long time regretting not telling him about the baby. She felt that was the great mistake of her life."

"Because maybe they would've married . . . and been happy?"

"Maybe. As it turned out, he died in World War II anyway."

"So it's like *do as I say, not as I do*. She didn't marry but insists that I must?"

"She wanted you to marry for true love, Daphne. Don't forget that. She never wanted to pressure you into marriage just for the sake of marriage. She simply wanted to pressure you to tune into your heart. She hoped you would allow yourself to fall in love."

"What if I don't know how? What if I'm so broken that I can't figure it out anymore? It might be too late for me."

He looked concerned. "Do you really believe that?"

Determined not to cry, she blinked back tears, but since he knew so much about Aunt Dee—and he was the only one who knew about the conditions of the will—she decided to fully open up to him. Suddenly she was telling him all about Ryan and New York and how he'd broken her heart and how much she'd loved him and how it had taken her ten years to recover from the pain.

"Dee suspected it was something like that," Jake said.

"And now—Ryan shows up out of the blue. And after a couple of days, he suddenly asks me to marry him." She was trying to keep the emotion out of her voice, pretending she wasn't nearly as disturbed as she felt.

"That's great. You should be happy, right?"

"I *should* be happy. But all I feel is confusion. And Aunt Dee's will just muddies the water even more. I honestly wish she'd bestowed her estate on all the relatives, splitting it evenly among all of us. Then I wouldn't feel so much pressure over this decision. I've never been good at important decisions. Haven't you noticed? I'm the queen of second-guesses."

"I don't see why you need to decide too quickly. You still have most of a year left. There's no real hurry. Not yet anyway."

She nodded. But looking forward to more tortured months like this—feeling desperate and torn and confused and pressured—well, she wasn't sure how much she could endure. And she decided, sitting there on the pleasant porch overlooking the pretty yard, she would be wise to come up with some kind of backup plan.

Chapter 23

Daphne waffled back and forth over the next few days. On Sunday, after having lunch with Olivia and Jeff and listening to them reminiscing about their wedding and how it was the happiest day of their life and how it took so long to plan everything, she had nearly made up her mind to marry Ryan. After all, wouldn't that simplify her life? She would have plenty of time to plan a perfect wedding. Plus she wouldn't have to spend the rest of the year in limbo, wondering whether or not she was going to be homeless. It seemed an easy way out.

But the next day, chatting with Mick in the garden, she was completely unsure again. Mick didn't like Ryan and he had no problem letting Daphne know. To make matters worse, he seemed to assume that Aunt Dee wouldn't approve of Ryan either. How he'd come up with this was a mystery, but she didn't take it lightly either.

Then she had a nightmare on Tuesday, so vivid and frightening that she woke in the middle of the night shaking and scared. It had been one of those life-threatening dreams where she was all alone and desperate. She woke up longing for someone to talk to, someone who could hold her and calm her and comfort her. The idea of having Ryan by her side was extremely tempting.

Then on Wednesday morning, after battling the feeling she was a complete and total fraud—who was she to give romantic advice to anyone—she compelled herself to sit down to write the *Dear Daphne* column again. But the first letter she read felt uncomfortably close to home. So much so she wasn't sure if she could answer it but knew she had to try.

> *Dear Daphne,*
> *Since I was a little girl, I've dreamed of being married. I've been dating the same man (Guy A) for more than seven years. I felt certain I loved him and that he loved me. But Guy A just can't seem to commit to marriage. I'll be forty next year and I don't think I can keep waiting like this. Meanwhile there's a nice man at work (Guy B) who has shown serious interest in me, plus he's the kind of man who could easily commit to marriage and family. However, I'm not really attracted to Guy B. But I suspect if I break up with Guy A and start dating Guy B, I will be married before I turn forty. So please tell me, do I break up with Guy A to achieve my dream of getting married?*
> *Indecisive in Indianapolis*

Daphne stared at the computer screen, wondering how her aunt would answer this one. Or maybe she wouldn't. Based on the number of letters received weekly, it was clear Aunt Dee could never have answered all of them. Perhaps this was one that should be set aside too. And yet this woman sounded so desperate. Kind of like Daphne. What would the wise Daphne Delacorte tell her? After several attempts and several deletions, she finally came up with a response.

> *Dear Indecisive,*
>
> *It sounds as if you've reached a crossroads. Based on your letter, Guy A might still love you, but he does not want to marry you. Guy B wants to commit to marriage, but you may not love him. The question is, what do you want? Do you only want love? Then stay with Guy A. Do you only want marriage? Then marry Guy B. Or do you want both? If you want both, I suggest you kiss both guys good-bye and just wait. Hopefully Guy C will show up, and he'll be a man you can both love and marry. And if not, you won't hate yourself for settling for less than what you truly want.*
>
> *Daphne*

As she hit Save she wondered why she couldn't be as strong-minded as Daphne Delacorte. If she could tell this indecisive woman to go for what she wanted and not settle for less, why couldn't she say the same thing to herself? Why couldn't she be simple and straightforward and to the point with herself? Make up her mind and stick to it? Daphne decided to actually write out the letter she'd made up in her head a few days ago. The words might not be exactly the same, but the basic question remained unchanged.

Dear Daphne,

*I was so wounded when the man I fell in love
with broke my heart that I'm afraid I've shut myself
off emotionally. I'm worried I'll never experience that
kind of true love again. Is it possible that even though
I'm only thirty-four, I might never be able to fall in
love again—with my whole heart? Will I be forced to
remain shutdown and single for the rest of my days?
Please, help me, before I settle for something I don't
really want.*

Hopeless on Huckleberry Lane

She took in a deep breath, and longing for Daphne Delacorte
to step in and write a sensible answer, she started to type—almost
without thinking.

Dear Hopeless,

*I suspect that everyone gets their heart broken at
some point in life. But a broken heart, like a broken
bone, will heal if it's treated properly and enough time
passes. I remember when I broke my arm when I fell
from a tree. The arm hurt so badly that even after the
cast came off, I babied and protected it because I was
worried I might injure it again. But the doctor assured
me the bone was stronger than ever—even stronger than
before I broke it. It took me a while, but eventually
I started taking chances with my arm. Soon I was
climbing trees again. It's time for you to take chances too.
Your heart is probably sturdier than you realize. Don't
settle for less than you deserve. And don't give up hope.*

Daphne

Feeling surprisingly optimistic, Daphne wrote responses to a couple more letters. These were simpler letters that didn't hit quite so close to home. She was satisfied when she finished the last of them, and she was just getting ready to send the new batch off to Jake when her phone rang. She'd been sort of expecting that Ryan would call her before the week was up. But so far he hadn't. And she didn't have his number or she might've called him and told him her answer—although she shouldn't because it changed from moment to moment. As she went for her phone, she decided that if that was him on the other end, she would gently but firmly decline his proposal.

But it wasn't Ryan. It was her dad. "I thought you and I could meet for dinner tonight," he said cheerfully.

"Sure. I was just missing you."

"Well, I've been running around like a turkey with his head cut off."

She laughed. "I thought it was supposed to be chicken."

"This is my version. Anyway, Karen's going great guns on selling my house, and I'm busy moving into the condo. So life has been a little crazy."

"I had a feeling the move had begun."

"Yes, I wanted to surprise you—I thought I'd be all settled in and I'd invite you for dinner before you figured it out. But everything takes longer than I expected."

She told him about driving by the house. "It was so sad seeing it like that—like it wasn't your house anymore."

"I'll be glad when it's not my house anymore. I'm perfectly happy at the condo. Well, I'll be a little happier when I get unpacked and settled. I couldn't even find a tie to wear to work today. But I like being there. It already feels more carefree. And hopefully the house will sell soon."

They agreed to meet at Midge's Diner at six. Then Daphne hung up and hit Send on her *Dear Daphne* column. As soon as she did, she realized the file she'd just sent Jake also contained her own letter, from Hopeless on Huckleberry Lane. There was no way to get the e-mail back, but she could at least warn him it was a mistake. She didn't want that letter to go out to the papers. So she shot him a quick e-mail, explaining that was a bogus letter and asking him not to read it.

As she closed down her computer, the doorbell rang and she was surprised to see Ricardo's mother, Maria Martoni, standing on her porch. "Hello, Mrs. Martoni," Daphne said happily.

"Please, call me Maria."

Daphne nodded. "Come on in, Maria."

"You're sure I'm not disturbing you?"

"Not at all. I just finished writing for the day. Can I get you a cup of tea or something cold?"

"No, thank you. This shouldn't take long. I would've called on the telephone, but I like talking to my neighbors in person."

They sat in the front room and Daphne, curious as to the nature of this visit, waited for Maria to continue.

"You might not know this, but your aunt, or maybe I should say your grandmother—"

"It's okay if you still call her my aunt. I still think of her as Aunt Dee."

"Oh, that's good. Anyway Dee was an active member of our neighborhood association."

"I wasn't aware of that."

Maria smiled. "Yes, well, Dee served as the secretary for our group for years and years. Ever since the association first started up, back in the eighties. Anyway, we have a meeting once a month. It's next week, and we wondered—and we hope you don't think it's presumptuous—but we hoped you might consider taking Dee's place."

"As secretary?"

Maria nodded. "She was so good at recording our minutes and sending them out to everyone. You know, she used to deliver them to all the neighbors. Over the years, most of us got e-mail. But she would still take copies to the neighbors who don't have computers. She said it was her way to catch up with them."

"That sounds like her."

"So, what do you think? Would you consider being our secretary, Daphne?"

"Sure, why not."

"Oh, thank you, thank you!" Maria stood with a big smile. "Everyone will be so pleased." She grasped Daphne's hand. "Your aunt would be proud of you."

"Thank you."

Maria gave her a curious look. "Do you mind if I ask you a question?"

"No, of course not. What?"

"Well, I noticed the young man at your housewarming party last week. The one who was staying so close to you. I believe his name was Ryan?"

"Yes. We were friends in New York."

"What I wanted to know is whether or not he's a serious friend. I mean a boyfriend kind of friend." She looked embarrassed. "Don't tell anyone, but I am asking for my son."

"Ricardo wants to know about Ryan?"

She waved her hand. "Ricardo hasn't said anything. But I know my Ricardo. I can tell he's had his eye on you."

"Really?" Daphne wasn't sure if this was just Maria's hopeful thinking or something more substantial.

"And nothing would make me happier than to see my Ricardo settled. He's too old to be a bachelor. Don't you think?"

Daphne shrugged. "I have noticed that Kellie at the diner seemed to have her eye on Ricardo."

Maria waved her hand. "No, no, Kellie is not right for him. Not at all."

"She's very pretty."

Maria shook her head. "Looks are not everything."

"No . . ."

"Don't tell Ricardo I spoke to you about this. He says I interfere too much."

Daphne couldn't help but chuckle as she walked Maria to the front door. Now why on earth should Ricardo say that?

"The meeting is next Wednesday at seven. At my house this month." Maria shook hands and thanked her again. "And remember, don't tell Ricardo about what I said."

"Don't worry, I won't." Amused that Maria seemed to have put her mother's stamp of approval on Daphne for her son, she vaguely wondered if Maria and Dad had been plotting behind their children's backs.

Perhaps there was something to be said for previous centuries when matchmakers or parents controlled the marital fate of their children. Maybe fathers or mothers really did know best.

Chapter 24

Daphne decided to do something she used to do when it was time to make a decision. Make a list. Usually she made a list of pros and cons. And because she was so good at seeing all the negative possibilities, the con side almost always won. Then she would make the "safe" decision to stay with the status quo, which was precisely why nothing in her life had changed over the past ten years.

On Thursday night, knowing Ryan would show up tomorrow to find out her decision, she sat with a pad of paper and pencil and wrote the pros and cons of marrying Ryan. To her relief, the cons truly did outnumber the pros. And perhaps the biggest, most glaring con was the fact that she simply did not want to marry him. It felt thrillingly liberating to look at those words—*I do not want to marry him!*

Of course, on the heels of this revelation came the nagging question—what if she didn't find anyone she wanted to marry, or what if no one besides Ryan wanted to marry her? Fortunately, she didn't need to concern herself with that now. Tomorrow she would tell Ryan her decision, she would wish him well, and then she would move on with her life.

Except that tomorrow came but Ryan did not. Daphne had purposely remained at home for the entire day, expecting him to show up. But when he didn't, she felt both vexed and concerned. She had no idea where he was or what he'd been doing all week, but it seemed uncharacteristic for him to be a no-show.

On Saturday, she was still concerned for Ryan and wondered if she should make an attempt to track him down. But at the same time she felt irritated. It seemed wrong and flaky for him to string her along like this after his proclamation of love last week. To distract herself, she got out her bike, which she had named Bluebell, and pedaled to town to get some groceries at The Apple Basket.

"I was just thinking of you," Truman announced as she came into the store.

"Really?" She smiled. "That's nice."

"So I'm curious, Daphne. You seem like such a nice person. Do you attend a church?"

"As a matter of fact, I do. Are you looking for a church to join?"

"No. I actually go to a pretty cool church. But I was thinking about how you're kind of new in town. I mean I get that you grew up here, but I know how you'd been in New York for a long time. And I thought you might be interested in the singles group in my church. That is, unless there's one in your church."

She smiled. "The one in my church is more for older people. Like my dad's age."

"This group is young. And they're fun." He gave her a shy smile. "You interested?"

"Sure."

"Great. It's at seven tonight. Want me to pick you up?"

"Tonight?"

"You've got plans." He looked disappointed.

"No . . . tonight's fine." She thought about Ryan but decided she didn't care. He was making her wait. If he showed up, she would make him wait.

She tried not to think about Ryan throughout the day. Yes, it was disconcerting. But she was determined not to obsess. And when Truman showed up at a little before seven, she cheerfully went with him to the singles group.

Once she got there, she was immediately dismayed by two things. For starters, it felt like everyone was younger than her. They all seemed fresh out of college, and although they were fun, like Truman had said, they seemed very young. Second, the males were outnumbered by females by nearly a three-to-one ratio.

Even so, she tried to act congenial. And she didn't even feel jealous when some of the younger women openly flirted with Truman. After all, it wasn't as if this was a date. He had simply invited her to his singles group. A singles group she wouldn't be coming back to—at least that's what she thought until the senior pastor got up to speak. Apparently Pastor Andrew didn't usually address this particular group, but since their usual leader was out of town, he'd offered to step in.

"As some of you know, I'm somewhat of an expert on being single," he began, and this brought a knowing chuckle from some of them.

Pastor Andrew wasn't particularly handsome, but he was nice looking in a short and slightly balding sort of way. And he had what Daphne would describe as a trustworthy sort of countenance. Also he had a nice, soothing speaking voice. But more than those characteristics, it was what he said that captured her attention. He talked about his own journey through singleness, sharing openly about some of the relationships he'd been in during his youth and into his twenties and thirties, and how he'd been hurt more times than he cared to think about it.

"I guess you'd say I was a slow learner. Because it wasn't until I hit forty, just a few years ago, that I figured it out. Or at least I got smarter. Now, I know none of you young ladies will relate to this, but all those years I was striving and trying to find the perfect relationship, searching for just the right woman, it felt like I had this biological time clock ticking away inside of me. I was absolutely certain I would never find true fulfillment or my complete purpose in life if I didn't find and marry my soul mate." He paused. "Anyone relate to that?"

Nervous twitters of laughter seemed to confirm this.

"And it was as I was turning forty that it really hit me. Oh, I'm sure I'd heard the message before. I'd probably even preached it myself. But it wasn't until that point that it all snapped into place and made sense. I realized with complete and utter clarity that I was looking for a human being to fulfill me and make me whole. When what I needed to do was to allow God to fulfill me and make me whole. Suddenly it was crystal clear that until I reached that place where God was making me whole, I wouldn't have all that much to offer to a soul mate anyway."

He looked around the room with a compassionate intensity, as if he cared about every single person there. "And so, on the eve of my fortieth birthday, I made a commitment to God. I would stop looking for my perfect match, and I would focus that energy on God instead. And as I made that commitment, I decided that I'd trust God to provide me with my soul mate when and if the time was right—and I would even trust him even if I never married."

He paused again and smiled. "That was back before I became the pastor of this church. And although I have to admit there have been a few times when I've been doubtful about this commitment, times when I've felt lonely or sorry for myself, for the most part, I've felt nothing but fulfilled and complete with God's perfect presence in my life."

In closing, he challenged them all to do the same. That instead of looking for soul mates, they should be looking for God to fill their souls. And everyone clapped when he finished.

Daphne couldn't help but notice, as soon as it was time to mingle and have refreshments, the flirting started right back up. Perhaps this was a message only a few could really absorb. But Daphne felt like some of it had slipped inside of her . . . and perhaps it would take root in time. Hopefully she wouldn't have to turn forty before she figured it all out.

On Monday morning, Willie showed up to paint the crown molding that had been missed. And while he was working, Jake called Daphne to discuss the *Dear Daphne* column. "Again, your answers all look very good, very compelling, but there is one particular letter . . ." He cleared his throat. "I'm not sure if you really want it sent out to the syndicates. It's from *Hopeless on Huckleberry Lane*."

Her hand flew to her mouth. "Oh dear! You didn't get my e-mail warning you not to read that one? That was a fake letter and response."

He chuckled. "I was hoping it was a mistake. Or else you might want to change the Huckleberry Lane part. Not that anyone would figure it out, necessarily."

"No, please delete that one. I don't want it printed."

"It's done."

"I'm glad you noticed. I'll be more careful in the future." Now she confessed to how she used to write fictional wedding announcements occasionally, just to pass the time. "But I never actually sent one to my editor."

"I couldn't help but notice that Daphne Delacorte created a rather intelligent response to that particular letter. I really liked the analogy of the broken arm healing up stronger. In fact, it's a shame we can't run those letters. It's a message some people need to hear."

"Well, maybe I'll get a chance to use the response with someone else's letter. I'll save it."

"Good idea. And while we're on this topic, I've been wondering how it turned out with you and Ryan. I don't want to be too nosy or be accused of acting like the enforcer. But as your friend, I'm curious."

"The truth is, I haven't heard from him," she admitted.

"Seriously?"

"Yeah. At first I was pretty mad about it. Then I got worried. But now I'm just moving on. Not really thinking about it."

"So if he'd shown up . . . or if he still does, which I'm guessing he will, what was your answer going to be?"

"I was going to tell him no thank you and then wish him well."

There was a long pause. "I think you made the right choice."

"I think my aunt would agree with you on that."

He excused himself saying he had a client coming in, and as she hung up, Mick's green truck pulled into her driveway. Smiling to herself to think of how many single men seemed to be coming and going throughout her world, she poured Mick and herself a cup of coffee and went out to greet him.

They visited for a while and he, too, inquired as to what had become of Ryan. Like Jake, Mick seemed relieved that Ryan had pulled a disappearing act. And Daphne assured him that she agreed it was for the best. "Although it was pretty aggravating."

"Better to be aggravated for a few days than miserable for the rest of your life." He handed her back his empty cup.

She laughed. "You got that right."

But as she was rinsing the cups in the sink, she noticed another nondescript sort of car pulling up in front of the house. It had the look of a rental car and, sure enough, Ryan was getting out of it. Stretching as if he'd had a long drive, he looked hopefully over to the house, and seeing her watching him out the kitchen window, he waved.

She went to the front door, stepping carefully over the drop cloth Willie had placed to protect the floor. "My apologies for the conversation you are about to hear," she called up to where Willie was perched on the ladder. "But Ryan's here and I'm about to send him packing."

Willie chuckled. "Good for you, Daphne. And if you have any problem with him, I'm happy to come down there and give you a hand. You're way too good for that young man."

Just then the doorbell rang and Daphne opened it with a stiff smile. "Ryan, what are you doing here?"

"I'm sorry I'm late," he said as he stepped inside. He glanced at the painting stuff and frowned. "Having it repainted already?"

"No. Willie just had a little finishing up to do."

Ryan looked up at Willie but didn't even say hello.

"Come into the front room," Daphne said as she led the way.

"Anyway, I was on assignment and it went on longer than I expected. I thought about calling to explain, but I really wanted to have this conversation face-to-face." Ryan smiled at her. "I missed you, Daphne."

She sat on the club chair, trying to think of a way to cut this short. "Have a seat," she offered. But he remained standing. "Or not."

"Daphne . . . before you answer, I want to ask you again. I want to do it better this time." And now he got down on one knee. "Daphne Ballinger, I love you. I have loved you for more than ten long years. I will always love you." He reached into his jacket pocket, removed a blue velvet box, and slowly opened it to reveal a very large diamond. "Daphne, will you marry me?"

Despite her best resolve, Daphne leaned over to peer at the diamond. "Wow, that's big."

"Will you make me the happiest man in the world and marry me?"

She reached out and pushed the lid of the little box, closing it with a snap. "No, Ryan. I'm sorry, but the answer is no. I can't marry you."

Ryan slowly stood, gazing down at her with a wounded expression. "Why not?"

She pointed to the couch. "Sit down."

Without arguing, he went over and sat.

"If you had asked me to marry you ten years ago and if you hadn't been married, I would've said yes."

"Then why not now?"

"Because now I know better. You and I don't belong together,

Ryan. You'll find someone who will be just right for you. But that's not me."

"But you loved me once, Daphne. I know you did. Why don't you love me now?"

She pressed her lips together, trying to understand him. And then a question that had been silently nagging her rose to the surface. "How did you find me here in Appleton?"

"Find you?"

"How did you know I'd moved back here?"

"Oh, that. Like I told you. I was at *The Times* interviewing for a job there. And I talked to Fiona. And she told me everything."

"Everything?" Suddenly Daphne remembered her own conversation with Fiona. She remembered in detail how she had stupidly bragged about inheriting her aunt's small fortune. It had been her way of feeling better about herself after Amelia had hurt her feelings.

"You know, that you were living here and that your aunt had died." He looked uneasy.

"And that I'd inherited a lot of money?"

He shrugged. "I don't remember that specifically."

"Well, I did tell Fiona I had inherited a lot. I'd actually bragged to her about it." She shook her head sadly.

"There's nothing wrong with that." He smiled again. "Why shouldn't you be happy about an inheritance?"

"Because it's not true."

"What's not true?" He tilted his head to one side.

"I haven't inherited a single cent, Ryan."

He looked confused. "So . . . what's all this then? Why do you have this house? And that car? And you're not working . . . and yet you've made all these costly improvements." He pointed toward the foyer. "Right now a guy's up there painting. And there's another one out working in your yard. How can you afford to pay these dudes if you haven't inherited some money?"

"My aunt's estate covers all the household expenses. But only for a year." Lucy hopped up into her lap now, purring as she rubbed her head against Daphne's wrist.

"Only for a year?" Ryan frowned. "How is that even possible?"

"It's the conditions of my aunt's will." She stroked the cat. "After a year . . ." She shrugged. "Well, unless there's some kind of miracle, which seems unlikely, everything will be turned over to a nonprofit organization my aunt has designated in her will."

"So you expect me to believe you only have this for a year?" He stood now, pacing as if he was anxious to leave. "And then that's it?"

"That's right. My aunt has generously given me the use of her possessions for a year. But I'm not allowed to sell anything or profit from it. My year will end in mid-May next year." She smiled. "To be honest, I was kind of miffed at first. But it's actually been like a much-needed vacation and I'm enjoying it."

Ryan ran his hand through his hair, an old frustrated gesture she'd nearly forgotten. But she could tell he felt cornered.

"So you see . . ."—she nudged Lucy onto the ottoman and stood, folding her arms across her front—"all this effort you've made, all this crazed talk of love and marriage, well, it was all for nothing, wasn't it?" She gave him a knowing look. "This game you've been playing with me . . . looks like you lost, Ryan."

His expression was a mixture of confusion and guilt, just like the little boy with his hand in the cookie jar. "But it just doesn't make sense. There's something you're not telling me. I know it." He pocketed the blue velvet box.

"Anyway, I won't keep you." She walked toward the door. "I'm sure you have places to go, people to see, the day is still young."

"I know what you're thinking about me," he said sharply. "But you're wrong, Daphne. Dead wrong. I proposed to you because I loved you."

"Really? So what if I'll be penniless and jobless and homeless next year? Do you still want to marry me now? And would you continue to support me and take care of me, for better or for worse, in sickness and in health, until death we do part?"

"Why are you acting like this?"

"Acting like what?" She paused by the door. "I'm simply talking about what we should expect in a marriage. Isn't that what we were talking about? Or have you changed your mind about marriage?"

"You're delusional," he growled. "And impossible."

She just nodded, opening the door for him.

"I came here to help you, Daphne. But why should I care if you turn out to be an old maid just like your pathetic old aunt?"

"And that just shows how totally clueless you are, Ryan." She wanted to add, "And don't let the door hit you on the way out," but controlled herself. However, she did shut it a bit more firmly than necessary, causing the leaded glass to rattle. Then she whisked her hands back and forth together as if slapping the dust from them. "Good riddance."

From up on the ladder, Willie clapped. "Bravo, Daphne. Good show. Really good show."

She jumped. "Oh! I nearly forgot you were up there, Willie. But at least I'd forewarned you. My apologies."

"And I'm sorry to have enjoyed that so much." He smiled sheep-ishly. "But I was kind of a captive audience. And you really did handle that nicely, Daphne. My hat's off to you."

She thanked him, then still feeling a little shaky but stronger than ever before, she went into her office and closed the door. She sat in her office chair and bowed her head, trying to remember Pastor Andrew's words about trusting God with her marital status.

As she prayed, she knew she wanted to trust God. She wanted to give up on this frenzied pursuit of a husband. But at the same time she was human. Very human. And she suspected her transformation wouldn't be instant. As much as she would like it to happen over-night, she had a strong feeling it would be a process. One little step at a time.

But sending Ryan on his way had been a good first step. A baby step of faith.

Chapter 25

On the Fourth of July, Daphne felt refreshingly independent. She was well aware that her unexpected sense of liberation had started with the rejection of Ryan's phony-baloney marriage proposal. Since that angst-filled morning, she had grown stronger and freer and more confident each day. And after making the decision to trust God for her future, whether or not she found her soul mate, she felt much more at peace too.

This new attitude seemed to permeate all areas of her life now, enabling her to truly enjoy even the simplest of pleasures. Whether it was rising early and slipping outside to watch the sunrise. Or riding her bike to Dad's condo and helping him unpack and organize. Or strolling through town and taking time to stop and visit with friends. Or picking a cherry tomato from her lovely garden and popping it right into her mouth and savoring the sweetness. It seemed that after so many years of barely existing, Daphne was finally truly living.

The best part of all this was that Daphne now believed that with or without her aunt's inheritance, she was going to be just fine. She just hoped that as her year in paradise drew to an end, about ten months from now, she would feel the same. She prayed she would.

"I can tell you're happy to be rid of Ryan," Olivia told Daphne as they sat on Daphne's front porch, sipping lemonade. Olivia had come over early to help get things ready for the July Fourth barbecue Daphne was hosting later in the day. But with most of the preparations done, they had decided to take a break. "I'm still feeling bummed that we don't get to have a wedding. I was imagining it in September, using autumnal-colored flowers."

Daphne laughed as she skimmed down the list she'd made for today's preparations, crossing off what they'd accomplished and circling what was still needing to be done. "I'm sorry to disappoint you, Olivia. But I know you wouldn't have wanted me to marry Ryan just so you could help throw a beautiful wedding."

Olivia's mouth twisted to one side, as if she wasn't so sure. "I do want you to be happy. But I don't see why your happiness couldn't include a wedding. I mean, eventually. Is that too much to ask?"

"Aren't you getting the cart ahead of the horse?" Daphne asked. "Planning a wedding before there's even a man in the picture? Sounds a little backward to me."

"I don't know. I remember hearing about this woman who had her wedding all planned out, even before she knew who she was going to marry."

"Well, that's just plain crazy." Daphne took a sip of lemonade and looked out to the pair of American flags she'd hung from her porch. Very festive.

"This gal had picked the date, bought the dress, reserved the church, had her bridesmaids all set, you know, the whole nine yards. She'd even ordered her cake and flowers, and those are perishable."

"Seriously? Had she sent out invitations too?" Daphne was imagining a sad bride with a church full of guests and no groom.

"I think she'd picked the invitations out. So anyway, just one month before her wedding date, she meets Mr. Right, and just like clockwork, he proposes and they have her dream wedding just like she planned—on the very same date. Can you believe it?"

"Not really." Daphne gave her a skeptical look. "So how did the marriage turn out? Are they still together?"

Olivia shrugged. "I don't know."

"Maybe the marriage only lasted a month," Daphne said in a teasing tone. "And maybe the bride had her divorce date all set as well."

"Oh, I don't think so."

"Perhaps you should do some research and find out."

Olivia chuckled. "Maybe I will."

"And I would greatly appreciate it if we could put any wedding plans for me to rest." Daphne smiled at her.

"Okay. Well, at least until we find Mr. Right. And even though I can admit that Ryan was most definitely not Mr. Right, you don't have to give up. And neither do I."

"What do you mean?"

"This town is crawling with Mr. Rights." Olivia got a mischievous look as she snatched the notebook from Daphne. "In fact, I think I'll make a list." She tore off Daphne's to-do list and handed it to her.

Daphne rolled her eyes, then downed the last of her lemonade and held the paper in the air. "While you're wasting your time on that list, I'm going to finish the tasks on this one."

Daphne returned to the kitchen, removed the hard-boiled eggs from the fridge, and began peeling them to make deviled eggs. Aunt

Dee used to say that the Fourth of July was not the Fourth of July without deviled eggs. And Daphne had to agree with her.

She was just starting to fill the empty egg-white halves when Olivia came back to the kitchen, waving her tablet victoriously. "I think our prospects of having a wedding are quite good."

Daphne just shook her head, keeping her focus on squeezing the yolk filling into the white ovals.

"Don't you want to see it? You don't want to check out all the Mr. Rights in Appleton?"

"Not particularly." Daphne bent over, continuing to squeeze. "I can guess who's on the list. And I can probably give you at least one good reason why every single guy you've listed there is not Mr. Right."

"Really?" Olivia sat down at the kitchen table. "We'll see about that." She started to read. Of course, she started with Ricardo, immediately asking what was wrong with him.

"Nothing is wrong with him, Olivia. But Kellie has her eye on him and I'm not 100 percent sure Ricardo doesn't have his eye on her as well. Have you ever watched the two of them talking at the diner? I'm not convinced something's not brewing there."

Olivia tossed her a look. "Fine. How about Mick Foster, then? I've seen him looking at you."

"And I've seen him looking at Julianne. And he probably looks at other women too. Mick is a flirt and you know it. He likes all women and it seems all women like him. That, in my opinion, is not Mr. Right. Not for me." Daphne turned the platter and continued filling.

"What about Jake McPheeters? He seems interested in you."

"Jake is a good friend. But I'm not convinced he and Gwen aren't getting back together." Daphne had already confided to Olivia about what she'd heard Jenna saying. However, she had not confided about how disappointed she'd been to hear that.

"I'd be surprised if that ever happened, Daphne. Those two seemed mismatched right from the start. Besides that, I heard that Gwen has been dating Frank Danson."

"Really?" Daphne tried not to appear overly interested.

"So maybe you shouldn't be too quick to take Jake off your list."

"You mean *your* list."

"I'm simply playing your secretary."

"Well, I hope you're enjoying your little game." Daphne wished Olivia would get this over and done with.

"Then there's Truman." Olivia giggled. "And even though he's a little young—"

"He's almost thirty," Daphne told her.

"Aha. So you're defending his age?" Olivia grinned. "That gives me hope."

"Just stating the facts." Daphne returned her attention to the eggs.

"And there's always Willie Troutman. I realize he's older, but he sure does seem to like you."

"I like Willie too." Daphne stood up straight. "But only as a friend."

"You are so picky." Olivia read off a few other names, pointing out various qualities and attributes in men she felt had potential. But as quickly as Olivia tossed them out, Daphne continued to shoot them down. Mostly for the fun of it and to enjoy Olivia's reaction. "You are hopeless," Olivia finally said.

"No, I'm not. I have great hopes. But it's like I told you"—
Daphne tore off some wax paper, laying it carefully over the deviled
eggs—"I am going to trust God for my future. If I'm supposed to get
married, Mr. Right will come along when the time is right. In the
meantime, I'm not going to worry about it."

"Yeah, yeah. I remember . . . Pastor Andrew's life-altering ser-
mon. You've already told me all about it." Olivia grabbed the pencil
and scribbled something down on her list. "Which reminds me, I
totally forgot to put Pastor Andrew on the list. You said he's single,
right?"

"Right. But as much as I respect him, I don't see myself with
him."

"Just because he's short and bald?"

Daphne put the egg plate into the fridge and then turned around
to give Olivia a warning look. "Okay, you've had your fun."

"Just trying to help."

"I know." Daphne smiled and stuck out her hand. "So, may I
have your list?"

Olivia looked surprised. "Sure. You really want it?"

Daphne nodded. "I promise to put it to good use."

Olivia blinked as she tore off the page and handed it to Daphne.
"All right then. I'm glad to see you're finally coming back to your
senses."

"I've got to check something outside." Daphne headed for the
back door with the paper in hand. Olivia followed, still talking
about her Mr. Right list and how Daphne should really study it
carefully.

"Maybe you could make columns next to each name," Olivia told
her. "You know to list their various qualities. You could have one for

good looks. One for compatibility. One for job security and so on. Then you could score each guy, maybe give them one to five points. See who gets the most points."

Daphne opened the barbecue, where she'd already arranged the charcoal and applied some lighter fluid. Now she lit a match, crumpled Olivia's Mr. Right list, and used the paper to light the charcoal. "Perfect." She turned to grin at Olivia. "Just what I needed to light my fire."

Olivia frowned as she watched her list going up in flames. "Glad I could be of help."

Daphne hugged her. "I know you mean well, Olivia. But honestly I'm happy as I am. Today is Independence Day and I just want to enjoy my newfound freedom and celebrate with all my friends and neighbors and family. Is that too much to ask?"

"No. If it makes you happy, I'll give you a break about finding true love." Olivia made a sheepish smile. "At least for today."

Daphne sighed. Maybe that was okay. Because really, that was all she could do anyway. All anyone could do was to live for today . . . and not worry about tomorrow. Because she truly believed that God was watching out for her. Perhaps Aunt Dee was keeping an eye on her too. Then as she closed the barbecue, she sensed someone else was watching her.

She glanced over her shoulder to see Jake. Dressed casually in cargo shorts and a navy T-shirt, he was leaning against the back porch stair railing with an amused smile playing on his lips—almost as if he'd been studying her.

"Hello, Daphne," he said warmly. "I hope I'm not too early."

"No, no, I think you're right on time." She giggled nervously as she remembered the list she'd just lit on fire. Hopefully it was safely reduced to ashes by now. And perhaps Olivia had been right. Maybe there was a future with this guy after all. Time would tell.

Dear Reader,

I hope you've enjoyed getting to know Daphne as much as I have. I love inventing characters whose lives are unfulfilling . . . or disappointing . . . or just plain stuck. I guess it's because it gives me something to work with—all things can do is get better. Or at least we hope they will. Also, it's a bit like real life. Because I think everyone gets stuck sometimes. And who hasn't wanted a second chance at some point?

Maybe that's why I love fiction so much. I get to create characters and situations and challenges—and make it as messy as I like. And then, just like that, I can start to clean it up and straighten things out. Sure, it might take some time and some work, but eventually I can give my character a wonderful second chance.

Now I realize (from personal experience) that life isn't usually as simple as a lighthearted novel. Maybe that's why fiction is so appealing. Because we all know that some of life's challenges aren't easily conquered. And occasionally a heartfelt prayer seems to take forever to be answered. Face it, sometimes life is just plain hard.

Even so, I continue to believe that God is the real giver of the best second chances. And I believe that just as Daphne gets the opportunity to change the general direction of her life, if we remain tuned in to God, he will show us the better way to go.

One of my favorite Scriptures is: "Trust in the LORD with all your heart, and lean not on your own understanding; in all your ways acknowledge Him, and He shall direct your paths" (Prov. 3:5–6 NKJV).

Thank you for reading the beginning of the Dear Daphne series. I hope you'll return to Appleton to see what's coming Daphne's way in the next installment. Until then, I pray that you will trust God to bring the second chances you are longing for in your own life.

I love to connect with my readers. Visit me on my website— www.melodycarlson.com.

Blessings,

Melody Carlson

Discussion Questions

1. Daphne had such high expectations for her life and her career in journalism. And yet at the beginning of the story, she seems to be stuck and discouraged. What do you think was the biggest reason for her state of hopelessness?

2. Appleton seems like such a charming town, and yet Daphne hadn't spent much time at home in past years. Why do you think she stayed away?

3. Some people snap right back after a soured romance. Why do you think Daphne had such difficulty in getting over her own brokenheartedness?

4. Daphne clearly needs people in her life, and yet she seems a little challenged in the area of relationships. Can you relate to this in any way? Explain.

5. What childhood factors have impacted Daphne's adult life the most dramatically?

6. Daphne knows that to secure her inheritance, she must get married. But do you think it's worth it? How would you react if you were in a similar situation?

7. Aunt Dee's true identity shocks Daphne and her father. Do you think Dee was right to keep her unwed motherhood a secret? Why or why not?

8. Daphne's experience with men is very limited (and somewhat jaded). If you were her good friend, what kind of advice would you give her in regard to dating and romance?

9. It doesn't take long for Daphne to have a short list of "available" men. Which guy do you think would be her best match? And why?

10. Do you think it was fair for Aunt Dee to put her odd conditions in her will? Why or why not?